BIRDIE SWITCHED ON THE LIGHT.

The woman lay on her back on the floor, her head facing the door. Her fair hair was tied into a loose plait. Her day clothes hung over the back of a chair nearby. White dress, white slip, cotton bra and panties. She was wearing pale blue pajamas. The jacket had been ripped open, the buttons scattered, to reveal small, perfect breasts. Her arms and legs were flung out at awkward angles, as if she'd been dropped onto the carpet from above. Birdie saw all this as though from a great distance. She saw the rolled-back eyes, the blue-tinged face, the dark pool of blood that soaked the carpet around the shoulders. Behind her, Alistair staggered. She put her hand back, pushed him out of the doorway.

That was a mistake, because then everyone saw, and the screaming started.

ALSO BY JENNIFER ROWE

Death in Store
Murder by the Book
Grim Pickings

COMING SOON:

Stranglehold

THE
MAKEOVER
MURDERS

Jennifer Rowe

Bantam Books
New York Toronto London Sydney Auckland

This edition contains the complete text of the original hardcover edition.
NOT ONE WORD HAS BEEN OMITTED.

THE MAKEOVER MURDERS

A Bantam Crime Line Book / published in association with Doubleday

PUBLISHING HISTORY
Doubleday hardcover edition / April 1993
Bantam paperback edition / June 1994

CRIME LINE *and the portrayal of a boxed "cl" are trademarks of Bantam Books, a division of Bantam Doubleday Dell Publishing Group, Inc.*

ISBN 0-553-29740-6

Published simultaneously in the United States and Canada

Bantam Books are published by Bantam Books, a division of Bantam Doubleday Dell Publishing Group, Inc. Its trademark, consisting of the words "Bantam Books" and the portrayal of a rooster, is Registered in U.S. Patent and Trademark Office and in other countries. Marca Registrada. Bantam Books, 1540 Broadway, New York, New York 10036.

PRINTED IN THE UNITED STATES OF AMERICA

RAD   0 9 8 7 6 5 4 3 2 1

THE

MAKEOVER

MURDERS

1

Margot Bell looked in the mirror and liked what she saw. She usually did at this time of day, when the lengthening shadows, the soft, golden light, and the promise of the night to come smoothed the tiny lines from beneath her eyes, warmed her fabled cheekbones, and filled her veins with champagne bubbles of energy.

The mornings were a different story. That was one reason why Margot preferred her guests (they were never called clients, or customers, of course) to arrive at Deepdene as the day ended. That way, she knew, they were seeing her, and the house, at their best—little imperfections invisible, glamour dazzling, under artificial light.

And this was important. It wasn't just a matter of vanity. It was business. Women paid thousands to put themselves in Margot Bell's hands for a fortnight, and for their money they expected, simply, a miracle. The Deepdene mystique was now well established, and the butterfly motif, so tastefully embossed on Margot's thick, cream stationery, so discreetly etched on the brass plate by the great iron gates that guarded the property, presented an irresistible promise to the select few who stepped nervously or boldly through the front door and felt the atmosphere of the house enfold them like a huge, silent, silken cocoon.

Margot smiled at her reflection. The butterfly had been one of Alistair's better ideas. The punters loved it. A shame that he, poor darling, still took it so literally, fussing futilely over hopelessly unpromising material, determined to reveal the inner beauty he claimed he saw in every woman who crossed his path, and give her the tools to keep it forever. It just wasn't cost-effective, all that individual attention. Margot had explained that to him, time and again. They could easily cut each group's stay in half—a week would be plenty, and they could charge the same. As long as every guest saw a definite change in her appearance—a definite improvement of course, simply accomplished by a good haircut, clever makeup, and some decent clothes—and as long as she got a good rest and a bit of pampering at Deepdene, she'd think her money well spent and go away happy. And the effect would last a good few months—long enough, anyway.

But Alistair was so committed to his original concept. Five years' experience, not to mention the few little money troubles the place was having at the moment, hadn't shaken him one iota. He was such a romantic—always had been. Sweet in a little hairdresser, lovely in a friend—gorgeous, really. But not so wonderful in a business partner. And there was a tiny touch of stubbornness in it, too, if one faced facts.

Margot frowned very slightly, and touched the shining wing of her own auburn hair where it curved into her cheek. Still, he was awfully talented. She'd never let anyone else touch her hair. He'd looked after it forever, all through her modeling days, and ever since. And the miracles he did with some of the guests —well, you had to hand it to him. But they couldn't go on as they were. He'd simply have to see . . .

The phone beside the bed buzzed discreetly. Margot took a final look at her reflection, sauntered across the room, and picked up the receiver. At the other end of the line someone caught his breath, and she smiled to herself. Sweet William.

"Margot, I have to talk to you."

"Are the guests all here, darling?" Margot spoke crisply. These days, it was wise to keep William on a short leash.

"Yes. They're here—all the real ones, I mean. The ABC woman hasn't arrived yet, but I wanted . . ." The voice wobbled and trailed off. She could hear him trying to control his breathing.

"Yes, darling?" Margot's voice was carefully formal. The poor boy was suffering, but one had to be cruel to be kind, really. A little dalliance was one thing, but he really had got himself into deep water, it seemed. She'd had no idea he'd take it all so seriously. Poor William. Poor, sweet little William.

She gazed through the window, narrowing her eyes, noting the mist beginning to rise and the pale trunks of the poplar trees shimmering in the fading light. The place looked beautiful. Peaceful and beautiful. Oh, everything would be all right. She would see to that. "Keep them happy, my pet," she murmured. "Tell Alistair not to mention the ABC woman for the moment. It has to be handled tactfully. I'll be right down." There was silence at the other end of the line. "Are you there, William?" she added sharply.

"Oh—yes."

"Well, will you do that, darling? I'll be right down."

"Yes. Margot? Margot, I have to talk to you. Alone. I really have to . . ."

Margot's eyes slid crossly from the poplars to the phone on the bedside table. "Look, William," she said, "you've got to be a good boy and stop badgering me. Now, I've told you—"

"Please, Margot, this is important. I . . ."

Margot shook her head and held the phone away from her ear. Her eyes drifted back to the view outside the window. The sky looked threatening. Please God it wouldn't rain again. They'd had enough rain to last all winter already. The grass looked beautiful—unbelievably lush and green—but the ground was soft underfoot, and the creek was high. It would be floods, next, and that would be the final straw. Locked in the house with William in this mood. And how disastrous if they had to cancel a fortnight. They'd never recover from the loss.

She put the receiver back to her ear and spoke into it abruptly, cutting through William's plaintive murmurings. "William, you've got to stop this. Enough's enough. I'm sorry you're upset, but you're a big boy, darling, and you have to face the fact that I mean what I say. Like the song, you know, William? We had great fun, but it was just one of those things? That's how it is. Now, let's just get down to business and concentrate on the guests. You keep them happy. I'll be with you in two ticks."

She put the phone down firmly before another flow of words could begin. Dear, oh dear. It really had been a mistake, the thing with William. Alistair had been right to disapprove. Alistair was very intuitive, sometimes. Gay men often were, she'd found. Sensitive. But William had been so sweet. So adoring. So grateful. So intense and protective. And those looks! Awfully appealing, at least for a while. But, let's face it, he was terribly stitched up. It made him a very good secretary, of course, but . . . well, novelty wore thin after a while. And then one looked for a little imagination in a lover. Sadly, William had become well—boring, really. And getting out of the affair had proved far more difficult than getting into it had been. Dear, oh dear. It would be such a shame to have to let William go. He was by far the best secretary she'd ever had.

Margot glanced once more at her reflection, shrugged, smiled, and left the room. She passed Alistair's door—he'd been downstairs for hours, of course —and made her way down the private stairs that led from their spacious attic apartments to the guest bedroom floor below.

Here the grandeur of the old house was apparent. The five guest suites were strung around a gallery from which you could look over cedar balustrades to the marble-floored vestibule below. A huge chandelier hung glittering in the center of the soaring ceiling. Warmth and soft light flooded every corner. Soft, pale carpet cushioned the floor. Margot paused for a moment at the head of the magnificent stairway, clearing her mind of all except the task ahead. The sounds of music and tinkling crystal drifted up to meet her. The timing was just right. It was always as well to make a proper entrance on a first night. She looked complacently down at her gloriously cut fine wool dress. Yes she'd been right to choose the white. The gray was very elegant, but William's carry-on was exhausting, and to sparkle in the gray she had to be feeling on top of things, absolutely.

Murmuring and occasional nervous laughter floated from the open doors of the sitting room. The guests were assembled and waiting. And the invited staff, presumably. Alistair, William, Angela the beautician, and . . . Conrad. Margot ran an experienced hand down the length of her body, from breast to thigh. It was a characteristic gesture with her before a performance of any kind—a mixture of caress, reassurance, and deliberate preparation. So a warrior might have crossed himself before going into battle.

She descended the stairs to the ground floor and

moved toward the sitting room, her high heels clicking as they struck the marble, a slight, practiced smile on her lips.

When she was a young girl, struggling to become established as a model, Mamie Spears, her rough, streetwise agent had given her a piece of advice. "For a fabulous entrance, my love," Mamie had said in that husky, cigarettes-and-brandy voice of hers, "just think to yourself three things: 'I'm beautiful, I'm successful—and I've got a secret!' Then you'll get them in every time." Margot had been much taken by this, and though of course she had left Mamie's agency for a more prestigious one as soon as her career began to prosper, she had never forgotten it. Since, what with one thing and another, and life being what it was, for her all three requirements of Mamie's adage were almost always true, very little imagination had been required to incorporate it into her standard public persona. She didn't even have to think about it these days.

She paused at the doorway, smiling, taking in the glow, the flowers, the firelight, the faces of four of the new Deepdene "guests" turned expectantly toward her, and the gratifying hush her entrance had caused. In the background, darkly tragic, William hovered. She quickly avoided his anxious eye and waved instead to Angela, who was cheerily smiling beside him, the inevitable apple juice in her hand. No complexion-spoiling alcohol for Angela Fellowes, who was a marvelous advertisement for her profession. She had only been with them a fortnight, but it was already obvious that she had been a good choice. What a sweet, chatty, wholesome, dependable, *earnest* sort of girl she was. With all the sex appeal and personality of a fence post, thought Margot complacently. She casually let her eyes drift further afield, to take in, without seeming to notice, the lounging figure by the fireplace.

Conrad Hunter was emphatically not sweet or chatty. And wholesome and dependable weren't the adjectives one would first think of to describe him either. Conrad was golden brown, with tawny fair hair that fell to his shoulders. His white shirt, sleeves rolled casually up, was unbuttoned just one button too many, his white trousers were just a little too tight, his white teeth were just a little too white, and he wore a gold stud in his left ear. He had long, narrow, heavy-lidded blue eyes, wide cheekbones, and a wide, full mouth. His voice was a languid drawl and he seemed to have only two main facial expressions—a sort of sulky, brooding look, which was his normal, or standard one, and a knowing, hungry smile, which he used when talking to women over fourteen and under sixty.

Margot had hired Conrad as Deepdene's new masseur against the combined outrage of both Alistair and William, who regarded him still, after a month, with the same astonished disgust they had shown on first meeting him. Well, let the boys fume, Margot thought now, dropping her eyes briefly to Conrad's long, strong, golden fingers curled around his champagne glass. He was a marvelous masseur, she could testify to that, and if the last two groups of guests were any indication, he was going to be a marvelous drawcard for Deepdene. Sublimely tacky, gloriously decadent, lovely to look at—the guests were putty in his hands, in more ways than one. And she herself—well, it had to be admitted that as an antidote to William's dark, sweet, clinging intensity, Conrad was hard to beat.

"Ah, Margot." Alistair, slim and fair and performing beautifully, moved quickly to her side and led her into the room. "At last!" He whisked a glass of champagne from a waiter's silver tray and placed it in her hand. "Everyone's looking forward to meeting you. Now . . . let me introduce you all round. This is Edwina. Edwina—Margot Bell."

Margot stretched out a slim hand to meet the other woman's firm grip. She was bad with names, and usually nicknamed the guests in her own mind to avoid mixing them up. But Edwina didn't need a nickname. Edwina she wouldn't forget. She smiled and murmured graciously, and appraised the material with interest. Strong, heavy face, thick iron-gray hair cut short, badly plucked eyebrows, caked-on makeup, and harsh red lipstick, bulky figure ill-served by a tight-fitting dull red woolen suit and gray blouse with an elaborate tie at the throat. On the plus side, milky white skin almost free of lines, judging by the neck, excellent teeth, intelligent, if rather cold, gray eyes, an assured manner, and a pleasant, practiced smile. Could be worse. The clothes were ugly, but obviously expensive. The delicate, spindly heeled black shoes that emphasized the heaviness of the legs above them were Italian. Edwina would do. She wouldn't be one of their greatest successes, but neither would she be a disaster. Fortunate, since although at discreet Deepdene first names only were used among the guests, Margot and Alistair both knew that Edwina Dwyer was to the outside world a person of some influence—destined, possibly, for even greater things—and it wouldn't do to disappoint her.

"I hope you'll find your stay here rewarding, Edwina," she said, smiling. "We're neighbors at dinner, I think, so we'll be able to have a proper chat then."

"That will be nice," murmured Edwina.

"Yes, well, I'd better move on. Do my duty, little speech and all!" laughed Margot, one woman of the world to another.

Edwina smiled faintly. Margot turned away, a trifle discomposed. A cool customer, this.

"Margot? This is Belinda. Belinda, Margot Bell." Alistair sparkled, laying a friendly hand on the floral sleeve of the short, dark woman next in line. She giggled nervously and Margot repressed a sigh. So this was Belinda. Darling Roberta's baby sister. Small, dependent, plump . . . Baby Belinda. And as unsatisfactory as Roberta had hinted on the phone. She'd been so tempted to say she was sorry, that the books were full, that much as she would love to help out an old modeling pal newly back home after years collecting husbands in Europe and now bent on doing a good sisterly deed . . . after all she hadn't seen hide nor hair of darling Roberta for—heavens, it must be twenty years! But there'd been that cancellation, and she and Roberta had been great pals in the old days, before she married that swine Julius and Roberta had disappeared to Switzerland with what's-his-name, who was supposed to have been a count but had turned out, Margot had heard, to be some sort of salesman. Margot sighed. Ah, the old days. No responsibilities to speak of, endless energy, all those lovely men beating down your door . . . presents and flowers, and naughty little secrets. Such fun!

Anyway, here Baby Belinda was, as different from confident Roberta as was possible—pathetically vivacious with a very slight lisp, swathed in ruched and pleated floral, anxious lines creasing her brow even as her mouth stretched in a nervous, too-wide smile. Her husband had left her, Roberta had said. And she looked it. You could always pick the dumped wives, Margot thought dispassionately. They had this fuzzy, disoriented, discarded look, like people who had been institutionalized, as if too many years with the wrong man had frayed their edges, and the experience of being thrown over, even by someone they'd grown to fear or dislike, or who had emotionally starved them for years, had knocked the stuffing out of them completely. Quite pathetic, really. But the more fool them for letting themselves get into such an ignominious situation. Roberta, she knew, would feel the same way.

She'd never let a man get under her skin. Belinda wore no wedding ring, and was booked in under her maiden name. That would be Roberta's doing. Trying to get her to have a bit of dignity, get the bastard out of her system. But Belinda was the doomed type. No one could help the Baby Belindas of this world, because they wouldn't help themselves. It was pointless even trying.

She disengaged herself from Belinda's small, eager hands, smiled vaguely at her chin, and moved on. Out of the corner of her eye she saw Alistair linger for a reassuring word and another little pat. Oh, how utterly predictable! Now he was going to make a pet of this Belinda and knock himself out for the whole bloody fortnight trying to make her think she was a raving beauty. He was quite impossible, really. A sucker for the runt of the litter every time. Why were people so unreasonable? She heard a rumble of thunder from outside and suddenly felt violently irritated. With the weather, with Alistair, with William, with silly little Belinda, with Roberta—with everything.

"I'm Josie. Pleased to meet you." The big, sandy, shapeless woman who was next in line held out a fat, freckled hand and beamed, showing a brilliant row of (surely capped?) teeth. "I like your place. Very nice." She sniffed and dropped Margot's hand to begin rummaging in her handbag.

"Thank you," Margot murmured graciously. She mentally cast up her eyes as the woman pulled out a huge handkerchief reeking of eucalyptus oil and blew her nose loudly. Surely she could have been spared a Josie this week. As if things weren't bad enough, with Edwina Dwyer to look after, and the ABC woman coming about the Deepdene program. Women like Josie were the worst possible makeover material. Big, fat, and formless. No shape anywhere, from head to toe. Not a bone, not an angle. Watery-pale eyes, short lashes, snub nose, undistinguished mouth. And that baby-fine, flyaway ginger hair! Honestly! And always, for some reason, loud and jolly with it. Jolly Josie. Jolly Jelly Josie. Yes. And always with a taste for lime green pants suits. And this one obviously had a heavy cold on top of it. Her nose looked red raw. Hopeless! Alistair really would have to be spoken to. After all, he took the applications. He saw the photographs. She'd tried over and over to impress on him that with women literally clamoring to get into Deepdene they simply didn't have to take the no-hopers. It was so bad for their image. Honestly—problems, problems! Sometimes none of it seemed worthwhile!

She lifted her eyes and over Josie's broad shoulder caught another glimpse of Conrad, propped negligently against the mantelpiece by the fire, one thumb caught in the waistband of his tight white slacks. Well, fortunately there were compensations.

"Margot?" Alistair had her by the elbow and was guiding her firmly on to the next waiting guest. "Margot, this is Helen. Helen, Margot Bell."

Margot's irritability ebbed, and interest took its place. She exerted herself. "Welcome to Deepdene, Helen," she smiled, using her best, "warm" social manner. Helen of Troy, she thought.

"Thank you," the woman before her said. Her voice was curiously toneless, her face almost without expression. She made no effort to hold out her hand. Margot exchanged glances with Alistair. A strange one, but oh, the material was there all right. Helen was tall, bone-thin, almost haggard. Her pepper and salt hair hung lank on either side of her face. She wore a shapeless two-piece garment in a mustard color that emphasized her gray pallor. Her shoulders slouched slightly. Her big, ringless hands hung awkwardly by her sides. Margot saw all this and dismissed it, concentrating instead on the magnificent bones of cheek and jawline, the wide mouth, the strong brows, the big, brilliant, deep-set eyes. For the first time that evening her professional instincts were aroused. A strange, striking face. Ugly now, but properly dealt with . . . She nodded with satisfaction. Helen of Troy. Alistair nudged her slightly and she became aware that the other guests, silly things, were darting smiles of veiled envy in Helen's direction. Her interest must be too obvious. She murmured something and moved on, casually sipping her champagne. One had to be careful not to put noses out of joint at this early stage. Though really, she thought impatiently, you'd think the meanest intelligence would understand her natural exhilaration at finding some material worth working on.

"We can do something there," she breathed in Alistair's ear as they moved away from the guests and headed toward the fire at the other end of the room, near the windows. She always made her welcoming speech and introduced the staff from there. It made a prettier picture. Conrad was still leaning against the mantelpiece, she saw, but now Angela had joined him, and was chatting animatedly, her glass of juice clutched firmly in the strong, brown hand with its short, scrubbed, healthy pink nails. Conrad was looking over her shoulder—straight into Margot's eyes. She felt a slight frisson of excitement, and resisted the temptation to wet her lips with the tip of her tongue.

"We can do something with all of them, Margot," Alistair was whispering reprovingly. It was an old argument.

"Oh, *something*, yes." She smiled charmingly at Angela, who nodded and waved cheerfully, glanced coolly at Conrad, who lifted a finger in casual salute. William, she noted, wasn't in evidence. Here, or with the guests. He must have slipped out. How unlike him. All routine was, for William, hallowed.

"Ready, Margot?" Alistair touched her elbow.

"In a minute, Alistair! Let me catch my breath,

won't you?" Margot snapped. "They're chatting on there. They'll be all right for a minute or two, surely. And anyway, William's not with us, is he? How can I introduce him if he isn't here?"

"They've been talking to William and the rest of us for half an hour, Margot, waiting for you, so it hardly matters, does it?" Alistair turned away. Oh, God, now he was going to sulk, thought Margot. Well, too bad! Let him.

Angela bent toward her. "I promised William I'd tell you he needs to talk to you before dinner, Miss Bell," she murmured diffidently. She eyed Margot's composed face, hesitated, then plunged on. "It's important, I think. He's *very* anxious about something."

Margot raised her eyebrows and smiled. "Anxiety is poor William's middle name, I'm afraid. As you'll learn, when you've been here a bit longer, Angela. But thank you. You can leave William to me, don't worry. I'll get to him in due course. After the guests have settled."

Angela, her duty to William discharged, relaxed and sipped her drink. "They seem a nice group, Miss Bell," she chirped. "Edwina has *wonderful* skin. The little dark lady—Belinda, isn't it?—yes . . . she's had such an *awful* time with her husband, poor thing. She was telling me . . ."

"Yes, well, not here and now, perhaps, Angela." Margot lifted her chin and smiled briefly and warningly enough to make Angela's perfect complexion flush brilliant rose.

"Oh, sorry," she whispered in confusion, and glanced guiltily at the guests, in case any of them showed signs of having overheard. Conrad raised an amused eyebrow.

"She was telling anyone who'd listen," he drawled. "One of those women who have to spill everything all over everyone they meet. What a turn-off. No wonder her husband dumped her."

"Conrad, you're *dreadful!*" whispered Angela, clutching at his sleeve and darting a delighted, scandalized look at Margot.

But Margot simply smiled and sipped her champagne, smugly aware of Alistair simmering beside her. How he loathed vulgarity, poor Alistair.

Conrad pushed himself away from the fireplace and stretched. "The tall one—Helen's got what it takes," he said. "Ve-ry odd lady, though."

Angela gave a little shudder. "I *know*," she whispered. "She's really strange. I tried to talk to her earlier, just being friendly. But she barely answered me. And she *stares*, you know? She gives me the creeps."

Conrad's wide mouth turned up at the corners.

Like a lithe shadow William slipped through the door and crossed the room to join them. Margot raised her eyebrows at him and he whispered an apology before moving to Alistair's side.

"O.K. Now we're all here, so let's get on with the show, Margot," said Alistair abruptly. "Drink up, and say your piece, darling, will you? We should go in to dinner."

Margot nodded, swallowed the last of her champagne, and turned, smiling, to face the rest of the company. But as she began her familiar welcoming spiel, she was aware that something was a little out of kilter. The room had seemed warm and inviting as usual when she came in, but now a tiny shiver crawled up and down her arms beneath the soft stuff of her dress. Her voice sounded highly artificial, brittle against the soft background music and the ominous rumbling of thunder outside. The faces turned toward her looked odd, as though the light had yellowed and the shadows deepened, making masks of them all. There was Edwina's watchful intelligence; Baby Belinda's strained vivacity; Jolly Josie's smug, red-nosed ordinariness; Helen's gaunt beauty. Beside her Angela, Conrad, William, and Alistair stood, presumably similarly revealed, as she must be herself. She tossed her head slightly, to clear it. What was wrong with her? How had the fancy of revealing masks popped into her head? And why did she find it so unnerving?

Because masks don't reveal. They disguise.

Outside, the poplar trees bent in the rising wind, the thunder rumbled, and the rain began to fall.

2

Verity Birdwood urged her battered car on through the pour-ing rain, praying there would be no more unpleasant incidents. The can of WD-40 that had bailed her out last time was almost empty, and she had no wish to be stuck out in this black wilderness with nothing but puddles and tossing trees to keep her company. The last leg of the trip to the river and the car ferry had been bad enough—negotiating that steep, narrow, winding, bush-lined road in the dark and the rain had been hair-raising, in her car, anyway. But on the other side of the fast-running river the road seemed to give up any pretense of order or discipline. The very bush and air felt different here, as though civilization itself had been left behind on the far bank with the general store, the phone booths, and the bobbing boats moored neatly in rows.

Some people might have found refreshment in this thought. But Birdie, hunched over the wheel of her struggling car, humming determinedly along with the Sunday night concert, peering ahead through her thick glasses at the small patch of glimmering wet road re-vealed by the headlights, found in it only gloom and a rising sense of panic. You couldn't trust a place, in Birdie's view, where you couldn't find an open coffee shop within five minutes' walk in any direction day or night. It just wasn't natural.

Mahler didn't help. At all. She clicked off the radio and checked the clock on the dashboard. Eight forty-five—damn, she'd miss dinner at this rate. She was starving, and from what she'd been told about this Deepdene place, the food at least was good. "Two weeks at Deepdene," her friend Kate Delaney had moaned enviously. "Two weeks of absolute luxury, with that gorgeous countryside all round you, and being *paid* for it—my God, and you're *complaining*! Some people don't know when they're well off! And they'll probably give you a free makeover, too, you realize. Birdie, you're so lucky I'd give my eyeteeth to . . ."

At that point she'd broken off to laugh at the look of disgust on her friend's small, pale, bespectacled face. "Oh, Birdie!" she'd teased. "Don't fight it! Look, Birdie, obviously you haven't read Deepdene's stuff. Don't you realize that this is your big chance to emerge from your chrysalis at last and find true beauty, truth, and happiness? Don't you . . . ?"

"I am going to this absurd beauty farm, Kate," Birdie had broken in repressively, "to work. To research a story some fool has decided will make good television, however that is defined. A flood-prone valley in winter is not my idea of gorgeous countryside, what's more. I would give a lot more than my eyeteeth not to be going anywhere *near* Makeover Mansion. And for your information, I don't happen to regard myself as a grub, whatever Margot Bell may think."

Birdie nodded vehemently to herself. She'd told Kate, all right. And it was indeed true she loathed the idea of the fortnight to come. She expected to be courted and patronized in turn. She expected to feel like a fish out of water, to be disgusted, alienated, and irritated.

The car plowed on through the rain. But mainly, Birdie thought bitterly to herself, and whatever else happens, there's one thing for sure. I'm going to be bored bloody witless.

She was to think of that afterward, and reflect that it just went to show that nothing in life was certain. The joke was on her, all right. But it was a long time before she would laugh about it.

Josie scraped the last smears of caramel from the sides of her bowl and licked the spoon approvingly. "Full as a goog!" she announced to the table in general, and patted her stomach, round beneath lime green jersey stretched to its limits. "What a relief! I expected to be half-starved on rabbit food here, didn't you, Belinda? Eh?" She nudged plump little Belinda beside her with a familiar elbow.

Belinda jumped, giggled, and rolled her eyes. "Oh well, no, I mean, I didn't really think about it." She flapped her small hands, and darted a look at Angela and the dark, silent William on the other side of the table. She made a face. "Too busy being scared to death, actually."

"Scared? Scared of what, for goodness' sake?" Josie snorted with laughter, sniffed, and stared.

Belinda blushed scarlet. There was a hunted look in her eyes. Her lips strained into an answering smile.

William spoke for the first time since dinner began. "Some people do feel nervous at first," he said gently, turning his somber gaze on her. "But there's nothing to worry about, Belinda, you'll see."

Belinda looked at him gratefully.

"That's right!" Angela chipped in cheerily. "We're all just here to *help* you, you know. And happy to do it."

Josie laughed again. "I should think so—God knows we're paying through the nose for the privilege."

Angela looked faintly shocked. This woman was definitely not the sort of client she'd expected to encounter at Deepdene. She glanced at the other end of the table, at Margot Bell, dealing elegantly with the high-powered lady with the good skin, bad makeup, and ugly, expensive clothes—Edwina, wasn't it?—and at Alistair, working hard to draw out that strange Helen, and thanked her own simple, healthy gods that tonight was the only night she'd have to socialize with the guests.

"It's not so much money," Belinda said, in a high voice. "I was just glad to get in. And I'm really going to make the most of it. I really am." She looked around defiantly, with the air of having got something off her chest.

"That's a *wonderful* attitude!" said Angela to her alone. She'd decided Josie was best ignored. "Isn't it, William?"

But William's attention seemed to have wandered again, and he just nodded absentmindedly. Angela sighed inwardly, and reminded herself that only an hour or so now separated her from her spartan room, her clean white sheets, and solitude.

Belinda gave a feverish giggle, and plucked at her regrettable floral. "Oh well, it was my sister Roberta's idea. She rang Margot Bell—they used to model together, you see—and got me in. She said if Deepdene couldn't make me pull myself together and get back to normal life, nothing could." She tried to giggle again, but her voice cracked and wavered. "She said it was my last chance," she finished, and bit her lip like a child. Tears were clustering in her eyes.

"What a cheek!" boomed Josie, looking down her

fleshy nose. "You should have told her to stick it up her bum!"

William looked solemn, Belinda gave a strangled sob, and Angela prayed for time to pass.

Edwina was concentrating on the lilting tones of Margot's voice to avoid thinking about the content of her conversation, which she found extremely irritating. She'd asked about the history of the Deepdene business more to avoid personal conversation than out of any real interest. Alistair Swanson, who seemed a pleasant enough fellow, and had been trying hard to converse with the silent Helen, had reacted with relief and said a few quite sensible things, but Margot had soon taken over, and it had all been downhill from then on. Mellifluous, Edwina thought to herself, listening to the rise and fall of the voice, and watching Margot's beautiful mouth moving opposite her. Has she had training, or developed it herself? It's entirely artificial, anyway. No one grows up talking like that.

She had been interested to meet Margot, as she was interested in everything very different from herself. Edwina had worked hard in her profession, and had succeeded beyond even her doting parents' wildest dreams. In the world of finance she was a well-known and widely respected figure. She was frequently quoted in the financial columns of the daily papers; she had sat upon many government advisory committees; her level head, her willingness to take a considered chance, and her ruthless streak were valued by the most archly conservative members of her male-dominated profession.

She was on the penultimate step of a very long ladder, and she knew it. In a year—eighteen months at the outside—the chief executive would move into gracious retirement, to enjoy his orange orchard, his yacht, his latest mistress, and the handful of directorships he would take on to keep his hand in and gratify his developed need for authority and long lunches. And Edwina was the obvious—some would say the only—choice as his replacement.

Edwina knew she deserved the job. She knew that there was no one better equipped to handle its complexities and responsibilities. She knew she was the obvious candidate. But she was too intelligent not to know also that there was one area in which her suitability could be questioned. The chief executive was the brains and experience behind the business, yes. Brains and experience she had. And in her present job, they were all she needed. But the chief executive was the company's figurehead, too. Image and presentation were a real issue. A man—well, a man had a decent haircut, shaved closely, cleaned his fingernails, put on an expensive dark suit, shirt, tie, pair of Italian shoes, and air of authority, and Bob's your uncle. But a woman was different.

Edwina's mouth tightened slightly as she thought just how different. She looked at Margot Bell, vapid nonsense dripping from her sensuous, painted mouth, cold narcissism glinting in those glorious, shallow eyes, and reflected calmly on the irony that this woman could teach her anything she needed to know. Never would she have believed it, in the old days at university, and in her first job, where dedication, hard work, idealism, and intelligence were the only weapons she saw as valid in the struggle to establish herself in her chosen field.

Every now and again, in those days, an invitation to a concert or to dine from some weedy youth she fancied she might grow to despise less on closer acquaintance would drive her to suspend her judgment and make an effort to acquire some feminine allure. She would, with a rising sense of helplessness, tread the unfamiliar territory of boutiques and trendy hairdress-

ers, spending her meager resources in panic and looking at the results later, at home, in humiliation and sick
despair. The memories of her own reflection in her bedroom mirror on those evenings, the startled, strained
looks on the faces of the weedy young men as she
opened the door to them, still to this day made her
blush and groan softly to herself through clenched
teeth.

As the years passed and her professional confidence increased, she became aware, with relief, that
such personal treachery was no longer possible for her.
She told herself she cared nothing at all for men's opinion of her sexual attractiveness, and in all but a tiny
corner of her secret mind where her adolescent self lay
hidden, this was true. She had never met a man she
would have wanted to marry. It had sometimes crossed
her mind, over the years, that if she had been a less
conservative person, in a less conservative profession,
she might have found a woman with whom she
wanted to share her life. But as it was, with one or two
notable and regrettable exceptions now firmly rele-
gated to the past, she had had no difficulty in putting
that part of herself aside, and concentrating on her
work with the passion she might otherwise have lav-
ished on a lover.

She dressed carefully, put on serviceable makeup,
and spent a great deal of money on clothes and shoes.
It was a uniform, she told herself. She was a professional. She had to look the part. She knew, though, that
what was good enough for second in command was
not good enough for the top job. For women there was
no real uniform. There was too much choice, too many
colors and styles, too much opportunity for error. She
knew, with her usual keen clear-sightedness, that she
was an expensively dressed frump. She knew that
other people knew it. She knew they saw it as a weakness, in a way they would never have considered had

she been a man. And that it gave everyone, from the junior typists to the managing director, the opportunity to patronize her in private, however respectful they may be to her face, and to undercut her authority in subtle ways over which she had no control.

It was typical of Edwina that, having come to this realization, she didn't waste time raging internally over the stupidity, unfairness, or inappropriateness of the attitude she perceived. She just saw it as a problem to be solved like any other, and calmly set about dealing with it in her usual manner—quickly, efficiently, and without emotion. Expert assistance was obviously required. Also discretion. Deepdene would provide both those things. And if she was to be wearied and irritated in the process—well, she'd been wearied and irritated in the cause of her career many, many times in the past, and she knew how to play her part in the game.

She smiled pleasantly at Margot, whose own confident smile widened in return. Patronize me all you like, you shallow, calculating bitch, thought Edwina dispassionately. You're a means to an end, and that's all you are. In two weeks I'll be able to forget that you, and this place, ever existed.

". . . so that's how it all began, didn't it, Alistair?" Margot was winding down at last. She spread her hands elegantly, taking in the elegant room, the silver and crystal, the formally clad waiter. "We had a dream, Alistair and I, and we made it a reality. We're very lucky. It's very, very hard work. We work our fingers to the bone. But we get by, don't we, darling?"

"Oh yes, Margot," Alistair replied dryly.

Edwina looked at him in amusement. He was obviously the workhorse to Margot's show pony in this partnership. Were the traces starting to chafe, perhaps?

"I thought there were to be five of us." Helen's voice came as a surprise. She had hardly spoken since dinner began, and the other three had become used to her silence.

Margot quickly recovered and flashed an approving smile at her. Coming out of your shell at last, the smile said. Good girl. You've got such potential, despite your off-putting manner.

Helen stared back stolidly. "I thought there were going to be five of us," she repeated. "That's what the brochure said."

Alistair turned toward her. "Our last guest hasn't arrived yet." He glanced at his watch, and then at Margot. "She's quite late. I hope she's O.K. The rain . . ."

Margot laughed. "Oh, darling, you old worry-wort. Of course she's all right. These people know what they're doing."

"What people?" Helen asked abruptly.

Margot's eyes flickered. "Oh, you know," she said vaguely. "Media types. Anyway—"

"You don't mean we've got a journalist coming, Margot? You assured absolute discretion." Edwina's face showed none of the alarm she felt, but her voice was cold.

Again Margot's eyes shifted. "Oh now, don't panic, darling. Our guests have all sorts of jobs, you know. I can't help that. But this girl's not a journalist anyway—a researcher, I think she said. That's all. She sounded charming. Anyway—"

"It's not a matter of panic, Margot," Edwina cut in, holding on to her temper.

"She's coming for the treatment, is she? Like us?" Helen was not to be put off.

"Of course." Margot glanced elaborately at her watch.

Alistair shifted in his chair. "Margot . . ."

"Lucky we didn't wait dinner, isn't it?" Margot went on breezily. "She is *awfully* late. Poor girl, she'll be starving. Ah . . .'' She smiled warmly at the waiter as he bore down on them carrying a silver coffeepot. "Thank you, Michael. Lovely coffee. Coffee, Helen? Edwina? Sugar? Cream?''

"Margot . . ." Alistair tried once again, but Margot stared him down, her eyes like cold green glass.

"Don't fuss, darling. Relax. All's well.''

There was a strained silence. Helen opened her mouth to speak. Edwina leaned forward, her strong brows knitted.

And then the doorbell rang. Loudly, and long.

Brisk footsteps echoed on the marble floor of the vestibule. Locks clicked like pistol shots as the front door was opened. Thunder grumbled. Rain splashed on the veranda. Voices murmured. Then the door was closed and the footfalls tapped toward the dining room doorway accompanied by a strange swishing and shuffling sound.

Margot lifted her chin, turned up the corners of her mouth, and waited. This could be a little awkward. If only Alistair wouldn't get himself in such a stew about these things. Now that he'd tumbled to the fact that she hadn't actually warned the guests of this Verity Birdwood's true purpose in being here, he was going to perform. He was going to say she'd deceived him, as well as them. Well, she would have told him, if she hadn't known he'd be a prig about it. And she hadn't told him an actual lie—just said to leave it to her. So he had, and she had acted as she thought best. It wouldn't have done to risk cancellations by actually telling people beforehand that this researcher was coming. Anyone could see that. Anyway, the ABC had been adamant that it must be business as usual while the researcher was there, and of course Margot had agreed, though naturally, as far as she was concerned, for the actual program it would be different. For lots of reasons she'd want to handpick the guests for that particular fortnight, whatever Alistair said. And what the ABC didn't know wouldn't hurt it.

She deliberately relaxed her shoulders. It would all be all right. Alistair would have to fall in with her. Things had gone too far. He'd have no choice. And the ABC had assured her that the woman they sent would be utterly discreet, and would fit in unobtrusively.

Mrs. Hinder, the housekeeper, appeared at the door in her decent black. She hesitated a moment. Her mouth looked oddly twisted, as if, Margot thought in momentary confusion, she had some sort of tic. Margot blinked once, and then Mrs. Hinder stepped to one side, revealing the figure behind her. It was small, and black, with huge, blinking eyes that stared blindly out through tangled hair. It was streaming with water. Steam rose from its noxious garments in a dank-smelling cloud. Weed and grass clung to its head and arms. It squelched as it moved. It showed its chattering teeth in what might have been a snarl, a smile, or just an involuntary spasm. Margot rose to her feet.

Mrs. Hinder gave a strangled snort and covered her mouth. "Fell in the creek, Miss Bell," she mumbled through her fingers, and snorted again.

"G'day," said Verity Birdwood. "The creature from the Black Lagoon at your service."

3

The bath was hot and fragrant. The towels were soft, thick, and white. The carpet was soft under Birdie's bare toes. The room was warm and faintly perfumed by the flowers and fruit that stood on the low table by the couch. The bed looked big, comfortable, and unbearably inviting.

Birdie blinked shortsightedly around her, considered the bed, resisted the temptation, and sat instead on the edge of the couch, feeling bruised and fragile, and wondering what to do next. She was wrapped in the luxuriously soft bathrobe Mrs. Hinder had left out for her. As far as she knew, she had nothing else to wear. The suitcase she had so foolishly attempted to lug with her across the creek was presumably bobbing along toward the sea with her glasses and handbag at this moment. Perhaps her car was, too. Served it right for balking at a bit of water, she thought bitterly. Death is too good for it. But she felt a pang of regret at the thought of it lying drowned, wheels up, on some muddy shore. Lucky I didn't go the same way, she thought then, and shivered at the memory of her feet slipping from under her, the heart-stopping fall into darkness, the icy, muddy, weed-filled water closing over her head. Stupid! She cursed herself to shut out the remembered fear. How unbelievably stupid to try to short-cut across a creek in the dark, in a strange place. Very clever, Sheena of the Jungle. Now you haven't even got a leopard skin to call your own. And you're blind as a bat, to boot.

There was a discreet tap on the door. Mrs. Hinder came in with a tray covered in silver dishes. "Thought you could do with a little something," she said, putting it down on the table in front of Birdie. "Kitchen's off, but I did the best I could."

"Oh—thank you *very* much, Mrs. Hinder!"

"Feeling better? You look better, I must say." The housekeeper bent over the tray, her lips twitching.

Birdie grimaced as she moved. "I'd want to, wouldn't I?"

"My George has seen to your car. Just pushed it to the side of the road, you know, to keep it out of trouble. And," the housekeeper added gleefully, "here's something that'll cheer you up! George found your bag beside the creek. You must have thrown it up, like, when you fell, and it landed on the bank. Soaked, of course. But look here . . ." With the air of a magician pulling a rabbit out of a hat, she produced a pair of glasses from her pocket. "Lucky you had a spare pair. And not a scratch on them."

"Oh, thank God!" exclaimed Birdie. She almost snatched the glasses from the woman's hand, and put them on. The world came into focus. The relief was inexpressible.

"We'll send your clothes out to the laundry tomorrow morning, love," Mrs. Hinder chatted on comfortably. "In the meantime Miss Bell's organizing some others for you. The dressers come in usually mid-week to advise the ladies, but out in the annex storeroom there's always some nice things—samples they leave, and that. Miss Bell will pick you out some and don't you worry, they'll fit as if you chose them yourself." She pursed her lips. "When it comes to clothes you can't fault madam, I have to admit, whatever could be said about her in other ways. Anyway, I'll bring the duds up presently, so you can go down to the drinks at ten, if you feel inclined—and I'll bring a nightie for you, too, and everything. You'll be all right." She considered Birdie appraisingly. "You look a bit peaky. You eat up, there, and have your tea while it's hot. It'll do you the world of good." She nodded maternally, patted Birdie's shoulder, and left her alone.

Birdie turned to her supper tray, feeling cosseted and comforted. She lifted the silver covers from the dishes, and her mouth started to water. Oh, delicious! Chicken soup, warm brown rolls and little curls of cold butter, scrambled eggs and smoked salmon, blackberry crumble and cream, a big pot of tea. And not an alfalfa sprout in sight. Mrs. Hinder, bless you!

She began to eat ravenously, with a growing sense of well-being. By the time she was halfway through the dessert, she was feeling positively jaunty. Amazing what food, shelter, and warmth will do, she thought. But there was something else that had livened her up. Something the housekeeper had said. Birdie's mind ran idly over the woman's conversation, and then she smiled to herself. Oh yes. "When it comes to clothes you can't fault madam, I have to admit," Mrs. Hinder had said archly, "whatever could be said about her in other ways."

A lot of begged questions there. Apparently if no man was a hero to his valet, no famous beauty-turned-businesswoman was a heroine to her housekeeper either. So there were undercurrents beneath the smooth surface of Deepdene, and the legendary Margot Bell had some chinks of human weakness in that flawless armor of hers. This story might turn out to be more interesting than Birdie had hoped. She might really go back to Sydney with something fascinating. Of course . . . Birdie ate the last spoonful of blackberry crumble thoughtfully and poured another cup of tea . . . it wouldn't be quite the story that idiot producer was expecting. But she'd cross that bridge when she came to it.

She smiled ruefully at the metaphor and picked up her cup. This time, though, she thought, I'll stay out of deep water. Warm and amused she leaned back and relaxed into the pastel embrace of the floral couch, only vaguely aware of the soft, steady fall of the rain outside, and the distant rumble of thunder.

"The schedules are all in the rooms, Alistair?" Margot looked sharply at her partner over the glasses she wore only when in her office, and when no one but William or Alistair, who didn't count, was there to see. They gave her a businesslike look Alistair usually found reassuring and impressive. Just now he found it vastly irritating. The woolly-headed nonsense she'd been talking on her reasons for not alerting this fortnight's guests to the presence among them of a TV researcher had been worrying enough. But her cool insistence that it was her decision to take, and that if he didn't like it he'd just have to lump it, really got on his nerves. She'd really been getting very high-handed lately. Treating him more like an employee than a partner. And now, of all times, that was simply not appropriate. He stared at her sullenly, not answering. She knew very well that he would have seen to all the usual arrangements.

Margot raised her eyebrows and ran a slim gold pen down the length of the paper in her hand. "Where did you put Roberta's sister—what's her name?—oh, Baby Belinda, yes, where did you put her? Oh, I see, 'Cleopatra.' God, Alistair, how appallingly inappropriate."

"Sorry if it offends you, darling. We were short on queens with fringes this fortnight. Anyway, I've got a few ideas for Belinda. She'll be O.K. Now, look—"

"Darling, don't give me a hard time!" Margot pulled off her glasses and blinked at him appealingly. "I'm sorry if I was naughty over the ABC thing, but everyone will settle down, really they will. And I've been having such a frightful time with all these bloody money worries—and with William, sweetie, you know I have." She threw out a hand impulsively and seized Alistair's fingers. "You were so right about William. I should have listened to you. I should always listen to you."

Alistair tried to maintain his uncompromising expression. He knew Margot of old. She could be so charming in this mood. And in one way she meant every word she said. Or thought she did. With Margot, manipulation was now so automatic that it was part of her personality. But he found himself smiling wryly despite himself. He shook his head. "You'll get us into trouble one of these days, you know, Margot, just bulldozing ahead like you do."

She almost purred. "Sweetie, I know. Forgive me." She checked her watch. "Ten to ten. Nearly time for night-night drinks. Thank God! I'm exhausted."

"I'm not surprised," Alistair said dryly. "Burning the candle at both ends, Margot, at your age . . ."

"What *do* you mean?" She bridled, but made no attempt to conceal her delight.

"You know very well. And how you can, I don't know." Alistair almost winced as Margot's naughty little girl look disappeared and forbidding hauteur took its place. He knew this wasn't the time. He knew nothing he said would make any difference. And he'd just made peace with her. He should leave it. But he was irritable and overtired and suddenly, tonight, sick to death of keeping Margot sweet, playing to her moods and controlling his own. Perversely he went on, watching, almost with pleasure, her expression darken. "William was bad enough. But this guy's a complete shocker, Margot. An oversexed, brainless, cold, vain, posing ponce! What are you thinking of?"

"Shut up, Alistair!" Margot was rigid with anger now. "You don't know a thing about it, and it's none of your business anyway!"

"It's my business when you make yourself a laughingstock throwing yourself at some slimy gigolo and neglecting everything else. I'm carrying the whole bloody show and I'm sick of it!"

"Is that so? Well, you know what you can do about it, don't you!"

Alistair's soft chin tightened. "If you mean by that, Margot, that I can get out," he said levelly, "you're forgetting, once again, that you're not my boss, or anything like it. We're partners, remember? This whole thing started with my idea—"

"And my money, Alistair." Margot's lip curled. "My money. I beggared myself for this place. I invested everything—"

"That's a load of shit, Margot, and you know it! You put in *some* of your money, and I put in *all* my money, and we borrowed the rest. Don't start reinventing the past, will you? You kept back plenty and you live bloody high on it, too. God, trips to Europe, clothes by the rack, Hollywood facelifts."

"You bastard!" Margot almost screeched. Her hand flew to her neck, tears starting in her eyes. "You promised never, never to . . ."

Alistair drew breath and abruptly calmed, realizing that he'd gone too far. They stared at each other, breathing fast. "Sorry, love," he mumbled at last. "Sorry. I shouldn't have said that. I lost my temper."

She looked at him steadily. Then, almost unwillingly, she began to smile. "And I didn't, of course, darling." She drew a long breath, and her smile broadened. "Look, let's forget it. Let's just forget it and don't let's fight. I can't stand it, darling, really I can't. We're both under terrific pressure, aren't we? This place . . ."

Alistair shook his head. His anger had evaporated, leaving him sick and empty and very tired, and grateful for her softness, genuine or not. "I can't understand it, Margot! How can things have got so bad so quickly? I mean, we were doing so well."

She grimaced, and gestured at the piles of bills on the desk in front of her. "Everything's gone up. I mean, this place is appalling to heat—and the food! It's costing us a fortune. And to get good staff out here you've just got to pay through the nose. Well, you know all that."

Alistair shrugged. "We'll have to cut back. Maybe Angela could go part-time. I mean, couldn't you do the makeup lessons, for example? Not the facials and manicures, Margot," he went on hastily, "just the makeup tuition."

Margot said nothing.

"After all, I do all the hair work myself," he went on carefully. "And the bookings, and the schedules and the running of the place and so on, and you basically only do the consultations. Monday's your only full day. I was thinking that since times were tight you might do more hands-on stuff. The guests would adore it, darling. And I mean, you'd probably enjoy—"

"Alistair, I do all the books, with only William to help," Margot interrupted stiffly. "I do the business, deal with the bank, and do all the PR as well as the Monday consultations, which are terribly draining, as you well know. By tomorrow night I'll only be fit for a massage and bed. If you want me to run myself into the ground . . ."

"Darling, of course I don't." Alistair felt himself

giving up. Again. "I was just trying to see a way around this thing, that's all." Oh, God, I'm whining now, he thought. Why does it always end like this?

"Alistair, I've told you the way around it. Cut the stay times to a week. Double the money coming in in one fell swoop!" Margot leaned forward, clasping her hands, her eyes wide and eager. "It would be easy, darling. They'll still come in droves, and pay the same, and we only really need a week. The second week is just—well, just . . ." She hesitated.

"Consolidation," said Alistair firmly, "and practice. Without the second week they'll forget everything we've taught them in no time, you know that, Margot. My whole concept depends on making a real difference. It's not just about doing women up and turning them loose none the wiser. We've been through all this. I won't change my mind, Margot. We'll have to find another way."

Margot put on her glasses and looked thoughtfully over them at him before dropping her eyes to the pile of accounts in front of her. "Well," she murmured, "I've said my piece. I've done all I can to convince you. We can't raise the rates for six months, since we've taken bookings for that long, and we can't hold out much longer. We'll just have to borrow some more cash."

"Will they give it to us?"

She shrugged. "The same people won't, but we might go elsewhere." She tapped her perfect teeth with the gold pen. "I've got a few ideas. Contacts help. The personal touch. We'll see."

"Margot . . ." Alistair hesitated. This would be tricky. "What about the rest of your money? Couldn't you see your way clear to investing that?"

She shook her head reproachfully. "Oh, Alistair, how can you ask? I haven't got enough for my own needs as it is, with interest rates so miserably low and inflation like it is. Everything's so terribly expensive, darling."

"You seem to do all right. I don't see why you can't consider it." He knew he sounded sulky. In fact, he hadn't realized till that moment just how much he resented Margot's private income. The money that bought her luxury, travel, and freedom. The money she guarded so jealously, and kept apart. The money that now could mean so much to Deepdene.

Margot's voice sharpened. "It's out of the question, Alistair. Our only hope is for me to go and put our position to someone and pray I still have enough reputation to get them to take the gamble."

"Banks don't gamble."

"No they don't, do they?" She smiled at him lazily and took off her glasses. "They like a sure thing. Like my weekly makeover plan. They'd see the virtue of that, all right. You know, I wouldn't be amazed if they made it a condition of any loan. That would be the only real way of making sure they'd get their money back, wouldn't it?"

"Margot!" Alistair felt himself flushing red with new, sick anger. "Don't play games with me. Don't you dare put any such thing to them, or I'll . . ."

She smiled again, but her eyes were very cold. "You'll what, my sweet? At this stage I don't think you're in a position to threaten me with anything at all. I'm the one with pull. I'm the only one who can get the money. No one knows you from a bar of soap, do they? As far as the world, and the bankers, are concerned, *I'm* Deepdene. You're nobody."

"Margot . . ."

She raised her eyebrows. "If you think, Alistair, that I'm going to see all we've worked for fall apart because you've got some airy-fairy, and I use the term advisedly, notions about making boring little Cinderellas into raving beauties forever, you're more feeble-minded than I thought. If you don't like it, buy me out."

Alistair gripped the edge of the desk with ferocious concentration. He was so angry he was seeing spinning points of light in the air between them. He forced himself to speak calmly. "You know I haven't got the money for that, Margot."

She smiled. "Exactly. And no one would lend it to you either, Alistair, because they know that without me Deepdene's nothing. Nothing. So make up your mind to it. Whatever you think, and whatever you want, things are going to be done my way from now on. And there's nothing you can do about it!"

There was a brisk tap on the door. It clicked open and Mrs. Hinder stood looking at them with undisguised curiosity.

"We're busy, Mrs. Hinder," said Margot repressively. "What is it?"

The woman drew herself up and sniffed slightly, making it clear that she registered the tone and resented it. "The poor little lady who fell in the creek wants a word with you before joining the other guests, Miss Bell."

"She's been properly looked after, I hope, Mrs. Hinder. It's very important to me that she be kept happy. Did you give her the clothes? Has she had dinner?" snapped Margot.

The housekeeper looked down her sharp nose at the back of Alistair's head and sniffed again. "Of course she's been looked after," she said. "I saw to it myself. Poor little mug. You wouldn't let a dog go through it, what she went through. Lucky George found her bag. Blind as a bat she is, you know, without her specs. Now, will I bring her down, or what? I've got to get going, you know. It's two hours past my time as it is. Not fair to keep George waiting round . . ."

"Yes, yes, all *right*, Mrs. Hinder." Margot ran an

impatient hand over her smooth hair. "It's only once in a blue moon we ask you, isn't it?" Her tone sharpened. "And while I think of it, could you please remind your husband to use the back entrance in future, when he comes to pick you up? I have spoken to you about it before, Mrs. Hinder."

Mrs. Hinder pursed her thin lips, but said nothing. Margot nodded slightly with satisfaction and rose from her chair. "I'll slip up and see Verity in her room, I think. 'Juliet,' wasn't it?" She looked at Alistair, raised her eyebrows at his stubbornly impassive face, and went to the door.

"George tells me that new guest house by the river'll be opening in the spring," said Mrs. Hinder conversationally, as she moved aside to let Margot pass.

"Oh yes?" Margot smiled graciously. There—the old biddy was coming around already. If only Alistair would realize that it paid to keep a firm hand on staff. They respected you far more for it in the end. Just because Mrs. Hinder had worked for the previous owners of Deepdene she seemed to think she had special rights in the place. But she soon came to heel when she was reminded who was boss.

"Yeah, saw it in the *Courier*. Big ad for local staff wanted, apparently. Housekeeper, handyman, waiters, maids—all that sort of thing." Mrs. Hinder nodded thoughtfully, gazing into space. "Nice place, that," she mused. "Wouldn't be surprised if they got quite a few takers. What with one thing and another."

Margot's smile wobbled just a fraction. "Oh yes?" she murmured. "Oh. Yes. Well, I'll just . . ." She slid past Mrs. Hinder and went out into the hall. Her footsteps hesitated for a moment and then they heard her high heels clicking as she made quickly for the stairs.

Mrs. Hinder allowed herself a small snort of triumphant laughter, then peered anxiously at Alistair, still sitting rigidly with his back to the door. "You all right?" she barked.

"Oh yes, thanks, Betty." He didn't turn around. His voice was exhausted.

In a moment she was beside him, her rough hand on his shoulder. "Ah, she's a vixen," she whispered. "I heard what she said. Don't let her get you down, love. She's all talk. You're worth a hundred of her and everyone knows it. Everyone round here, anyhow."

"That's the point, Betty." Alistair rubbed his eyes with the back of his hand. "Outsiders don't know me from Adam, just like she says." Thunder rumbled outside and the lights flickered. He glanced impatiently at the curtained window. "Oh, damn this rain. Damn every bloody thing!"

She squeezed his shoulder and primmed her mouth in silent, frustrated sympathy.

Rain pattered on the veranda roof and he lifted his head again to listen. "What does George say?" he said at last.

She knew what he meant. "Creek'll be overflowing by midnight if this keeps up. And it's the same all up the coast, according to the report. They'll let the dam spill soon, George reckons."

"Oh, blast and damn!"

"It's a bugger," she agreed. "Still, you never know, it could clear up."

"It could." Alistair stood up wearily. "Well, Betty, you'd better get on or George'll be after me." He glanced at her anxious face and winked. "Don't worry, I'm fine, Bet, really. Margot doesn't mean half what she says. You know that."

The woman turned to go. "Be that as it may," she said darkly, "that lady'd do better to put a leash on her tongue. She pushes people too far, and one day she'll be sorry for it. That William's a basket case."

"Always was, wasn't he?" Alistair followed her to

the door. "You wouldn't really go for the house-keeper's job at the new place, would you, Betty?" he asked abruptly.

She grimaced. "Nah—s'pose not. Not after all this time. But madam gets you down. You've got to face it, love, she's hell to work for and she gets worse instead of better. You couldn't blame me for thinking about it, or anyone else on the staff."

He sighed. "No, I suppose I couldn't. But I don't know what we'd do without you, Bet."

Her hard face softened. "Oh, you'd get by," she muttered. "But anyhow, you won't have to, will you? I don't like madam, and madam doesn't like me, but I love this old place. Twenty years in November I've been here, you know." She turned away from him. "And you're not so bad," she threw back over her shoulder. "It's not so hard putting up with you."

He smiled for the first time. "Thank *you*, Mrs. Hinder."

She nodded, and left him standing there.

4

Upstairs, oblivious to the existence of any problems other than their own, four women contemplated the fortnight to come.

Behind the door marked "Marie Antoinette," the woman Margot had nicknamed Jolly Josie snuffled and plumped herself down on the softly cushioned couch. She blew her nose and pulled at the neck of her jersey. She felt sticky and uncomfortable. Maybe she had a temperature. No, she was all right, but the pants suit was too hot and heavy. She should have showered and changed after dinner. The air-conditioning in this place kept it like a sauna. No time to do anything now. Drinks at ten, and they'd been asked not to be late. She started to read again the typed sheets that detailed her daily regime. Monday: 7:30 A.M. breakfast; 9 A.M. facial; 10 A.M. hair consultancy with Alistair; free time; 1 P.M. lunch; 2 P.M. makeup consultancy with Margot; free time; 4 P.M. massage; free time; 6 P.M. cocktails; 7 P.M. dinner; free time; 10 P.M. group chat with Margot before bed. Tuesday: massage, makeup lesson, ·free time, lunch, rest period, wardrobe consultancy, manicure, free time, cocktails, dinner, free time, group chat with

Margot before bed . . . By the look of things she was going to have heaps of opportunity to get to know Margot Bell. Heaps of opportunity. Her lips curved into a malicious smile that sat oddly on her plump face. What Glen would think if he knew she was here! Would she ever tell him? Probably not.

She thought of her husband now, already changed into soft blue pajamas and dressing gown, watching TV in the bedroom while the housekeeper engaged for the fortnight dealt with the older children and tidied up. He'd be at peace with the world now, Glen. No anxiety about her—happily holidaying on the Gold Coast, as far as he knew. Tomorrow morning he'd slide the Jag out of the driveway and cruise to work, well fed and pink, smoothly besuited, smelling of Aramis and toothpaste. A big, successful, organized, self-made man with enough years of hard work and worry behind him for the fruits of success still to taste sweet and clear on his tongue with every new day.

Josie threw the sheets of paper onto the coffee table, lay back on the couch, and gazed at her reflection in the gilt-framed mirror hanging over the desk on the wall opposite. Her face, inscrutable, stared back at her. The lighting was soft, the apricot tones of the walls flattering, the reflection kind. But nothing could disguise the effects of years of work, worry, weather, and neglect on the fine, fair skin. Nothing could return the fresh impression of prettiness to the blunt features that had never been more than pleasant, plump, and cheerful, even in youth.

She looked a good ten years older than Glen—maybe fifteen, she thought. People were always surprised when they met her. You could see it in their eyes. Expecting someone as sleek as Glen, she presumed. As sleek as Glen, as sleek as the house they lived in, as sleek as their three children, all at private schools now and mixing with the kids of the rich, learning to say "napkin" instead of "serviette" and be embarrassed by the tinned spaghetti she still sometimes fancied for lunch.

She wasn't really worried by that, by the kids. They loved her, she knew. They knew how she'd worked for them over the years. They remembered her cooking, cleaning, sewing, bathing them, feeding them, tucking them in at night—all on her own, mostly, with Glen working long hours, or so he said, and often not home till late at night. She'd got cranky sometimes. Who wouldn't, with money so short and three active kids to see to? But they'd been happy. And so had she, never regretting a thing. Never doubting for a moment that all her sacrifices were worthwhile. Putting herself last, always, while her youth wore away, in the absolute certainty that she was valued and loved for herself, not for what she looked like or the clothes she wore. Well, so she had—that had been proved to her, absolutely, only six months ago. But not in the way she would have chosen.

And now she was here, under Margot Bell's roof, a valuable, paying guest, about to learn, with Margot's help, how to be beautiful. What an irony. Josie smiled into the mirror and ran her tongue over her teeth thoughtfully. It was a habit she'd developed since she'd had the two front ones capped. She loved the smooth, even feel of them. She glanced at her watch. Nearly time to rejoin the mob for cozy chats before bed. Josie snuffled again. Dreary lot, they were. From what she'd seen so far, there wasn't a single person with a sense of humor in the place. Still, social life wasn't what she was here for, was it?

Glancing at the mirror again, she pushed at her straggly hair with an impatient finger. Then, deciding that nothing more was to be done, she picked up her big, sensible handbag already bulging with the handkerchiefs, eucalyptus drops, wallet, keys, credit cards, letters, jewelry, and other things she felt she needed with her for convenience or safety, packed Alistair's program for her beautification carefully inside, and tucked it securely under her arm. The door to her room, she had noted, could be deadlocked. But presumably the staff had master keys, and you could never be too careful in a place like this. She didn't want anyone poking through her things.

As she turned off the light and shut the door she was aware of a tiny tingle of excitement, a feeling she hadn't experienced in years. She was going to enjoy the next two weeks. Indulge herself thoroughly, for once. No one knew she was here. She'd given a false name and paid with a bank check, so no one need ever know. It gave her an extraordinary sense of freedom—and power. She could do anything. Be anything. She felt the tingle again and grinned to herself, running her tongue over her smooth, white teeth. Time to spread your wings, Josie, she said to herself. Now it's your turn to fly.

"Cleopatra" 's unhappy occupant dabbed feverishly at her smudged lipstick, and plucked at the bodice of her floral dress. It made her look like a pouter pigeon. She was going to be late for the ten o'clock drinks. Why on earth hadn't she got herself organized earlier? Her hands were sweating, her heart was beating fast, and she hardly recognized the wild-eyed face staring back at her from the bathroom mirror. Should she take another pill? What if she had a panic attack in front of everyone? God, they might throw her out! Then what would Roberta say? Her heart thudded sickeningly at the thought.

"Now, I've set it up for you." Roberta's voice, clipped and authoritative, with that very slight Italian accent, echoed in her mind. "I've told Margot you've had trouble with your husband. All right? Could happen to anyone. God, she's ta-taed two husbands herself —she knows men are bastards. So if anyone asks you, just stick to that. No need to go into anything else. Margot won't ask, anyway. You're just my baby sister Belinda to her. She didn't even know I had a sister till a month ago, and she's not going to ask any questions. She's much too interested in herself to worry about what you've been doing, bless her. Understand? . . . For God's sake, are you listening to me?"

Belinda's hand twitched convulsively and the lip-stick smeared again. She almost cried out. This was like those nightmares she always had, about trying to get ready for something and everything going wrong and time running out. But this was real. Real! Roberta's voice began again: "Will you pull yourself together! What's the good of dwelling on it? Just put it out of your mind. Have a bit of spunk! What's the matter with you?" And then the dark look, the Italianate shrug, the resigned sigh. "Oh, why do I try? It's always been the same, hasn't it?"

"Yes," Belinda said aloud, to the mirror. It had always been the same. She could see that now. The therapist had made it so clear. It had been the same with Mother, before she died, with Roberta, with Lisa, her friend at school—with everyone. Others had led, she had followed. Her weakness had fed their strength; their strength had drained her. Her incompetence had encouraged petty tyranny in those she loved. Petty tyranny in those she loved had driven her to incompetence, the only escape route, the only way to prove to them and to herself that she was an individual at all.

When Roberta disappeared overseas she'd been bereft, at first. And then, slowly, she'd started to feel free. She still remembered the first flutterings of the feeling. Free. For the first time in her life. Eighteen, in her own flat, alone. Disappointing and irritating nobody. And then came John. It had been so wonderful at first. But after a few short months, the pattern had started again. The dark looks, the strained patience, the nagging, the silence. In two years he was gone. And this time there was no fluttering feeling. There was no fight left in her. Only the need for shelter, at any price. And what came after—the final loss of control, the darkness . . . well, that was all part of it.

Roberta said it was bullshit. Roberta said everyone's destiny was in their own hands, and there was no getting out of it, and no excuses. No wonder she thought so highly of Margot Bell. They were very alike. They should have been the sisters. Belinda had thought that instantly, as soon as she'd heard Margot's strong, musical voice, felt the cool, confident pressure of her hand, saw the familiar look of veiled impatience and contempt in her eyes. In that moment of meeting, the faint, vague stirrings of hope that had accompanied her preparations for Deepdene had stilled and died. It had always been the same, for her. It always would, while people like Margot and Roberta were running things.

Belinda blinked at her reflection and backed away from it. She was late. She should go down. Right now. Or *should* she have one of her pills first? She plucked nervously at her necklace, pulling the fine string roughly against her skin. It broke, and hundreds of tiny blue beads rained onto the marble floor. She stood and stared, openmouthed, as they fell, bouncing gaily, catching the light as they rolled to every corner of the room. Then she raised her eyes to the mirror again and watched, almost with surprise, the hot tears of humiliation and rage begin to spill at last down her newly powdered cheeks.

Edwina stepped into the hallway in businesslike fashion and turned to make sure her door was securely fastened. She smiled slightly as she contemplated the nameplate adorning the gleaming cedar. "Circe," eh?

How extremely, embarrassingly absurd. But then . . . her smile broadened and she chuckled to herself.

She turned back toward the stairway and was disconcerted to see someone standing motionless at the head of the stairs, watching her. It was that tall, silent woman, Helen. Where had she sprung from? It made her uncomfortable to be caught giggling at nothing like that. Blast these thick carpets. You couldn't hear people moving around at all.

She strode briskly down the gallery, turned to the right, and reached Helen's side. She nodded cheerfully. "Laughing at the name of my room," she remarked. It was boring to have to explain, but it wouldn't do for this stranger to think she was soft in the head at this early stage.

Helen nodded. Her big hands gripped the balustrade.

"It's 'Circe,'" Edwina went on, eyeing Helen's rather crumpled mustard-colored skirt and resisting the temptation to smooth her own impeccable gray. "I was thinking that as most of the men I know are in fact swine, it was probably more appropriate than I'd thought." She smiled again at her little joke, but no answering smile warmed Helen's gaunt, pale face.

Oh, God, Edwina thought. What's up with her? She nodded again, more curtly this time, and began to walk down the broad stairway. To her surprise Helen fell silently into step beside her. Their feet made no sound on the carpeted stairs, and Helen said nothing until they reached the marbled vestibule below. Then she paused, looking toward the lighted sitting room where, presumably, Margot Bell and the other guests were waiting. "Do you believe that journalist's here for the treatment?" she said abruptly.

Edwina frowned. "She'd better be."

"Yes." Helen's face showed no emotion. "I

wouldn't have come if I'd thought there'd be—anyone like that."

"Neither would I. Who would?"

Helen appeared to consider this seriously. "Oh . . . I don't suppose some people would mind," she said at last. "Some people might like it. Being on television; getting their name in the paper. Some people like that sort of thing, don't they? Some people go out looking for it. People who've never had it."

Edwina shrugged. She felt acutely uncomfortable. Behind her she heard a very slight movement. She turned her head quickly and saw William, Margot's dark young secretary, standing rigidly in the doorway of the office on the other side of the vestibule, staring at them. His eyes were in shadow, but the knuckles of his hand shone white as he pressed them against his teeth while, with the other hand, he still gripped the knob of the door as if incapable of further movement. He made no sign of recognition or acknowledgment. Just stood there, dumbly looking.

Edwina felt her scalp prickle. She slowly turned back to the gaunt woman beside her.

Helen had noticed nothing. She was still staring at the half-open door of the sitting room. "My room's called 'Eve,' " she said dully, and the ghost of a smile flickered across her face. "That's got its ironies, too."

Edwina looked at her and could think of no suitable response, since the obvious question was clearly out. She cleared her throat. "Well, let's go in, shall we?" she said finally. And led the way, with relief, into the room.

The scene that greeted them was peaceful. Alistair Swanson was squatting by the fire at the far end of the room, pushing logs into place with a brass poker. On a couch to the right of the door Josie, still encased in her lime green pants suit, and looking very hot and heavy, sat sipping tea beside a small, bespectacled woman with an untamed bush of chestnut brown hair that clashed oddly with her ultra respectable silk shirt and softly tailored trousers. Margot was facing them, beautifully posed in an armchair upholstered in dusty pink. A silver tea and coffee service was set out on a low table in front of her. She smiled warmly at Edwina and Helen, and beckoned.

"Come in, darlings, and make yourself comfortable. You know Josie, but now meet Verity. An orphan of the storm—but safe and dry at last." She laughed. "Now, we're always very casual at this time of night. No staff. Just us. All very casual. Will you have some tea? Coffee? Or a drink?"

"A whisky and water would be nice, thank you," said Edwina, nodding in Birdie's general direction then decisively moving away from Helen and seating herself in an armchair that stood slightly apart from the others.

"Of course. Alistair?"

"Coming right up." Alistair rose to his feet and moved to a side table where crystal decanters and glasses stood waiting.

"Helen? Coffee? Tea?"

"Black tea, please. I don't drink coffee."

Margot nodded graciously and bent over the teapot. Edwina watched Helen hover awkwardly in front of her and then back away to a chair in the corner, fine china cup and saucer clutched in one hand, carefully not looking at the occupants of the couch.

The fire crackled cozily, and shadows flickered on the soft pink walls. An attractive scene—a perfect setting for Margot Bell, composed and beautiful in white, a wing of shining hair swinging forward as she poured hot water into the teapot. But the atmosphere in the room was not restful. There was a brittleness to Margot's voice, a tension in her posture, that was reflected in every other person there—except perhaps the little woman Verity, who seemed quite relaxed and composed. She looked harmless enough, but appearances could be deceptive, and she could still well present a danger, Edwina thought. Margot Bell was not a woman to be trusted, obviously, and her vague assurances regarding this Verity's presence had not engendered confidence.

Alistair brought Edwina's drink and retreated to the fireplace again. He was pale and drawn, and while he attempted to smile at her as he passed over the glass, the stiffness of his lips made the smile look false, and she felt the tremor of his fingers against her own. What on earth was up with him?

"Still raining," Josie remarked, cocking her head. "Looks like it's set in." She sniffed and opened her handbag, releasing a gust of eucalyptus. She extracted a big white handkerchief with which she wiped her already pink nose.

"Oh, *isn't* it a terrible bore," said Margot lightly, looking away. She tapped her fingernails on the teapot and glanced at her watch.

As if on cue there was a clattering scurry outside the door and Belinda sidled into the room, anxiously smiling, murmuring apologies, plucking at the neck of her dress and looking everywhere but at Margot. She looked around desperately for a chair, darted for the couch, and was perched uncomfortably between Josie and Birdie by the time Margot had started speaking.

". . . all very casual, darling." Margot began her patter again, her voice sharp with irritation. "Tea?" She glanced quickly at the door which was swinging open again. This time it was William who slipped into the room, looking strained and glassy-eyed. Perhaps she wasn't expecting to see him, because her lips tightened and a slight frown appeared between her eyebrows as she turned again to the teapot. "Belinda?" she repeated curtly. "Can I offer you some tea? It's been a rather busy day for all of us, hasn't it, so if you could just . . ."

"Oh . . . no . . . or . . . well, if everyone's having one . . ." Belinda's eyes were wide and frightened. Edwina watched Josie cock her head and stick out her bottom lip in mild, amused contempt. The Verity woman by contrast looked interested. "I broke my beads," Belinda gabbled, again plucking at the neck of her dress and looking around. "Sorry to hold things up. If I did. I mean . . ."

Margot held out a brimming cup. "Sugar?" she asked curtly.

"Oh. Yes, please. Three. No! Two."

Margot raised her eyebrows and added two lumps of sugar to the already overfull cup. She waited, hand outstretched. Bitch, thought Edwina.

Crimson in the face, Belinda scrambled awkwardly to her feet and trotted over to take the cup. She began to make her way back to the couch. Her hands were trembling uncontrollably. Tea slopped into the saucer with every step she took. She looked desperate. She's going to spill the lot in a minute, Edwina thought, and found herself leaning forward, dreading the moment.

From his place by the doorway William took a hesitant step forward, his brow wrinkled in concern. But Alistair was there before him. Shooting a cold glance in Margot's direction he took the cup from Belinda's hand and guided her to her seat. "Not that I've made a better job of it," he said lightly, smiling at her and nodding at the teacup, now swimming in a puddle of pale brown tea that nearly filled the saucer. "The cup was much too full, wasn't it? Do you want me to get you another one?"

"No. I . . . I don't really want tea any more. Thank you," she whispered. He smiled at her again and took the cup away, placing it carefully and deliberately on the table in front of Margot, where it sat in the middle of the elegant tea tray incongruously slopped and disreputable.

Margot looked furious. Birdie was riveted. Beside her she could feel Belinda trembling slightly all over, like a leaf in the wind. No wonder. She was vulnerable, defenseless, and obviously disturbed, and exactly the type to bring out the worst in a bully like Margot Bell. Interesting how her vulnerability also brought out the protective instinct in the two men present, despite the fact that Alistair was plainly not interested in women in the conventional sense, and William, for all his dark beauty, was himself a bundle of nerves for some reason and, anyway, hardly the caveman type.

Margot didn't like it. You could see that. Presumably she was used to being the center of male attention herself. And she probably didn't like being cast as the Wicked Witch of the West by implication, however much she acted like it.

5

As if Margot had read Birdie's thoughts she took a little breath, lifted her chin, and smiled ruefully. "It *has* been a very busy day," she said to the company in general, and her eyes made it clear that this was to be taken as a dignified apology for her flash of temper. "And, Verity, how are you feeling, darling? No harm done? We'll look out some more clothes for you tomorrow morning."

As Birdie had already been through all this with Margot earlier in her room, she imagined this was simply an effort to change the tone of the conversation. If so, she was happy to cooperate, this time. She smiled pleasantly. "I'm much better, thank you. I've got a few bruises and I'll probably be a bit stiff tomorrow, but it's marvelous to be warm and dry again. The best thing was Mrs. Hinder's husband finding my bag so I could have my spare glasses. The clothes and things don't matter, but I wouldn't have wanted to spend the next fortnight half-blind. I can't see a thing without my glasses."

"It must have been quite frightening," said Edwina, also apparently willing to contribute to the rehabilitation of the atmosphere. "Are you a strong swimmer, Verity?"

"No I'm not. But it wasn't really a matter of swimming, anyway," Birdie said, again feeling a jolt in her stomach at the thought of the churning, weed-filled water closing over her head. "The stream wasn't so deep—it was just rushing very fast, and full of sticks and branches and things. It was really a case of fighting your way to the edge without getting swept away." Despite herself, she shuddered.

The other women in the room stirred and looked at her as if realizing for the first time that her mishap could have ended in disaster instead of embarrassment and inconvenience.

"You could have drowned," Belinda breathed beside her. "How awful!"

The others murmured sympathetically and Birdie shifted uncomfortably in her seat. Their concentrated attention was getting her down. "Oh well," she said, with a breeziness she was far from feeling, "my guardian angel must have been working overtime."

"If there *were* such things as guardian angels," William droned mournfully from his place by the door. He blinked at Birdie from under his black eyebrows. "But there aren't," he went on thickly, ignoring her startled expression. "You just take your chances against the odds. You were lucky. Some people aren't so lucky. They get snatched away—just ripped away—from life in the middle of everything. Whether they're good or bad, or sad or happy. There's no sense to it." He shook his head. "No sense."

"Darling, you're so *black*," remonstrated Margot, waggling her fingers at him playfully.

William gave her a look of burning reproach. "I'm just saying what's true. I know what I'm talking about. I've seen it. My mother was killed in a car accident when I was only ten. She was lovely—kind and gentle and full of love." His dark eyes filled with tears and he caught his bottom lip between his teeth. Birdie heard Belinda beside her catch her breath in sympathy. She herself felt merely acutely uncomfortable. It was obvious that William had had at least one drink too many. Probably quite a few.

"Ah—well, we . . ." Alistair began, but William was too fast for him.

"I had a feeling, you know," he went on loudly, and now the slur in his voice was unmistakable. "I had a feeling something awful was going to happen. I begged her not to go out that night. 'Stay home with me, Mummy,' I said. I remember it so clearly. But she just laughed. She laughed. And she went out—and died. And I was left alone." He bent his head and pressed his knuckles to his eyes. The effect was extremely melodramatic. Almost absurd, thought Birdie. There was something forced about it, despite the man's obvious sincerity. What was he trying to achieve by all this? He was clearly drunk, but . . .

William looked up again. "My mother's death was an accident," he said, very slowly and deliberately, "but it's not always an accident, or an illness, that kills people before their time. Sometimes someone else takes their life from them. Just like that. For no reason but evil and madness. I—I've seen that, too. I've thought a lot about it. It couldn't be part of a big plan. That couldn't be God, or fate. There's no rhyme or reason to it." He frowned out into the room, his sensitive, fine-boned face transformed by a sort of feverish urgency.

"Oh, God, darling, don't let's get all deep and depressing," trilled Margot, looking at him steadily. "Let's—"

"I know about this." William was insistent. "I know. I've seen it, in my own life. Someone—a mad, evil person—killed someone I loved very much. It was just this time of year, ten years ago . . ." His voice

trembled, and for a horrible moment Birdie thought he
was going to cry. Beside her Belinda quivered. Across
the room Edwina frowned in fascinated concern. Even
the silent Helen had turned an impassive face to watch.

"*William!*" Margot's voice rose slightly, but she
failed to pierce his self-absorption. He stood there beside the door, slim and dark, hands in pockets, shoulders slightly hunched, glaring around the room as if
waiting for the assembled company to argue with him,
or challenge him.

"William," Margot repeated, more gently and per-
suasively this time. "Darling, it was awful. It was an
awful thing. But there's no point in going over it again,
is there? You just make yourself miserable. Let Alistair
make you a drink, now, my sweet, and don't let it get
you down. It was a long time ago. It's all over."

"It's not, you know." William continued his survey of the room, and his eyes were burning. "It's over
for Lois, and for those other poor women. But for me,
and for the other relatives, it won't be over till we're
dead ourselves." He finally turned to her. His shoulders slumped.

"Darling, I know." For a moment Margot's expression softened to a genuine tenderness. He responded,
flicking his silky hair back from his high forehead with
a nervous shake of the head, dropping his eyes to the
rug at his feet. Alistair went across to him, took him by
the arm, and led him to the bar, murmuring earnestly.

Margot turned to the absorbed company. "It's an
awful thing to talk about," she said slowly, lowering
her voice and choosing her words with care. "But so
you'll know . . . William did have a real tragedy in
his life ten years ago. A very dear friend of his was
killed. You may have read about it. She was murdered,
quite brutally and senselessly. With several other
women in Woollahra and Double Bay, in a terrible se-
ries of deaths that—"

"Not the Gray Lady murders?" Birdie sat forward in her seat. "God! Lois. Lois . . ." She clutched at her hair and tugged at it in concentration. "Lois . . . Freeman. Lois Freeman. The fifth victim. Was she William's friend?"

William had spun round from the bar as soon as the name was mentioned. Now he shook off Alistair's kindly restraining hand. "She was my *fiancée!* We were going to be married. You remember!" he whispered fiercely. "You remember her name, at least. More than most people do."

"I remember too," said Josie slowly. "I remember it well. The papers were full of it. Six women, wasn't it? Strangled, and then . . ."

"I found her. Lois," whispered William. He swayed, his hand on his forehead. "She was just lying there, on the grass. Her lovely, soft face was all twisted up, and her clothes pulled around. The buttons of her cardigan were dotted all over the grass like little red buds. And her neck was all red too . . . red . . ."

"Please." Belinda's voice was faint. "Please. It's awful. Don't let's talk about it any more."

"I agree," said Margot crisply. "Let's drop it now, shall we?"

"It was a woman, wasn't it? They caught her in the end," Josie went on relentlessly. "Put her away for life in the loony bin." She glanced at William. "That ought to give you some satisfaction," she added, "though I can't see all this psychology stuff myself. She was sane enough to cover her tracks, wasn't she? She killed six women before they got her. Strangled them with a stocking and then stuck a pair of scissors in their necks. An eye for an eye, a tooth for a tooth, I say. Mad or not, they should've hung her."

"Please stop!" Belinda put her hands over her ears.

"I can't agree with you there, Josie," said Edwina calmly from her armchair. "I remember the case quite well too. The woman—Laurel Moon, her name was— was obviously not responsible at the time she did those murders. She ended up killing her own aunt and then trying to kill herself. That's how she was caught. She had blackouts, heard voices—the lot. A whole battery of psychiatrists testified to the fact she needed help, not punishment."

Josie narrowed her eyes and primmed her mouth. "A lot of people I know'd say—" she began aggressively.

"A lot of people I know would say that life in an asylum for the criminally insane was punishment enough for the worst crime." Helen's flat voice cut through the bombast like a knife through butter, and Josie fell silent. Birdie wondered again at the power that lay behind Helen's shabby facade. Her self-containment was formidable.

Margot took a deep breath. "I don't know about everyone else," she said, pushing the tea things about on the tray with slim fingers that seemed to tremble slightly, "but I'm absolutely pooped. Time for my beauty sleep. So . . ."

"They've let her out, you know." William lurched from his place against the wall and loomed over her, clutching his drink. He met her startled gaze and drank thirstily.

"What?" Margot's cool was finally shaken. She looked wildly up at William, and shook her head in bewilderment. "What?"

"Laurel Moon. The madwoman who killed Lois. They've said she's cured and let her out. She's walking round free as a bird. Free as a bird. D'you know that? Been out for six months. I heard earlier tonight. I tried to tell you about it. But you wouldn't listen, would you, Margot? You never listen anymore. Not like before. Then you listened to everything. Now you won't listen to anything. Margot . . ."

He stretched out a trembling hand. Margot stood up abruptly, rattling the tea tray as her knees bumped the table. "I must get some sleep," she said rapidly, and made for the door, leaving William staring helplessly after her. At the doorway she turned. "Good night, all," she said, and flashed a strained smile around the room. "See you all in the morning. Big day tomorrow. This time tomorrow night you won't know yourselves. Alistair, you'll look after . . . everything . . . won't you, darling?" She disappeared with a wave, and they heard her shoes tapping rapidly on the marble as she made for the stairs.

As soon as she had gone, William seemed to crumple. He gestured feebly around the room. "I'm sorry to . . . to have brought all this up," he said. "I'm sorry. It's just that it was such a shock. An old friend of Lois's and mine rang up and told me. And it brought it all back, you see? It knocked me around. I've probably"—he glanced at the almost-empty glass in his hand —"probably had a bit too much to drink. Sorry. I . . . I wasn't well for quite a while after Lois was killed. I've never really got over it." His lips trembled.

Without hesitation little Belinda stood up and went toward him. She put her hand on his arm. "Of course you haven't," she murmured. "Of course. And of course we understand how upset you must be. You *should* talk about it, you know. It helps so much to talk about things that worry you. Doesn't it, Verity?"

Birdie, astonished at being so appealed to, nodded.

"So, you come with me now and we'll find the kitchen and I'll make you a nice cup of tea," Belinda continued calmly. "Then you can get off to bed, and you'll feel much better. O.K.?"

William looked exhausted. He nodded dumbly and let her lead him away. They made an incongruous pair, he so tall and slim and Byronically good-looking, Belinda like a little floral dumpling by his side. But in another way, Birdie thought, they were the only natural partners in all the company—both lonely, unhappy, and both obviously tender-hearted in the face of another's distress.

"Well," said Josie archly once the door had closed behind them. "Our little Belinda's not wasting any time, is she?"

The others looked at her in silence. She ran her tongue over her smooth, white teeth and her eyes shifted from one face to another. "Well," she said defiantly, at last. "Sorry I spoke!"

Edwina rose from her chair. "I think I'll go to bed now," she said to Alistair. He nodded and smiled absentmindedly.

Birdie stood up too. Obviously the drama was over for tonight. Suddenly she became aware of how tired she was. The thought of that big, soft bed upstairs was very tempting. She said good night and left the room with Edwina. They crossed the vestibule to the stairway together.

"Well, the fun starts tomorrow," she said to break the silence as they started to climb the stairs.

Edwina smiled rather stiffly and didn't reply. At the head of the stairs she paused. "I go this way," she said, pointing to the left.

"And I go the other," said Birdie. " 'Juliet,' would you believe. Well, see you in the morning, Edwina."

The tall woman hesitated, then seemed to make a decision. "I heard you were a journalist, Verity," she said carefully. "I was rather taken aback by that. My privacy is important to me. I hope that's understood." She looked down at Birdie, unsmiling.

"Of course it's understood, Edwina." Birdie attempted to meet her companion's eyes without actually having to bend backward. There were times when being short put you at a tremendous disadvantage, she thought resentfully. She attempted to look sincere. "I'm here to be done over, just like everyone else. And I don't gossip." So that was why the woman was being so snippy with her. No harm in reassuring her. There'd be no reason whatever to mention her in research—or any individual guest, come to that. That was why Birdie had at last agreed to Margot Bell's demand that she didn't admit to anyone her real purpose in coming here. The trouble was that now she would have to go through the ludicrous makeover process herself, to establish her bona fides. She knew that for the purposes of the story it was just as well, but she dreaded the very idea of people talking at her about the way she looked. It made her feel panicky. As it was, in these elegant, borrowed clothes, she felt strange and uncomfortable, as if she wasn't quite herself.

"Actually, I'm dreading the whole thing," she said abruptly, wondering instantly why on earth she was confiding in a complete stranger.

Edwina looked at her gravely for a moment, and then her face broke into a frank and very charming smile. "So am I," she said. "Oh, God, so am I."

They both began to laugh, and Birdie felt her spirits rise. Here, at least, was someone she could talk to.

They heard footsteps and voices below and looked down to the vestibule. Alistair, Helen, and Josie were moving toward the stairs. As Birdie and her companion watched, Belinda and William appeared from the back of the house and joined the others. Without a word Birdie and Edwina signaled their good nights and turned to go. Neither had any wish to participate in more dramas tonight.

But once safely back in "Juliet," hearing at first the vague sounds of voices saying good night, the shutting of doors, and finally only soft, warm silence within and the steady falling of the rain without, Birdie began to feel restless. She couldn't bring herself to take off her clothes and put on the cream silk pajamas laid out on her bed. And the bed itself had ceased to look inviting. The overwhelming fatigue she'd felt earlier had completely disappeared. She had nothing to read but the glossy fashion magazines provided by the establishment, presumably to inspire the guests; nothing to write on but the few sheets of thick, plain, pale pink stationery that lay beside the bed. But she had lots to think about, and it was only ten-thirty—an absurd hour, in her view, to retire to bed.

She could watch an old movie on TV. She considered the discreetly concealed set opposite the couch carefully, then dismissed the idea. Why watch TV when there were other things she could be doing? After all, she was supposed to be researching this place. Who said she had to do it in daylight?

She went over to the window and drew back the curtains. Her room was at the front of the house, on the left-hand side facing out. It must be, then, just about directly above Margot's office. She tugged at the windows ineffectually for a minute before realizing that they were sealed shut. It was so the air-conditioning would work effectively, she supposed, but the room suddenly seemed claustrophobic now that there was no possibility of leaning out and breathing the fresh air.

It was dark and starless outside. The rain had eased a little, but still fell softly and steadily like a fine veil on the other side of the fixed glass. The tree silhouettes she could see against the slightly paler sky were still. The wind had dropped, then. The faint rushing sound she could hear must be the creek, swollen, churning, and muddy, maybe even now spilling over its banks and seeping out onto the sodden ground on either side. She winced, and decided. Enough was enough. She'd go downstairs and have a look around. She had to get out of here.

6

Birdie closed her door quietly behind her and looked around the gallery. No one was to be seen, and all the doors were shut tight. She looked over the railing to the vestibule below. Again, no one about. But there was a light burning down there somewhere, and she thought she could hear the faint sound of voices. Maybe from the office. She began to wander the long way round the gallery to the head of the stairs.

The room next to hers, over the front area of the vestibule, was marked "Cleopatra." She noticed with mild amusement the little sprinkling of tiny blue beads that lay on the carpet before the door. Elementary, my dear Watson. This was poor Belinda's room. All was quiet within. Maybe Belinda had treated herself to a sleeping pill. Or maybe her good deed with William had helped settle her nerves.

Further on, occupying the other front corner, was "Circe," Edwina's retreat. Faint music drifted through the heavy door. Edwina, at least, had been in the mood for an old movie.

Next to Edwina's room, rounding to the back section of the gallery, was "Marie Antoinette." Josie.

"Wasn't she the French piece who told the mob to eat cake, or something?" she'd chortled, as she and Birdie drank tea with Margot in the sitting room. "Suits me, eh, Verity? I've got through a bit of cake in my time." Her doughy face grimaced with laughter as she played the jolly fat lady. But her eyes, turned on Margot's barely concealed disdain, did not laugh. Water was running in Josie's room. Sounded like she was having a bath, no doubt reeking of eucalyptus oil. She'd told Birdie there was nothing like eucalyptus oil for a cold. Her handkerchiefs were all sprinkled with it. Hadn't done much for her so far, Birdie thought. Except to make her smell like a koala.

So the suite corresponding to Josie's on the other side, the one called "Eve" must be the strange Helen's. Birdie had Helen on one side, and Belinda on the other. Very jolly.

There was no room opposite the head of the stairs. Rather, there was a little sitting area, a huge stained-glass window that looked out over the back of the house, and, in one corner, a door discreetly labeled "Staff Only." Birdie opened it softly. Beyond the door was a staircase leading up to the top floor, where Margot and Alistair had their apartments, and down, presumably to the staff quarters and therapy rooms in the extension at the back of the house proper. Birdie peered curiously up the stairs, but they turned, and she could see nothing but a soft light shining from above. Downstairs there was only darkness. She closed the door again. Sadly, she could hardly find an excuse for exploring that way.

As she was turning to go Birdie caught sight of a pale pink envelope lying on the corner table beside one of the armchairs in the sitting area. She moved closer and peered at it. It was Deepdene stationery, like the stuff in her room. On the outside of the envelope was written, in scrawled capitals, DEEPDENE—URGENT. Nothing else.

Birdie picked up the envelope. It was sealed, and it felt as though there was a single sheet of paper inside it. What on earth was it? Who did it belong to? It looked a bit like a prop in a child's game of Spy. She shrugged and stuffed it in her pocket. She'd ask someone about it tomorrow.

As she walked downstairs, resisting the urge to tiptoe, reminding herself that she had every right to do what she was doing, Birdie heard the rumble of thunder. More stormy weather. This was getting ridiculous.

The chandelier over the gallery had been extinguished. The main lights had also been turned off in the vestibule, and the corners were in shadow, but two lamps made pools of soft, golden light on either side of the staircase. Margot's office was dark, and she could no longer hear the murmur of voices she had noticed on her way down. Whoever it was must have given up and gone to bed.

Next door to the office, toward the back of the house, was another room she hadn't yet seen. Perhaps this was the "Library and Music Room" described in the brochure. Well, only one way to find out. Birdie turned the knob, stepped into the dark room, turned on the light, and then jumped violently. The room was inhabited. Alistair and William sat there on either side of a dying fire, looking round at her in amazement, their mouths open.

Birdie gasped and felt herself stagger stupidly. She'd been taken completely by surprise. "Oh—sorry," she heard herself squeak. "Didn't know anyone was here. I . . . er . . . thought I might get a book to read. Mine all went—in the creek." Listen to you making excuses, she thought contemptuously to herself. Didn't you decide you didn't *need* an excuse to have a poke around?

Alistair stood up and swept a hand around. "Help yourself, Verity. You want a book, you've come to the right place."

Birdie looked, and was impressed. Books did indeed line the room, floor to ceiling.

"They came with the house," Alistair explained. "Most of them, anyway. This was a guest house before we came, and the owners bought up quite a few whole collections from deceased estates over the years. There's a lot of junk, but most people can find something they're interested in here. There's a whole set of Dickens. There's Agatha Christies by the dozen. And Barbara Cartland, and Raymond Chandler and *Biggles!* And there's D. H. Lawrence and *War and Peace*, *Portnoy's Complaint*, Sylvia Plath and *Lolita*, a book on basket-weaving—and three different versions of the Bible. Oh, we cater for all tastes here."

"Great!" said Birdie sincerely. She made for one of the shelves, and then hesitated. "I'm not disturbing you?"

"Oh no," said Alistair, apparently just as sincerely. Birdie got the impression that the tête-à-tête with William had been rather wearing.

William himself sat motionless in his armchair, making no effort to join the conversation or even disguise his obvious continuing distress. Belinda's therapeutic cup of tea had not, apparently, done its work. Alistair had been trying brandy, by the look of the two glasses on the table between their chairs, but in Birdie's opinion William had had more than enough alcohol, tea, and sympathy for one night.

She remembered the envelope she had found, and pulled it from her pocket. "I found this on the floor upstairs," she said, handing it over to Alistair. "Someone must have dropped it."

"How odd." Alistair turned the envelope over in

his pale, slightly freckled hands. "Looks like a kid's writing. I wonder whose it is?"

"You could open it," Birdie prompted. "It's addressed to Deepdene. It's on your notepaper. And it is marked urgent."

"Yes." Alistair looked doubtfully at the envelope for a moment and then shrugged. "Why not?" He slipped a finger under the flap of the envelope and tore it open, pulling out a single, folded sheet of pink paper. His eyes flicked over it, and his mouth opened slightly. "God, what . . . ?"

"Let me see." Birdie held out her hand and he passed the paper over to her automatically, realizing a little too late that this mightn't be a good idea.

Two lines of straggling capitals trailed across the page.

" 'You think I don't know you,' " Birdie read aloud. " 'You think you're safe. But nowhere's safe from me.' "

"What?" William struggled to his feet, his face white. He snatched the note from Birdie's hand and read it. He rounded on Alistair, his eyes wild, his forehead and top lip gleaming with sweat. "I told you!" he shrieked. "I told you. It's her! I knew it! Oh, God!" He began to shake uncontrollably.

Birdie tore her eyes away from him and looked blankly at Alistair. "What's he talking about?"

William gasped, and started to laugh hysterically. "That's what they all say," he choked. "What's William on about? Stupid William. Silly William. He had a nervous breakdown, you know. He's been drinking. He's upset. Don't listen to him. Well, now you know. Now you'll find out. She's here. Laurel Moon. She's here!"

Alistair licked his lips and briefly pressed his fingers to his eyes. When he took them away his face was calm. He took William's arm. "Will, this note could mean anything at all, mate," he said firmly. "It says nothing about Laurel Moon, or whatever her name is. Now, think about it. It's probably just a joke. Look, it's silly." He crumpled the note and threw it into the fireplace. William gave a shuddering sigh and watched with glazed eyes as the paper caught fire, flared up, and became a wafer of gray ash in a moment. "There. It's gone," said Alistair. "Now, stop thinking about all this stuff, William. Go to your room, take a sleeping pill, if you want to, and get some sleep. And don't try to talk to Margot again. She'll go off the deep end if you do. Leave it to me. Right?"

William nodded dumbly. He looked exhausted.

"O.K.," said Alistair, still in that calm, firm voice he seemed to have summoned up from somewhere for this emergency. "You don't tell Margot about this letter; you don't tell anyone. I don't want you scaring the guests—*any* of them, William—with this. Is that understood?" He waited for a second nod, then nodded himself with satisfaction. "Off you go, then. I have to have a few words with Verity. Or do you want me to come with you?"

William shook his head. "I'll be all right," he said dully. He turned and trailed out of the room, shutting the door behind him.

Alistair breathed a sigh of relief, and slumped down into his chair. "Oh, Lordy!" he groaned. He leaned back and closed his eyes.

Birdie sat down in the chair William had vacated and waited patiently. After a few moments Alistair's fair eyelashes fluttered, his eyes opened, and he made a rueful face at her. "You've had a great introduction to Deepdene, Verity."

"Yeah," said Birdie cheerfully. "Half drowned, lost all my clothes, found an anonymous threatening letter, seen someone go half off his head . . ."

"It's not always like this," Alistair began earnestly, and then laughed. His laugh was a little hysterical but very infectious, and Birdie herself could see the humor of the situation. She leaned forward.

"Look," she said. "Forget the ABC for a minute. I'm not going to rush back to Sydney with notebooks full of this stuff, if that's what you're afraid of. It's not what I'm here for. But I'm bloody curious, all the same. You can understand that, can't you? What gives with William? Why does he say Laurel Moon is here? Is he crazy?"

"No. He's a good bloke, Will. Very sincere sort of bloke. Works like a dog. But he always was a bit neurotic. You know . . . nervy and a bit paranoid. God, you can understand it. He came home from work one night late and found his fiancée's body, you know, after that madwoman had finished with her. Strangled, her clothes all torn and pulled around, with a pair of sewing scissors stuck into her neck. Just lying there under the clothesline in the dark. Been there for hours. You can imagine. Flies and ants—and birds . . . ugh!" Alistair shivered and rubbed his eyes again. He looked drained and tired, and his pleasant, slightly chubby face was shadowed with lines of strain. "The thing is, he's been . . . um . . . having a difficult time lately anyway, and apparently today—this evening, actually, just before drinks at six—this woman rang—Joyce, a friend of his fiancée who he's kept in touch with over the years. According to William, she said she'd just met, quite by chance, at an afternoon tea party, an old schoolfriend who now works for the Corrective Services department. This friend told her that Laurel Moon had been pronounced cured and quietly released six months ago."

"It's been ten years," said Birdie thoughtfully. "I guess in that time . . ."

"Oh, yeah. The poor woman was obviously right out of it, and if she's better now, or they've got her on some kind of medication that keeps her stable, well and good. But of course this Joyce was very fond of Lois, William's fiancée, and she doesn't see it like that at all. And neither does William."

"I guess not. But I still don't see . . ."

"No. I haven't got to the bizarre part yet. Joyce didn't just ring to tell William about the release. She rang in a panic. Her friend apparently went on to moan and groan about the unfairness of life in general because while she herself had to struggle and work her fingers to the bone to make ends meet, Laurel Moon was being looked after well and truly. The family has money, apparently, and to help her get herself back to some sort of normal life, they decided—guess what?"

"To send her to Deepdene." Birdie had been waiting for this. No wonder William was beside himself. But . . . she frowned at Alistair. "But you'd know. I mean . . ."

Alistair shook his head. "We wouldn't know," he said decisively. "Discretion's everything here. Guests pay up front, often with a bank check. They can use any name they like, can't they? That's not our business. William knows that. They send a photograph with their application, but he never saw Laurel Moon, even a picture of her, so he doesn't know what she looks like. And I certainly don't."

"So you could really have her booked to come here, and you'd never know," said Birdie slowly. "I don't think I've ever seen a picture of her anywhere either. They kept her right under wraps, didn't they? She could be here now. One of us. That's what William's thinking, isn't it? Because of that note. He thinks Laurel Moon wrote it. But why would she?" She was almost talking to herself now, but Alistair nodded vigorously.

"That's the point. It's crazy. Why would she draw attention to herself? And as I said to William before you came in, if the poor woman's come here, she's come for help. She's cured. The experts have said so. William mightn't like it, but he'll just have to be professional and get on with his job. No more of that terrible stuff earlier. He deliberately brought it all up, you know, to try to surprise her into identifying herself. Well, all he did was get himself into a state and upset everyone else!"

Birdie thought of William's white, sweating face as he read the note. "He—William—didn't just look upset, though, in here before. He seemed terrified. Why terrified?"

"Oh . . ." Alistair raised his hand helplessly, and let it drop again. "He—well, all those interviews and things he did after Lois was killed. He tried to organize a vigilante squad to hunt the killer down, said whoever it was should be killed in the same way . . . the sort of thing people say when they're in shock. He had a nervous breakdown soon after. His picture was plastered over every paper in town, and he was on TV, too. He was the only relative to talk, and he made a fantastic fuss. Don't you remember?"

Dimly Birdie did remember. She usually shied away from seeing or reading interviews with grief-stricken, shocked people. They were too harrowing, and served no useful purpose. But casting her mind back to the coverage of Lois Freeman's murder, she did now recall a thin, dark tragic young face, eyes black holes in a white face. So that had been William.

"William has got it into his head that Laurel Moon would have seen his picture, and heard what he had to say, and have lived with it all the time she was locked up. And he thinks she's after—revenge." Alistair almost blushed. "I know it sounds terribly melodramatic," he said apologetically, "but William's like that —especially if he's had a few drinks."

"She was caught red-handed, though," said Birdie. "She was actually *seen*. And she confessed, for God's sake. William's carry-on had nothing to do with her being locked up."

"Exactly what I said to William," Alistair sighed. "I said it in twenty different positions. But he won't be told. He thinks if she's coming here, she's coming for him. And when you brought in that note—oh, that was all we needed! Now he's convinced that Laurel Moon is not only on the premises, but out to get him."

Birdie looked into the fireplace, where the pale pink note had crumbled into a heap of gray ash amid the broken coals. "I wish you hadn't burned it," she said, pointing. She frowned, trying to recall the exact words. When she did, a shiver ran down her back. *You think I don't know you*, the note had read. *You think you're safe. But nowhere's safe from me.* She repeated the words to Alistair. "You can see where he'd be a bit concerned," she said lightly.

"It's rubbish!" snapped Alistair. "It must be! It wasn't addressed directly to William, anyway. I refuse to believe . . ." His voice trailed off.

"Then where did the note come from?" Birdie persisted. "Who did write it? And why? And look, even if Laurel Moon didn't write the note . . . she could still be here. And if she is here, who is she?"

At about two in the morning, the rain started again in earnest.

Mrs. Hinder, warm in her own bed five kilometers from Deepdene, heard it and nudged her unconscious spouse. "Hear that, George?" she said. "We're for it now." George grunted patiently and patted her flannelette-encased thigh before heaving himself over to face the silent wall. "We're for it now," Mrs. Hinder repeated to herself sturdily. "Ah, well."

The rain beat steadily on the sodden paddocks, through the bare branches of the poplar forests, into the swollen creek. It beat on the Deepdene roof, and

sheeted against its tightly sealed windows. Birdie
heard it, grumbled to herself, and turned over, pulling
the blanket over her head. Alistair, dozing fitfully,
heard it and cursed. Margot didn't hear it. She was by
then deep in drugged sleep, her face still shimmering
with the high-tech miracle cream she never failed to
apply, no matter what upsets or delights had marked
the hours before bedtime.

In the staff annex at the back of the house the rain
gurgled and sang in the downpipes, splattered heavily
from the overflowing gutters onto the paving below.
Angela slept on undisturbed, composed and rosy in her
narrow white bed. Conrad, in the room next door, lay
frowning with his hands behind his head, listening.
And on the other side William tossed in the grip of a
nightmare in which black water rose relentlessly
around his pinioned body, lapping his chin, soon to
engulf him.

7

Birdie was drowning. Water rushed over her head, pressing her down. She struggled violently to get to the surface, but she could see it only vaguely, wavering above her head. She'd lost her glasses. The water pressed her down. She couldn't breathe. Then she realized the water was warm, and pink. It shouldn't be warm. Shouldn't be pink. It wasn't water. She wasn't drowning. She was suffocating! She was blindly suffocating, her arms pinned to her sides, soft encasing fabric binding her. Vaguely smiling faces floated above her through a haze of pink transparent silk. Terrified, she tried to call out, to make them hear, but could only wheeze faintly. Her throat ached with the effort. Her heart was pounding. Then faintly, in the distance, she heard the chimes. Soft and sweet. Was this death? The chimes grew louder . . .

Birdie opened her eyes and lay panting, drenched in sweat, the bedclothes tangled around her. The alarm clock beside the bed went on chiming, softly, sweetly, but very insistently. She rolled over, grabbed her glasses from the side table, and slammed at the clock viciously till it stopped. Then she fell back, exhausted.

The dream was still vivid in her mind and she tossed her head on the pillow to try to dispel the horrible feeling it had given her. The claustrophobia, the help-lessness . . . ugh!

She struggled painfully from the bedclothes that bound her. She ached in every muscle. The bangs, bruises, and strains of her adventure in the creek had left her body feeling as though it had been run over by a truck. Shower, dress, go downstairs to breakfast. Breakfast served seven-thirty to nine. So she had an accident in the creek and lost all her stuff and got a few bumps and bruises. So it was raining. Still raining. So what? So this place gave her the heebies. So—and she uncompromisingly faced the fact that this was at the heart of it—so she didn't want anyone messing her around, taking her over, making her into some pa-thetic, painted copy of the conventional idea of beauti-ful. Well, so what? That was no reason to go to pieces. This was all just routine. Just a job, like any other job. Shower, dress, go downstairs to breakfast. Tour of the house at nine. Two hours of free time from ten. First appointment, facial with Angela at midday.

She slowly stripped off the borrowed silk pajamas and threw them on the bed. Then she hobbled, stiff and naked but at least her own woman, into the bathroom.

Breakfast was a nervy, awkward affair. Alistair and Edwina ate their fruit, drank their coffee, and disap-peared just before eight to begin their hair consultation, leaving an obviously crabby Margot Bell—who had al-ready crossed swords with both Mrs. Hinder and one of the maids, to everyone else's embarrassment—tête-à-tête with the mute Helen. Margot's solution to this was to pick silently at a piece of dry rye toast, making no attempt to speak to her companion or, indeed, any-one else.

At the other end of the table Belinda nibbled at a

croissant and chatted nonstop to William, Josie, Birdie, and anyone who would listen. Her nervousness seemed, if anything, to have worsened overnight, as had Josie's cold, which made them both less than ideal breakfast companions.

But fortunately none of them seemed to want to linger. Margot left first, her face still like thunder. Then Josie and William went off to the office to ring Josie's children before they went to school and Helen and Belinda drifted off soon after. By eight-thirty Birdie was alone at the table. Heartily relieved, she settled back in her chair, poured herself another cup of coffee, and ate the last croissant, spreading honey on it with a lavish hand in the secure knowledge that no one was there to notice.

At nine, Margot Bell took her on the promised tour of the establishment. It wasn't a particularly pleasant experience. She was obviously still in a foul mood, and trying most unsuccessfully to hide it. She smiled constantly, with cold, snapping eyes belying the show of teeth and the upturned lips. She talked continually, with a hard edge to the practiced, melodious voice.

". . . a hundred years old," she was saying now, as they walked toward the back of the house. "Very ramshackle when we came, you can imagine. And things to be mended all the time. You know how old houses are. It all costs a fortune!" She sighed and flicked an exquisitely cared-for hand to the left. Rubies set in thick gold flashed on her fingers. And what do you cost? thought Birdie. She followed Margot through a dark storeroom and into the kitchen. Betty Hinder sat there at a big pine table with her shoes off, having a cup of tea. She looked surprised to see them. Birdie grinned at her in a friendly way.

"Having a tea-break already, Mrs. Hinder," said Margot coldly and turned away from her. "As you see," she went on to Birdie in a high, artificial voice, "very modern, but still quite homey. I think that's very important. The live-in staff, except for my secretary William of course, eat here most of the time, and make their own little snacks here and so on. I don't allow food in the bedrooms. And occasionally a guest might find her way here too. So I styled it to suit."

"It's nice, isn't it, Mrs. Hinder?" said Birdie, not wanting to join Margot in ignoring the housekeeper.

"Very nice," agreed Mrs. Hinder firmly. "Mr. Alistair has very good taste. And he had the sense to talk to me about it before he went ahead. So it works well."

A spot of natural red appeared on each of Margot's impeccable cheekbones. She looked furious, but wisely said nothing.

"How many staff do you have here then, Margot? How many live in?" Birdie thought it prudent to move the subject on from interior decoration at this point.

"Well, other than Alistair and I, who have our apartments on the top floor of the house, only William, Angela the beautician, and Conrad the masseur live in. You met William, of course, at breakfast. Oh—yes, and last night." She hesitated, compressed her lips slightly.

"He was a bit upset," Birdie remarked, watching her. It had occurred to her that Margot's bad temper this morning could easily be connected to William and his obsession with Laurel Moon. If he had disobeyed Alistair and told Margot about the anonymous letter, for example . . . "Is he all right this morning?"

"I haven't had an opportunity to speak to him yet. Poor old William!" Margot Bell spoke dismissively, and there was no extra cloud on her brow as she spoke. William had decided to be discreet, then.

"That William's a basket case if you ask me," Betty Hinder piped up maliciously. "And he's drinking too much."

"William has had a very sad life, Mrs. Hinder," retorted Margot. "He lost—"

"Well I lost my mum at sixteen, and buried a child myself." Betty Hinder gripped her teacup, her eyes glittering. "And I don't go moaning and whinging around the place looking for sympathy, do I? That Lois woman was twice his age, anyhow. What was he doing getting engaged to someone old enough to be his mother?"

"He wasn't really engaged to her, Mrs. Hinder," snapped Margot. "They were just close friends. William overdramatizes. He admitted to me that he'd asked her to marry him but obviously she was a sensible woman because she just treated it as a joke between them."

"Oh well. Some old biddies have more sense than others, I s'pose." A wicked smile crossed Mrs. Hinder's face. "Anyhow, he's kept it up, hasn't he? He likes them old, I reckon, because they remind him of his mum."

Margot turned away. The two spots of bright color burned on her cheekbones. She met Birdie's fascinated eyes and spoke directly to her in a high, tight voice. "William, Conrad, and Angela are the really vital members of the team. Their rooms are in the staff quarters in the annex. I'll show you that in a minute. Mrs. Hinder lives nearby. The chef comes in for lunch and dinner only. Then there is Michael the waiter, two maids, who also come in by the day . . ."

"One now," mumbled Betty Hinder, shoulders hunched over her cup. "Worse luck. Don't know how I'm supposed to cope. Or how we'll get a replacement." She looked directly at Birdie. "One of the maids —pretty little thing, efficient too, for once—got her marching orders this morning."

"Oh—yes, I gathered that. Why?" Birdie couldn't think of anything else to say.

"She was impertinent!" snapped Margot. "I really don't think it's relevant to our discussion though, do you, Verity?" She strode to the door. "Thank you, Mrs. Hinder," she said icily, without turning around.

Betty Hinder gave Birdie a broad wink. Then she settled back, smiling, and poured herself another cup of tea.

"The annex, of course, is all new. We demolished the old guest house additions to put it in. They were very rubbishy, as you can imagine." Cheeks still flushed from the brush with her housekeeper, Margot pushed open a door at the back of the house to reveal a modern, white-painted, brightly lit space furnished with green-covered couches and armchairs more casual in appearance than those in the front rooms. Double glass doors at the far end led into what was obviously the pool and recreation areas, and a narrow corridor ran off to one side. Margot strode toward it. "The treatment room corridor. If you'll come this way . . ."

There wasn't much to see. Sealed, streaming windows on the left, firmly shut doors on the right, soft beige carpet underfoot.

"You'll see all these rooms as your treatment progresses today," Margot remarked ominously. "Hair, massage, beauty therapy, makeup . . . storeroom at the end here."

Birdie regarded the closed doors curiously. No sound met her ears from any of them. She wondered how Edwina was getting on with Alistair, and Josie with Angela. She wouldn't like to be working close to Josie today. Having breakfast with her was bad enough. The corridor turned to the left to make an L-shape, and Margot indicated four more doors, again firmly closed. "Staff bedrooms here, three occupied, at present, and one spare. Very occasionally Mrs. Hinder or one of the others decides to stay over, if the weather's a problem."

"Like now," Birdie remarked conversationally,

looking out to the sodden courtyard and garden beyond the windows.

Margot looked and shrugged. "It's such a bore!" She turned away impatiently. "I'll show you the pool and so on on the way back," she said. "But first I must get you some more garments to tide you over until your own things come back from the laundry. They're so appallingly slow sometimes."

"Oh, no, look, really . . ." Birdie began. But Margot was already unlocking the storeroom door.

"You can hardly wear *those* things again today, can you, darling?" she drawled. "And you'll want to look your best for tonight. Now . . ." She switched on the light and Birdie blinked, her thoughts immediately flying to her friend Kate. The storeroom door faced the main corridor, but the corner room inside was far bigger than Birdie had expected, because it borrowed space from both legs of the L. It was an Aladdin's cave of goodies that would have made Kate drool. There were boxes of silk underwear, fine tights in every conceivable shade, scarves and shawls, racks of shirts, tops, trousers and dresses, coats, skirts and jackets, lotions, potions, creams, hair products—and at the business end of the scale, boxes of tissues, cottonwool balls, eye pads, disposable latex gloves, hair removal creams and waxes, huge bottles of cleaning fluid and bundles of pale pink towels and rather worn-looking protective gowns, strings neatly tied. The whole effect was very disturbing, as far as Birdie was concerned. The paraphernalia of professional beauty care—ghastly in its reverberations of gross overintimacy with other people's bodies mixed with slick surface glamour.

Margot began flicking through the clothes racks, pulling out garments apparently at random and throwing them over her arm. Occasionally she turned and gave Birdie a sharp, appraising look, then went back to her task without comment. Birdie watched her in alarm. Surely the woman didn't expect her to try them on now?

But to her relief Margot seemed to have no such thought. She finished what she was doing at the racks, seized some underwear and tights from boxes marked "petite," and glanced at her watch. "We have to fly, darling," she said. "I'll have these taken to your room and you can see what you fancy. Then you can change before your treatments begin. All right?" Without waiting for an answer she led the way from the room and began walking quickly back up the corridor with Birdie almost trotting beside her, painfully aware of her stiff muscles.

"Just a quick look at the pool and spa, darling, and then I'm frightfully sorry but I'll just have to get on with my work. It's *such* a rush, the first Monday of a fortnight. I don't know how I stand it, really."

Birdie felt an impulse to apologize for taking up her time, but controlled it instantly. For God's sake, the woman had been slavering at the mouth to get her here. And she'd insisted on conducting this tour personally. Anyone else would have been infinitely preferable as far as Birdie was concerned. Even the lugubrious William. At least the woman had calmed down a bit since they began. She obviously liked to show off the place. Feet slipping slightly in her soft, borrowed shoes, Birdie reluctantly followed her guide through the double doors that led from the annex sitting area to the swimming pool, squash court, spa, and all the various other amenities. She hoped she wouldn't have to inspect everything individually.

"You can also reach this area through the massage room, for the guests' convenience," Margot began. "But we wouldn't want to disturb Helen, would we, so I brought you the long way. Now—the pool is heated, of course, floodlit at night with . . ."

Her voice ran on. Birdie's eyes glazed over.

• • •

At ten Birdie was released. Margot was committed, she said, to an hour with William in her office to check through accounts. She would leave Birdie to wander at will, and read over the brochures and information William had prepared for her—statistics and so on, and a bit more detail about the services Deepdene offered.

"We gave you the 'morning free' Monday timetable, darling," she went on, flicking a tiny speck of powder from her immaculate cream sleeve. "It means a busy afternoon for you, but it's the one we thought would be handiest for you, on your first day, so you can get your bearings and start on your notes and so on." She lifted an elegant, proprietorial hand and just touched Birdie's mop of chestnut curls. "Lovely strong hair, darling," she said vaguely, then peered directly into her face. "And *glorious* eyes. But I really would consider contact lenses. We must talk about it."

"Sure," said Birdie politely, feeling a wild impulse to spit in the cold, green gaze. She made her escape and headed for the kitchen. A bit too much pine and aluminum for her taste, but at least it wasn't pink or antique. She cadged a cup of coffee and a biscuit from the now bustling Mrs. Hinder, admired the herb garden which was that formidable person's pride and joy but was at present barely visible through the streaming kitchen window, and decided to hide herself away in the library for an hour or two.

She found Edwina sitting there reading a John le Carré thriller. She'd had her hair done. The whole style had been softened and the gray was now merely interesting streaks in a golden-brown base. Birdie noted with interest that the cleverness of the cut seemed to have optically reduced the heaviness of Edwina's jaw, and highlighted her deep-set eyes. The change was quite remarkable.

"Your hair looks great," she said sincerely, and Edwina looked self-consciously pleased.

"Yes, I thought it did," she said, stroking the soft feathers of hair at the back of her neck. "He's a good hairdresser. Haven't you started yet?"

"No. I don't have my first thing till twelve. Then it's all go throughout the afternoon. What do you have next?"

"Massage. At eleven." Edwina looked uncomfortable. "I'm not looking forward to that. I've never had one. Have you?"

"No."

They looked at each other gloomily. In both their minds the image of Conrad standing expressionless over their prone and less-than-perfect bodies rose up like a specter.

"Will we be able to leave our underwear on, do you think?" asked Edwina plaintively.

"Oh, God! Surely!" Birdie was horrified. This was a problem she hadn't even considered.

Edwina sighed and went back to her book.

Birdie sat down and swallowed the last of her tepid coffee. She decided that for the sake of her mental health she'd better get to work. She turned reluctantly to William's notes, then remembered she hadn't asked Margot for a notepad and pen as she'd intended. Wearily she hoisted herself out of her chair again, wincing as her bruised body protested. She left the library, and made for the office next door. It was just ajar. She raised her hand to knock.

"So that's it!" she heard Margot saying sharply. "That's the end of that."

William's gentle voice murmured something indecipherable.

"You're a sweetie, William. I don't know what I'd do without you." Margot's voice had softened. Birdie hesitated. Maybe she shouldn't interrupt.

Outside there was a sudden crack of thunder and the sound of the rain increased to a furious drumming.

"My God! This bloody rain!" shouted Margot. "Look, William, go and put those things away now, darling, will you? I'd like to give you some letters and I want to try and catch Edwina before she goes for her massage. Hurry up, now. I have to be with Helen in . . . God . . . twenty minutes! God I hate these Mondays! It's absurd, what I go through!"

There was another murmur.

Birdie knocked.

"Yes?" The voice was imperious now. Birdie pushed open the door. Margot gave her an impatient smile. "Yes, Verity?"

"Could I have a pad and a pen, please?" Birdie came straight to the point. "All my stuff got lost in the creek."

"Darling, of course. William! Get Miss Birdwood what she wants. Quickly now."

William, standing by his own desk at the side of the room, looked flustered. His hands were filled with folders and a large checkbook. He looked at Margot resignedly, dumped his burden in the center of the desk, and started to leave the room.

"William, wait! Now, don't be a martyr, darling. I'm sorry. What was it you wanted? Last thing."

"Just this check here, Margot. June 10. Cash. Twelve hundred and seventy-three dollars fifty. You didn't do the stub."

Margot tapped her teeth with her slim gold pen. "That was . . . that was . . ." She shut her eyes. Then they snapped open. "Silver. Ted Silver. Generator, pool filter—odds and sods," she announced triumphantly.

He made a note and smiled gratefully at her. You'd think, thought Birdie, she was doing him a favor by doing her job.

"William will look after you, darling," Margot

said, flashing her teeth. "You won't mind if I get back to it, will you? I'm just flat-out today!" She began sorting through the six or seven sheets of paper on her gleaming desk.

"Yes, I can see that," said Birdie. "All go, isn't it?"

Margot darted a quick look at her, but Birdie preserved a bland expression and, satisfied, returned to her labors. Anxiously, William guided Birdie from the room. He, at least, knew trouble when he saw it.

"Margot does have a lot of correspondence," he babbled nervously, as they hurried toward the back of the house. "She knows so many people. Some of them are quite famous, you know. Film stars and MPs—all sorts. Sir Arthur Longley, for example—an old, old friend of Margot's." He glanced quickly at Birdie to see if she was listening and was suitably impressed.

"Isn't he dead?" asked Birdie dryly. Her legs were aching, and she didn't feel like humoring anyone just at the moment.

William looked hurt. "Well he's dead *now*," he admitted reluctantly. "But that only happened about a year ago. And before he died he used to write to Margot every single month without fail. Imagine! A rich, famous man like that!"

"Wonderful!" Birdie made an effort to look encouraging. From what she remembered, Sir Arthur Longley had been a pompous old fart who, after thirty years of ferocious money-making, had devoted his declining years to the indulgence of his twin obsessions—berating the country's young for its moral turpitude and blowing his own trumpet at every opportunity. Both these hobbies must have proved expensive, for his widow and his creditors had discovered to their chagrin, upon his sudden demise on the golf course, that Sir Arthur's debts had thoroughly outweighed his assets. But after all, Birdie didn't have anything against poor William. If he chose to enjoy basking in Margot

Bell's reflected glory, however tawdry, that was his funeral.

They reached the storeroom door. William paused and looked at his fingernails. "Have you by any chance said anything to Margot about—you know—last night?" he enquired, elaborately casual.

"No. Have you?"

"No. Alistair said to leave it to him. But I don't think he's said anything."

"Probably just as well. She doesn't seem too happy. He's probably waiting for the right moment."

"Probably." William suddenly darted off to the right and plunged into a cluttered office opposite the kitchen. He came out with two pads and three pens, and pressed them into her hands.

"Is that your office?" asked Birdie curiously.

"Oh no. I sit with Margot. This is Alistair's. We keep the stationery stocks here. Help yourself if you want anything else. Everyone does. Alistair doesn't mind. He's doing hair all day today, anyway. Eight till six."

"Long day for him."

"Oh yes!" William nodded earnestly. "The first Monday's a long day for all of us. Alistair's appointments are two hours instead of one, and he always takes every bit of his time with every lady. He's such a perfectionist. That's why he has to work straight through without a break. But it's very satisfying. Everyone's a new person by the six o'clock drinks."

"Oh. Well, that should be interesting. I'll look forward to that." Birdie looked at him. "You're feeling better about things this morning, I gather?"

He nodded, and looked a trifle shamefaced. "It was the shock," he mumbled. "Joyce did give me an awful shock. I overreacted. I hope you won't . . . ah . . . feel you need to say anything to Margot. Or write about it for, you know, the ABC or anything." His face

brightened. He'd found the phrase he wanted. "It was
. . . off the record, you know?"

"Oh, sure." Birdie nodded seriously, to stop herself from snorting with laughter. God, this place was
like the Mad Hatter's tea party.

"Well . . . um . . . I'd better get back. Margot's
due at the makeup room in ten minutes. See you!" William turned and beat a retreat at a loping run.

Birdie peered through the storeroom and into the
kitchen. Betty Hinder was no longer there, but a
woman in white with bright red hair was industriously
chopping up chickens at the sink. Lunch was obviously
in preparation. Birdie trailed back to the library. She'd
work a bit and then go up to her room and change her
clothes like a good girl. No point in upsetting Margot at
this early stage.

Edwina's chair was empty. She must have gone to
prepare herself for the rigors of Conrad's ministrations.
Birdie shuddered at the thought. She opened one of the
folders she'd been given and stared at the butterfly motif that adorned the thick, white paper inside. They
took all this so seriously. She briefly wondered what
had upset Margot Bell so much this morning. She'd
been furious, that was obvious. One maid's cheek?
Surely not. That sacking would have been a symptom
of the disease, not a cause. What then? She didn't seem
to have been told about the anonymous letter, so it
couldn't be that. And it wasn't William that was worrying her. Despite her mood, she was being quite sweet
to him today. And he was quite pathetically grateful
for small mercies.

Margot's heels clicked past the door toward the
annex. Someone was walking with her. William? No—a
heavy high-heeled tread, and a low murmur. Edwina.
Birdie smiled to herself. Ah yes, Margot had wanted to
catch up with Edwina. She was obviously a great one

for getting to know people who might be useful to her later.

Birdie read for a while, took a few notes, then put down the folder and walked over to the window. She tugged at it absentmindedly, but of course it didn't move. It was a constant impulse she had in this house, she realized. To go to the windows, in any room, and try them. Just in case. But all were sealed tight. So the elements stayed out, she thought, and the people stayed in. Warm, dry, snug—and safe.

Safe. The word hung in her mind as she returned to her chair. She stared again at the butterfly motif. Thought of Margot, right now working on Helen in the makeup room, painting on the glow, taking out the shadows, Angela creaming, patting little Belinda's anxious baby face, Edwina laid out stolidly in the massage room, Josie joking with Alistair while he wrestled with her fine, flyaway hair. Only she was still waiting. She shivered, and then shook herself impatiently. What was wrong with her? Jittery, that's all. Jittery for no reason.

She turned back to the folder and opened it. But within five minutes she was back at the window. Staring out. Listening to the rain. Her hands pressed against the glass.

8

High noon. *The beauty therapy room. Shoes off, glasses off,
shirt off, pink smock on,* Birdie braced herself as the
chair reclined, shut her watering eyes against the
bright, bright light. *What am I doing here?*

Pink haze. Angela, crisp, flawless, earnest, bending
over her, smelling of soap, baby powder, and lemon.
Her voice, running like a brook . . . "A *little* bit dehy-
drated here on the cheekbones, aren't we, Verity? . . .
Cleanse, tone, and moisturize. *Twice* a day, no matter
what else happens. Once we're into our thirties it's *so*
important to . . ."

Creams, face packs, scented steam, soft, strong fingers, damp pads on the eyes, cutting out all light, all
sight, all thought. The voice rippling on, so soft, so
sweet, so insistent, like the chime of the alarm clock
upstairs. ". . . and we all *deserve* that little bit of time,
don't we, Verity? We owe it to our bodies . . . eight
full glasses of water a day . . . and do you manage
much exercise? . . . oh, I *know*, all my ladies are so
busy . . . I find *meditation* . . . now I'll just tidy up
those eyebrows . . ." *Ridiculous. This is ridiculous!*

One o'clock. *Dining room. Lunch.* Josie, almost

shy, looking five kilos thinner and ten years younger
despite a voluminous batik dress, with her hair feathered softly into her pink cheeks; Belinda glowing and
giggly, flirting openly with William, the lines on her
forehead magically smoothed by the laying on of Angela's and Conrad's hands; Edwina buttering bread,
handsome face closed against compliment or question;
Margot, serene at the head of the table. No Alistair, no
Helen. He's doing her hair. Can't get us all done if he
doesn't work through lunch. Drinking soup, leek soup,
bemused; face tingling, bizarrely soft, naked. *Soon this
will all be over.*

Two o'clock. Massage room. Conrad, dazzling in
white, tanned arms, wolfish smile; pink towels, pink
table, scented oil, warmth, music. *God!* ". . . Just here,
sweetheart, head flat on the couch . . ." *No way out.*
". . . and relax . . . no worries . . . arm up . . .
arm down . . . I'm going to use a warm pack now
. . . a lot of tension there . . . breathe . . . relax . . .
feeling good?" *Resistance is useless.* ". . . oh yes, that's
better . . . that's it . . . relax . . . mmm . . ." *Think
of nothing.*

Time blurring.

Three o'clock. Makeup room. Margot Bell. In her
hands. Helpless, unprotesting, blind without your
glasses. Your blemished, imperfect face her canvas. *Lie
still. Stare ahead. Think of nothing.* Foundation, powder,
paint. *Your mother's dressing table, all those years ago.
Small, freckled, and skinny in your pajamas, you gaze at her
sitting there, radiant, leaning forward to put black stuff on
her eyelashes. The room smells of roses. She's like a film star.
You move forward to touch the smooth, shimmering green of
her dress. In the mirror your own face pops up beside hers. It
must have happened a hundred times before, but this one
time something clicks. At that moment you suddenly understand why people always say you look like your father, except
for your eyes. You'd never really thought about it before.*

Now you know. The world shifts a little. Your father beams proudly from the edge of the bed, lacing his shoes. He's small, plain, and clever. He worships her. You slip away from the mirror, out of the room.

Margot's shallow green eyes, perfectly shadowed, outlined, and colored in, are intent above you. "Now I'll just . . . a tiny spot of concealer here, and here, and here, see? And here, of course, and . . . ah, now isn't that better? . . . Look up . . . look down . . . Now you consider those contacts, darling. It'll make all the difference in the world . . . such glorious eyes . . . no point in hiding your best feature . . ." *Only feature, you mean.* ". . . Tomorrow Angela will show you how . . ." *Think of nothing.*

Four o'clock. Hairdressing room. Alistair tired but still able to muster a smile for his last customer of the day, running fingers through the mass of chestnut curls, pulling gently, thoughtfully. "All this weight— we don't need that . . . how about . . . ?" *Nod. Smile. Agree. Anything you like, Alistair. Whatever you think.* Wash, condition, cut . . . damp brown semicircles falling on the shoulders of the smooth pink smock, heaping in drifts on the floor, on the arms of the chair. So much hair. So much time. Gone . . . A shocked, familiar-unfamiliar painted face staring out from Alistair's mirror, while his gloved hands paint bizarre-looking color on the wisps and strands of hair that poke through the holes in a sort of shower cap. Alistair's laughter. "Don't look so worried, Verity. It'll look great. Great . . ." *How could you let him do it? Why didn't you stop him? He's overtired. He's made a terrible mistake. You're scalped. You're a freak. It'll take months to grow back. Back to work in a fortnight . . . impossible. You'll have to hide out . . . say you're sick. You caught something. Something infectious . . . hepatitis . . .*

.   .   .

"Five past six—late as usual!" Alistair opened a cupboard by the door and pulled out a jacket hanging there. He shrugged himself into it and glanced at the silent figure still sitting in the chair. He yawned and smiled. "Ready for a drink?"

Birdie nodded obediently. Her hand went involuntarily to the nape of her neck, and stroked the white, soft skin there. It felt so odd. She barely recognized her own reflection. The cut had made an enormous difference. The color too. She stared. After a moment she became aware that Alistair was hovering by the door, his finger on the light switch. Of course. Drinks at six. She pushed herself from the chair and followed him out of the room. She felt as though she were floating. The silk of her trousers fell smoothly, whisper-soft against the insides of her thighs, the backs of her knees. The tunic top with its high, Chinese collar was weightless. Her head felt unimaginably light. Could hair weigh so much?

In the annex corridor she blinked. It was dark outside. Rain beat on the iron roof and streamed down the windows. Across the courtyard light poured from the kitchen, and in the dark, wet mass that was the herb garden, the odd leaf gleamed silver.

They hurried through the annex vestibule and into the house proper. The smell of cooking drifted from the kitchen, mixing with the scent of polished wood, open fires, and flowers. "Poor old William, I always end up leaving him to cope," said Alistair. "Always late. Still, it's not so bad tonight." He seemed distracted. He had something on his mind. Birdie remembered, with wonder that she'd forgotten: William. The threatening letter. Margot Bell. Laurel Moon.

The marble-tiled hall was flooded with light, the chandelier brilliant above the stairs. The murmur of conversation drifted from the sitting room. Alistair paused and looked at his companion quizzically. "You O.K.?"

"Sure!" Birdie gnawed at her lip and then grimaced. "Actually," she said gruffly, "I'm a bit spaced out. I'm . . . ah . . . not really into this sort of thing."

He put a warm hand on her arm. "You'll recover," he teased gently. "And you look great! Come on. Let's get in there and see how the others got on."

Josie, Belinda, and William turned to look as Birdie and Alistair came into the room. They were all clutching drinks, and the two women looked bright-eyed and expectant. Belinda, rosy and now possessed of a charming and entirely appropriate mass of dark curls that flew around her face and strayed over her forehead, looked very pretty indeed.

"Well, look at *you!*" boomed Josie, beaming. "Don't you look marvelous! A hundred percent! What a difference!"

"Thanks very much," said Birdie tartly.

"Oh, not that you looked that bad before!" Josie's plump face crimsoned slightly. She guffawed uneasily and slapped at her cheek. "Dear oh dear, foot in mouth disease again, Josie." She buried her nose unhappily in her drink.

Belinda giggled and darted a look at William. But he was oblivious to her. Handsome face intent, he was engaging in some sort of silent communication with Alistair.

Birdie saw that the object of their attention was Conrad, who was leaning casually against the mantelpiece, drink in hand. In her confusion she hadn't even noticed he was in the room. The firelight flickered on his white clothes. And Helen was standing beside him. Birdie caught her breath. It was astounding. The woman was transformed. Her hair swung smooth, thick, and burnished, just grazing her jawline. Above the ugly stuff of her dress the extraordinary face, all hollows and bone, stood out like a carving. The magnificent, deep-set eyes glowed under strong, arching brows.

Conrad jerked his head slightly in greeting. His eyes flicked appreciatively over Birdie's body, and he smiled. She nodded, felt herself grow warm, then hot, under the thin silk, and desperately resisted the urge to fold her arms protectively across her chest. Conrad transferred his gaze to Alistair. His grin became more fixed. He held Alistair's eyes, as if daring him to speak. Fairly obviously, his appearance in this gathering was unexpected. Some hallowed routine had been disturbed. Nothing else could account for Alistair's startled, then deliberately bland, expression or William's barely concealed agitation.

"Drink, Verity?" murmured Alistair, turning to her finally.

"Scotch, please. Just with ice." Birdie stood uncertainly in the center of the room as he left her. She didn't fancy joining either of the groups on offer. She glanced at her watch. Ten past six. With a bit of luck Edwina would come in before she had to make a choice. She was Margot's last appointment for the day, and obviously Margot had decided to make the most of their tête-à-tête. Still, Edwina shouldn't be long. They'd been told tactfully that Margot never came to drinks on Day One. She found the day so *draining*, she needed to be a little quiet before dinner. So she'd have to let Edwina go soon, or she'd miss out on her rest and go completely down the drain.

Alistair brought the drink and Birdie took it gratefully, smiling her thanks. Maybe the alcohol would help steady her down and stop her feeling like Alice down the rabbit hole, she thought. But the first gulp disabused her of this hope. Her head swam slightly.

"Ah Edwina, at last!" said Alistair, looking over her shoulder. Birdie turned around.

Edwina stood tall and handsome by the door, smiling slightly and holding herself very straight. Strangely enough she looked at first glance as though she was wearing less makeup than before. The caked, heavily powdered look and the thick red lipstick had gone. But her cool gray eyes looked wider and brighter; her cheekbones seemed to gleam in the light; her generous mouth curved in a slight smile. In a way it was a subtle difference, but its effect was powerful. She no longer looked uncomfortably and determinedly painted and covered up. She actually looked more herself, and more in control, not less.

Birdie considered this phenomenon and its implications, and with the consideration came a grudging respect for Margot Bell. The woman was an egomaniac—spoiled, selfish, and not, in Birdie's terms, intelligent, though with plenty of rat cunning—but in her area she was obviously a real professional. She'd taken each of these women and treated them according to type and temperament. She'd really given them something they could live with as themselves, instead of painting on masks for them to hide behind. Always assuming, Birdie added hastily to herself, that they wanted to go in for all that makeup and stuff. Which presumably they did, since they were paying a fortune to find out about it. She herself, of course, was here on business. It had nothing to do with her.

Edwina accepted the drink Alistair brought her and moved slightly self-consciously to Birdie's side. "I like your hair like that," she said, as casually as if Birdie had simply changed her parting from one side to the other. No foot in mouth disease for Edwina.

"You look marvelous," Birdie countered.

They stood in uneasy silence for a moment, sipping their drinks. Then their eyes met, and they grinned almost guiltily at each other. "Pretty good, eh?" muttered Edwina. "Better than I thought." She glanced around the room. "In fact we all look so much better, it's almost embarrassing. God, look at Helen!"

"I know. She's a raving beauty. Margot must have loved working on her. She's got a face like a model."

"Or Katharine Hepburn, or someone like that. Look at Conrad turning on the charm, will you? Surely he doesn't expect to get anywhere with Helen."

"Maybe he likes a challenge." Birdie shrugged. "Well, anyway, that's stage one. Margot bows out now, doesn't she? Angela takes over from tomorrow, and teaches us mere mortals how to get the same effect. That should be fun."

"Oh, Lord, I forgot!" Edwina raised her voice. "Alistair!"

Alistair turned from his conversation with the bubbling Belinda to look at her inquiringly.

"Margot asked me to tell you she's waiting in the beauty therapy room for her neck massage. She has a headache," said Edwina rather dryly. Birdie smiled to herself. Edwina didn't take kindly to being used as a messenger by Margot, apparently.

Alistair looked blank. He raised his eyebrows at Conrad, still standing with Helen by the fire.

"Nothing to do with me, man," drawled Conrad. "Madam canceled out the usual spot. Maybe she's decided to use Angela today, if she's in the beauty therapy room."

William and Alistair exchanged those bemused glances again. William frowned. "Oh no, she'd never do something like that without telling me," he said slowly. "She never changes the routine without letting me know. And anyway, she knows Angela always swims from six to six-thirty. Angela's not available to do a neck massage now."

Conrad yawned and stretched. "William," he drawled, shaking his head, "you spend too much time working on that damned timetable. Loosen up a bit.

Variety's the spice of life." He grinned insolently. "Margot obviously thinks so, anyhow. The same old routine over and over again leaves her cold."

It was fairly easy to see he wasn't just talking about the running of Deepdene. Birdie saw William turn crimson, heard Alistair's voice rise animatedly, babbling about Angela and her evening swims and her meditation beforehand and what a health fiend she was and how she wouldn't be too pleased at having to give it up. Poor Alistair. Somehow one felt that covering up awkward social situations caused by Margot and her amors had become second nature with him.

"But Angela *has* gone swimming," William blurted out, still blushing but obviously determined to put Conrad in the wrong. "I saw her going through to the pool just before I came in here."

"Well, did she say anything about seeing Margot then, William?" asked Alistair.

William stared at him. "Of *course* she didn't," he snapped huffily. "I've told you that. I just saw her, anyway. I didn't speak to her."

Josie snorted through her handkerchief. "Margot won't be too happy then, will she?" she chortled to Alistair. "Us all guzzling our drinks while she cools her heels."

Alistair smiled. But it was a halfhearted effort. You could understand why, Birdie thought. Having seen Margot Bell in a snit that morning, sulky, throwing her weight around—and sacking that maid for cheek without a second thought—she wasn't surprised Alistair was worried. The last thing he needed was another display like that from Deepdene's star attraction.

She watched him put his drink down with a casual air and wander to the door. "I'll see what's up," he said, and disappeared. They heard him striding rapidly toward the back of the house. Obviously he was going to get Angela out of the pool and into Margot's neck massage as fast as was humanly possible.

"Poor bastard," Edwina murmured beside her. She drained her glass. "Does this mean we don't get another drink?"

"Let's ask William," Birdie whispered back.

"If it's not in the rule book he might say no. Conrad's a better bet. After all, we're on intimate terms after today. It's the least he could do."

"God, don't remind me. But I don't think he's supposed to be here. He and William might come to blows over the decanters."

"William, then."

"O.K."

They sauntered over to the drinks cabinet where Belinda and William were murmuring together. Belinda, Birdie noted, had her hand on William's arm. His eyes were downcast, the long, black lashes showing to great effect. Josie, excluded from their conversation, was standing rather uncertainly over to one side, sniffing and fingering her empty sherry glass. Birdie nodded to her and was appalled to see her move forward eagerly. It was one thing to feel sorry for Josie from the sidelines. Quite another to have to deal with her face to face.

"I'm glad someone's not backward in coming forward!" Josie nudged Birdie conspiratorially. She stuck out her tongue and made little panting noises, then roared with laughter. William and Belinda turned to look. Belinda giggled breathlessly, her eyes wide.

"We were wondering if we could have another drink, William," Edwina said firmly.

"Oh, sure, of course. Sorry about that. I should have asked." William smiled briefly, took the glasses, and began to pour the drinks with hands that trembled a little. "We're a bit disorganized tonight."

"When you've done that, William," said Belinda,

rather overloudly, her face pink, "do you think you could find me that book you were talking about? From the library?"

"Yes. Yes, of course." William glanced at her quickly. He handed over the drinks and nodded earnestly at Edwina. "Please help yourself to another when you're ready, won't you? At least—I'll probably be back by the time—anyway . . ." He glanced again at Belinda. "Ready?" he said.

They scuttled from the room, followed by Josie's knowing guffaw. She threw a handful of stuffed olives into her mouth and chewed vigorously. "This *is* all a bit disorganized, isn't it?" she boomed to Conrad. "For a place that sets itself up to be so posh?" She sniffed, and pulled a handkerchief from her handbag in a waft of eucalyptus. Birdie turned aside. If she didn't come out of this experience any the wiser about the ways of beauty, she was certainly going to come out of it with a cold, if Josie had anything to do with it.

Conrad shrugged and grinned, but didn't reply. None of this was anything to do with him, it seemed. He leaned confidentially toward Helen and spoke to her in an undertone, obviously asking if she wanted another drink, for she held up her half-full glass and shook her head.

But Josie wasn't going to be ignored. "I'm surprised Margot Bell'd rather have Angela than you to rub her neck, Conrad," she called, almost kittenishly. "I'd have thought you could supply all the variety she needed, wouldn't you, Verity?"

Birdie muttered something about Margot having a headache and concentrated on her drink. Conrad blinked lazily and turned his back.

Josie's fine skin stained pink, registering the snub. "If you ask me," she said loudly, "it's that letter she got at lunchtime that's given her a headache."

Birdie went very still. "What letter?" she heard Edwina ask curiously.

"Oh, I thought you'd have seen what happened! This letter I found." Josie lowered her voice. "I found it in the ladies' loo after lunch, propped up against one of the mirrors. It said 'Deepdene—Urgent' on the envelope. It was one of the pink envelopes, like in our rooms. *Well*"—she looked around to make sure she had their attention—"I gave it to Margot Bell when she came out of the dining room and she opened it, and you should have seen how she reacted! Of course I tried to see what was in it, but she folded it up and stuffed it in her pocket so quick I didn't get much of a chance. I did see a few words, though." She looked at them avidly, willing them to ask her to go on.

Edwina gazed vaguely at some point over Josie's shoulder and turned away. She wandered over to an armchair, sat down, and began rather pointedly flipping over the pages of a magazine. Josie stared after her, mouth slightly open. Birdie touched her arm. "What were the words?" she asked, trying to look suitably and innocently agog.

"It was all in capital letters," said Josie flatly, turning her pale eyes back to Birdie's face. "And I saw 'bitch,' and Margot's name, and 'you'll pay.' It was a blackmail letter, I'm sure of it. She went as red as a lobster when she read it." She looked sideways at Conrad and went on in a piercing stage whisper. "A woman like that . . . she'd have a lot of nasty little secrets, wouldn't she?"

Helen's glass clinked onto the mantelpiece. She muttered something to Conrad and blundered out of the room, looking at no one. Edwina didn't raise her eyes from her magazine, but her hands were still, and she was frowning. She's had it with the lot of us, Birdie thought. And she's getting worried about being involved in some scandal. For someone in Edwina's position, Birdie knew, the faintest breath of odd or shady dealing, even by association, would be a big professional problem.

There was an awkward silence. Josie blew her nose defiantly. The rain pattered steadily on outside. Birdie cleared her throat.

"Still raining," she said finally.

"Cats and dogs." Josie's eyes darted from Conrad to Edwina. "Lovely, isn't it? Did you hear we're likely to be flooded in?"

"*What?*" Birdie pushed at her glasses, appalled. She felt, rather than saw, Edwina put down the magazine and stare.

"Oh yes," Josie went on with some relish. "The housekeeper told me. She says it could happen any time in the next few hours, when the spill from the dam comes down the creek. She's expecting to have to spend the night here because of it. She stayed to serve dinner. The rest of the staff have been sent home early so they won't get stuck."

"What about us?"

Josie shrugged and grinned. "It's happened before, it'll happen again, Mrs. Hinder says. Won't matter to us, will it? We're stuck here anyway. No need to go anywhere, have we?"

Birdie looked over to Edwina's chair. Edwina was sitting upright, with an alert, determined expression on her face. Obviously she was considering her options, and the idea of getting out of Deepdene while she could was preeminent among them. But as Birdie watched she grimaced, and settled back. She was being mature, resisting the impulse. How many times that night, Birdie was to think later, she must have regretted that decision.

Conrad pushed himself away from the mantelpiece, put down his drink, and strolled to the door.

"Back in five," he said, to no one in particular, and left the room.

"I see," chortled Josie. "Well, that puts us in our place, doesn't it? Think we've got bad breath or something, Verity?" She filled her mouth with olives, chewed and hesitated. Suddenly she felt desperately for her handkerchief, sneezed convulsively, and immediately began to choke.

Birdie banged her ineffectually on the back as she wheezed and coughed, bent almost double. Grab her round the diaphragm and pull, Birdie thought. Or will she cope without that? What if I do it and she doesn't need it? What if I don't do it and she chokes to death? With enormous relief she saw Alistair come hurrying into the room. He was flustered and out of breath but coped admirably with Josie's paroxysms. Soon she was sitting down, pink in the face and with streaming eyes but reasonably composed, sipping at a glass of water.

"Angela's changing now," chattered Alistair, straightening his tie and running a hand over his ruffled fair hair. "There's obviously been some sort of mix-up. Anyway, she'll see to Margot." He was trying to appear casual and urbane, but looked frazzled. My God, what a life he leads, thought Birdie. Margot's got him by the balls like she's got everyone else.

Alistair looked around with surprise, as though noticing for the first time the absence of half the company. "Where is everyone?" he asked.

As Birdie opened her mouth to reply, William and Belinda appeared at the door, pink-cheeked and smiling self-consciously. There was no sign of the book they had ostensibly been fetching, Birdie noted.

"Belinda, you *do* look gorgeous!" Alistair beamed at her. She sparkled back at him, shaking her curls, and looked sideways at William, who nodded gently.

"Look, I think champagne's in order, don't you?"

said Alistair impulsively. "Why not? William, will you get the glasses? I'll be back in a tick."

He bustled out through the door of the dining room, leaving it ajar. The smell of cooking drifted into the room. Birdie sniffed appreciatively. She realized she was starving. She ate the two olives left in the bowl Josie had been ravaging. They didn't help. William was pulling champagne flutes from the drinks cabinet, and placing them carefully on a silver tray. Despite his quivering hands he seemed much calmer tonight. Belinda stood beside him, whispering and fluttering, and he occasionally looked at her and smiled. Birdie wondered whether William and Alistair knew about the second threatening letter. It was impossible to say. But as Margot had been tied up all afternoon, it was quite likely she hadn't had a chance to tell them about it. When she did, William's present mood could change dramatically.

Alistair returned with the champagne. The cork slid from the first bottle with a gentle pop under his expert hands and he filled the glasses, handing them around with a smile. William tossed another log on the fire. An air of celebration unaccountably filled the room. And right on cue Conrad and Helen appeared, arm in arm. She was smiling, for the first time that Birdie had noticed since she arrived at Deepdene. Her cheeks glowed, her eyes shone. She looked ravishing, despite her clothes. Where had they been? Anyway, whatever Conrad's been saying to her out there it's really brightened her up, Birdie thought, gulping champagne and feeling her head swim in response. A bit of flattery from a good-looking man goes a long way, it seems, when you're not used to it.

She looked again at the two of them, standing drinking from the slender crystal glasses. They were an absurd couple, but in one way they looked absolutely right and familiar together. Why was that? Then she realized. They looked exactly like all those magazine photographs of superb, aging actresses arm in arm with pretty young men of dubious morals. Helen must see that Conrad's a spiv, she thought. But maybe that doesn't matter. Maybe the admiration's what counts. And the admiration, what's more, of a man who's probably had hundreds of women and doesn't hesitate to come on strong. Maybe that's more of a turn-on and less of a threat for someone like Helen than the bumbling advances of the good, less expert, less dangerous sort of man. Fascinating.

Birdie sipped, musing. Chatter flowed around her. William was talking to Belinda and Alistair, his face animated as they laughed with him. Yes, he'd come a long way since last night. Last night it had been hard to imagine why Margot Bell would ever have taken him on as a secretary, let alone into her bed, however good-looking he might be. But tonight you could see his charm. Belinda was a goner, anyway, that was clear. It had happened fast. Like ski lodges, conferences, and ships, thought Birdie dreamily. They seemed to accelerate things. You got to know people very, very quickly when you were cut off from the outside world.

"I'm starving, aren't you?" Edwina's voice penetrated her thoughts. Birdie looked around and grinned. Edwina had obviously decided to overlook her encouragement of Josie's gossip. That was a relief. She'd have missed having someone to talk to. "Starving and half pissed," she said. "Thinking about ski lodges and ships."

"Ships?"

"Yes, I . . ." Birdie's voice trailed off. She cocked her head, listened, frowned. "What's that?"

"I don't . . ." Edwina's startled eyes met hers. "It's . . . Alistair, what's . . . ?"

But Alistair's shocked expression showed that he had heard it now. And within a split second so had everyone else. The screaming, shrill and terrified, piercing the sound of the rain, caught half-spoken words in their throats, widened their eyes, and filled their ears. With a curse Conrad threw open the door into the hall. And the sound, shriek upon shriek, crashed into the room, echoing in waves around them, louder and louder. Gasping and shocked, pushing and panicked, they rushed out to meet it.

9

Monday was the first day of Detective Sergeant Dan Toby's new health regime. He'd promised himself over the weekend that this would be so, and had gamely stuck to his plan, from the early morning walk, through the muesli breakfast, to the fruit at morning tea, the salad sandwich for lunch, and the mineral water and plain digestive biscuit midafternoon. Now he sat with gurgling stomach contemplating the rainy darkness outside the office window, pushing the tin of tuna he had purchased for dinner around on his desk with a blunt, discontented finger. There seemed no point in going home. He couldn't have a beer. He'd thrown out the last of the chocolate. There was bugger-all on TV. He knew in his bones that the tuna salad he'd planned was not going to eventuate. He'd end up eating the fish out of the can with a spoon and drinking the juice. He could do that just as well here.

He glanced across the room to where Detective Constable Milson sat typing up one of his meticulous and stultifyingly boring reports. Even the back of the man's head irritated Toby. Milson's neck was pale, skinny, and stiff. His ears stuck out slightly. Toby narrowed his eyes. His stomach rumbled. The typing stopped, and Toby quickly looked out the window. When he looked back, Milson had swung round to face him. "It's after six, sir," Milson said pointedly.

"I know that, Milson, thanks," growled Toby. He began to shuffle the papers on his desk, pushing the tin of tuna to one side. "I've got work to do. You go, by all means."

"Oh no." Milson turned back to his typing. "I'd rather finish this."

Oh yes, you crawler, thought Toby savagely. And you like to leave after me, don't you? So if the Super comes in he can see just how dedicated and busy you are—in contrast to yours truly. I know your little game, Milson. Well, tonight I'm outwaiting you, if it takes till midnight. Hope your bloody lovebirds starve.

The phone rang. Toby snatched up the receiver. "Yes?" he barked, his eyes still fixed to the back of Milson's head. A faint voice squeaked in his ear. "What? Can you speak up?"

"Dan!" The voice was louder now, but panicky and high-pitched. "Dan, I need help here. Dan? Are you there?"

"Who is this?" bawled Toby. Milson swung round in his chair to stare.

"For God's sake, Dan, don't play silly buggers with me. It's Birdie!"

"Birdie! Where are you?" Toby grinned, put a hand over one ear, and squinted with concentration. Milson tightened his thin lips, ostentatiously turned back to his desk, and began to type furiously. He'd many times made clear his opinion of Verity Birdwood and her absurd dabblings in detection. It infuriated him that Dan Toby, who was forever grumbling about the woman's cheek and the trouble she caused, gave her in fact such a long rope. The old man knew exactly how he felt. It had occurred to Milson, indeed, that Toby encouraged her at times simply to spite him.

"Milson, stop that noise, I can't hear!" roared Toby. He glared at Milson's hunched and insulted back for a moment and then spoke slowly and clearly into the receiver. "Now. Say it again. Milson was being rowdy. Where are you?"

"Dan. I'm at Deepdene. You know, Margot Bell's place? Near Windsor. The makeover place."

"God, finally decided to smarten yourself up, have you? Catch a man before it's too late? Glad to hear it."

"Dan! God, Dan, this isn't a joke. You've got to listen and get us some help. She's dead. Margot Bell." Birdie's voice crackled on the line.

"What?" Toby sobered immediately. "How?"

"She's been murdered, Dan. We just found her."

"For . . . Why are you ringing me, Birdwood? Are you nuts? Get onto the local cops. Do it now!"

"I've *rung* the local cops. I got a recorded message! I couldn't believe it! It said to ring Windsor."

"Well, *ring* Windsor!"

"They're engaged. They've been engaged for five minutes! I know your number, so I rang you. Dan, you've got to get us some help! There's a killer here. It could be anyone. Margot Bell's lying here going stiff, with a pair of scissors in her neck, and . . ." The line crackled and hissed.

"*What!*"

"Yes, and Dan, it's still raining! It won't stop raining!"

Toby thought quickly. He'd never heard Birdie like this. She never lost her cool. What was she doing babbling about the weather? "Listen, Birdie," he snapped. "Don't worry. I'll fix everything. You just get everyone there together, and don't let anyone touch anything. Hear me?"

"Yes." The word was like a sigh on the line.

"I'm going to hang up now, Birdie," Toby said firmly, "and get someone over there. Just sit tight, all right? Someone will be there. In"—he looked at his watch and made some quick calculations—"in about an hour. O.K.?"

"All right. Tell them to hurry."

"Don't worry," he said briefly, and cut the connection, his mind racing. Something, some idea or memory, fluttered at the edge of his mind and he shook his head slowly, trying to capture it. He looked up to meet Milson's cold, curious stare. "Look up the number of the Windsor police, will you, Milson?" he snapped.

Milson raised his eyebrows but wasn't going to risk a snub by asking any questions. It was obvious that Toby was off chasing some hare that woman Birdwood had started. Milson would hear about it in due course. Probably when the usual chaos resulted. But at least if the flurry was at Windsor he wouldn't be personally involved. And for that he was devoutly grateful.

"Cheer up, Milson. Couple of days in the country'll do you the world of good." Toby, in high good humor, stuffed a last corner of hamburger into his mouth and nudged his poker-faced companion. "Sure you don't want a chip?"

Milson shook his head and bent further over the wheel. Rain beat on the windscreen. The narrow strip of asphalt directly in front of them was black and glossy in the headlights for a few meters, then disappeared into gray nothingness.

"Bad luck for you you were working late tonight, eh?" Toby continued relentlessly. "The Super would've had to nab someone else to go with me, wouldn't he, if you'd gone home earlier?"

"I don't mind, sir," said Milson tightly.

"Ah, but you do mind, Milson. And why

shouldn't you?" Toby sniggered, munching chips. "It's dark, and it's wet, and it's late, and you'd like to be home watching the telly instead of driving me out into the sticks. I can understand that, son. Police work's a bugger, isn't it?"

"I don't mind," repeated Milson, goaded beyond endurance. "I still don't see why Windsor can't handle this. But that's for the Super to decide, of course."

"Yes, it is." Toby licked his salty fingers and crumpled up the chip bag. His stomach felt warm, full, and satisfied for the first time in twenty-four hours. He smiled complacently. A shame about the diet. But of course emergencies did occur and then a man just had to grab what he could to eat while he got on with the job. It just couldn't be helped. Never mind. Next week, perhaps. "And he felt that with Windsor tied up with storm damage and the bus smash, we had to pitch in. Fair enough, isn't it? Windsor thinks so anyway, Milson, if you don't. And Margot Bell's a pretty big deal as far as the press goes. The old bugger would have taken that into account as well. Won't do us any harm to collar whoever did her in."

"If we do," muttered Milson, staring straight ahead. "Sir. And if she's really dead. We've only got Verity Birdwood's word for it. The whole thing might be a wild-goose chase."

"No." Toby sobered, thinking of Birdie's panicky voice on the phone. "I don't think it's a wild-goose chase."

They drove in silence down the winding road that led to the river and the car ferry. They were alone on the road, it seemed. The bush on either side of the asphalt at first rose dark and sodden, closing them in, and then began to fall away steeply. Toby found himself gripping the sides of his seat as Milson negotiated the hairpin bends with something less than his normal prudence. Perhaps he shouldn't have needled him quite so much. "Take it steady, Milson," he was driven to protest at last.

Milson raised his eyebrows and slowed a fraction. "Sorry. I thought you were keen to hurry, sir," he murmured.

"I didn't say I was keen to die. Right, now, there's the ferry down that way. Another twenty minutes and we should be at Deepdene, according to the map." And thank heaven for that, Toby added to himself.

"If the road's passable," commented Milson, looking down his nose at the ferry plying slowly toward them across the broad expanse of rain-beaten water. "This place is flood-prone."

"Which is precisely why we have brought a four-wheel drive vehicle, Milson. Just leave the worrying to me, will you?" All the same, after a minute or two Toby, elaborately casual, reached for the two-way radio and reported their whereabouts. He wasn't usually so punctilious, but there was something about the black, rippling river that unnerved him. And Birdie's description of Margot Bell's dead body reverberated unpleasantly in his memory now that he was getting closer not only to the scene of her murder, but, presumably, to her murderer as well.

The confidently promised twenty minutes had lengthened to forty by the time Toby and Milson's car crawled up the Deepdene driveway, its serried rows of bare-branched poplars towering above them on either side. The last kilometer, plunging deep into a pitch-black valley, had been the worst, and the sight of Birdie's battered VW abandoned by the side of the road above the swollen creek had done nothing to reduce Toby's feeling of foreboding.

Deepdene blazed with light. Rain fell about it, translucent in the beams streaming from every window. The valley was filled with the sound of water dripping, pattering, rushing. But the blazing house was silent, doors and windows shut tight, holding the valley out, and its secrets in.

Toby glanced at his companion. Milson was a cold fish. Nerveless, he would have said. But now he sat unmoving at the wheel, making no attempt to cut the ignition, his face lit from the side by the glow from the house, the shadows of rain playing on his cheek. Toby found he wasn't too keen on the idea of hearing the reassuring drone of the engine die either. And the tight-shut house with its garish lights beating from within did not beckon. He ran a tongue over his dry bottom lip, caught himself doing it, and was suddenly disgusted. What stupidity! A few trees, a bit of rain, and a bunch of women—what was there to be scared of in that lot?

"Report in, Milson," he said roughly. "Let's get this show on the road, eh?" He heaved himself around and fumbled in the backseat for his raincoat. It was only a few steps to the door but he had no intention of spending the next few hours damp and steaming. Fired with newfound determination as he was, he was already struggling into a second recalcitrant gray plastic arm when he became aware of the fact that Milson was having trouble.

"I can't get through," said Milson, turning a long pale face toward him. He held out the microphone for Toby to see, as if that would help. "Nothing but static." He pushed at the receiver with impatient bony fingers.

"Blast and damn! Bloody thing!" Toby brushed Milson away and tackled the two-way radio himself. Nothing. Nothing but static. Bloody gadgets always broke down just when you needed them most. He sat there in his raincoat, fuming, and then realized what the trouble was. "It's the valley," he said slowly. "There must be a blind spot here. Two-way's useless."

"There's someone there," said Milson flatly, staring past him. Toby turned his head toward the house. The huge front door was slowly opening. A crack of light fell onto the veranda paving and inside a shadowy figure hovered, waiting.

Toby's spine prickled, and he cursed silently. He turned furiously on his silent companion. "God almighty, what are we doing stuck out here!" he barked. "We'll ring from the house. I'll get in there and you bring the stuff. And get a move on!" He wrenched open the car door and heaved himself out into the blackness and the rain. Resisting the impulse to run, he jammed his hands into his coat pockets and strode, head down, toward the house in what he hoped appeared a manly and purposeful fashion.

The door swung wider as he approached. He stepped onto the streaming veranda and in four strides was over the threshold and into the house. The door was gently closed behind him and he stood still, blinking and dripping, momentarily dazed by the pink and golden light and the closed, scented atmosphere that enveloped him.

"Detective Sergeant Toby?"

He focused on the woman speaking to him. She was shrewd-eyed and sensible-looking, dressed in neat black. Her appearance reassured him considerably.

"Could I take your coat, sir?" she said calmly, and did so, thus simultaneously and tactfully establishing her position as a member of staff, and protecting the marble floor from further puddling as well. Obviously a woman to be respected—and cultivated.

"Thank you. And you are?"

"I'm the housekeeper, sir. Mrs. Hinder. Betty Hinder. Would you like to go through?"

Toby glanced at the door. "My constable's still outside, Mrs. Hinder. If you wouldn't mind opening up again?"

He watched as she again pulled open the huge

door to disclose Milson, his hand just raised to knock. Milson's jaw dropped a little in shock, and Toby snorted with ill-natured laughter. "In you come, Milson," he said. "But give Mrs. Hinder here your raincoat first, will you? No sense in messing up her nice clean floor." He smiled winningly at the housekeeper, who unfortunately showed no sign of being disarmed.

"Mr. Alistair, the rest of the live-in staff, and the guests are in the sitting room, sir," she said, as Milson struggled from his coat and moved himself and the bags he'd brought from the car into the vestibule. She nodded toward a big door on the left of the hall. "The policeman from Windsor is . . . um . . ." For the first time her aplomb faltered.

"He's where he should be, with the deceased, I presume," Toby rumbled. "And the doctor?"

"The doctor—Dr. Thoms, I believe—is with him too. Quite keen to be leaving, the doctor is," Mrs. Hinder offered, unbending a fraction. "He says he's wanted in town."

"Mmm. I daresay. Well, we'll put him out of his misery right away, I think. Will you do the honors?"

She hesitated. "Mr. Alistair did ask me, when you arrived, to . . ."

"That'll be all right, Mrs. Hinder. I don't think we'll trouble anyone else just at the moment. Now, if you'll be so kind?" Toby held out a massive arm, inviting her to lead the way. The housekeeper stiffened slightly, then nodded and began walking toward the back of the house. Toby kept pace with her in easy strides. He was feeling better. This was familiar territory. He looked keenly at the woman beside him. She put up a good front—a very good front—but her hands were clenched into tense fists, worry and upset lurked behind her eyes, and lines of strain tightened her thin mouth.

"Worked here long, Mrs. Hinder?" he asked casually as they passed through a doorway and entered a dimmer, more cluttered region, very obviously the engine room of the house. He glanced left at a storeroom or pantry and beyond that a big, gleaming kitchen through one door. To the right there was another door, marked Office. But surely there'd been another, much grander office to the right of the front door? Maybe that was just for show.

"Twenty years," the woman said briefly. "Twenty years in this house." She opened a door directly in front of them. It must have been the original back door of the house, but now led to a modern annex, clean-lined and spacious, all pale carpet and palms and big, multipaned windows. Rain drummed unmuffled on an iron roof above their heads.

"Must have been a shock to you, then, all this." Toby watched her closed face tighten even more as she nodded. She turned down a corridor with windows on the left, and closed doors on the right, then stopped so abruptly that Milson, behind her, stumbled. "There it is," she said unnecessarily.

The second door from the end stood slightly ajar, and outside it stood a young uniformed policeman and a short, middle-aged, rather choleric-looking individual in a crumpled suit. Both men stirred and straightened on seeing the newcomers. The policeman looked mightily relieved, Toby noticed with amusement. The good Dr. Thoms must have been giving him a hard time.

Mrs. Hinder was staring straight ahead. "I'm just glad it happened in the new part," she said suddenly, and then glanced at Toby. "I mean, if it had to happen at all. You know." She wiped her hand quickly over her mouth and took a step backward.

He nodded. "I'll take over here now, Mrs. Hinder. Thank you. Could I ask you to go back and join the others now?"

"When will I tell Alistair, Mr. Alistair, that you'll . . . ?"

"I'll be with you as soon as I can," Toby said firmly. "This Mr. Alistair—he's the general manager or something, I presume?"

She drew herself up slightly, with some return of her former controlled dignity. "Mr. Alistair is the owner," she said reprovingly.

Toby's face showed his surprise. "Didn't Margot Bell own this place then?"

She flushed. "Oh no! Well, not by herself, anyway. People thought that, because she was the one that got all the publicity. But they bought this place together, Mr. Alistair and Miss Bell."

"I see. They were joint owners."

"But it's just him now, isn't it? Because she's dead." The woman looked again down the corridor, toward the half-open door.

"I suppose so." Toby looked at her thoughtfully. "Thank you, Mrs. Hinder."

"Thank you, sir." She turned and walked quickly back the way they'd come, her neat black shoes making no sound on the thick carpet.

Toby jerked his head at Milson and together they went forward to meet the two men waiting for them. The young policeman held back as they entered the room, and once inside Toby understood why. He'd investigated plenty of violent deaths in his time, but the first sight of Margot Bell's body, spotlighted by the strong lamp trained on her from above, was to stay with him for a long, long while.

Stretched out like a human sacrifice, perfect white arms trailing, she turned a grotesquely straining face toward the ceiling. Thick pads obscured her eyes, and blood soaked and spattered her pink robe, pooling dark and sticky at last on the white vinyl tiles of the floor, soaking another pink gown that lay there in a sodden heap. In her throat the silver scissor handles glinted in a tacky, overflowing well of red, their points buried deep, pinning her to the pale pink reclining chair on which she lay. He stared, fighting the nausea rising in his throat, shocked not only by the sight, but by a totally unexpected sense of déjà vu. He'd seen this before. He'd seen a picture of this, or something very like it, before. But how? Where? He heard Milson's hiss of indrawn breath, and at the same moment the memory hit him like a blow to the stomach.

Toby drew breath and forced his eyes away from the winking silver circles. "How long ago, would you say?" he asked the disgruntled little Dr. Thoms, who seemed to be the one person in the room absolutely unaffected by the sight of the body.

The doctor clicked his teeth impatiently. "You know in these conditions I can't be exact," he said. "About two and a half or three hours, let's say."

"She was strangled." Toby bent forward toward that terrible face, fighting the instinct to recoil, and with a fingernail touched the limp, blood-soaked leg of a pair of panty hose that still lay wound around the corpse's neck.

"Obviously." The doctor frowned. "But that's not what killed her. She appears to have been strangled from behind with one leg of a pair of tights to the point of unconsciousness, then attacked with the scissors, so that the windpipe was severed, causing suffocation. The blood loss is consistent with that. It would have taken a minute or two for death to occur." He fidgeted. "The PM will establish what happened. Hard to be exact under these conditions."

"Yes. You said." Toby wouldn't be hurried. "Would the person who stabbed her have been spattered with blood then?"

"Could have been. There was a spurt of blood, as you can see. This cloak affair—the same as the one the deceased's got on, as you see"—the doctor indicated the blood-soaked garment on the floor with a fastidious foot—"could have been worn to protect the murderer's clothes. He almost certainly would have got blood on his hands, anyway. Could have got it all over him, for all I know. Impossible to be exact . . ."

"In these conditions—yes, I heard you the first time." Toby was getting tired of Dr. Thoms. "You said 'he.' You're saying that a woman wouldn't have had the strength for the job?"

"Why not?"

"Well, you made the suggestion, Doctor. I merely . . ."

The small man drew himself up indignantly. "Mr. Toby, I made no suggestion whatever, and I certainly hope that I won't find myself quoted as having done so. I used 'he' as a generic term. Any human being of average strength would be perfectly capable of having done this. Is that clear?"

"Perfectly. Was she drugged?"

"How would I know?"

"You're the doctor."

"Not a witch doctor, Mr. Toby. I do not claim, nor am I expected to have, magic powers. All your questions will be answered, almost certainly, by the postmortem. Now, if you don't mind, I have to go. I'm wanted in town. The constable here brought me in his car, and is going to drive me back, I believe." Dr. Thoms looked severely at the young policeman, who nodded and blushed and looked anxiously at Toby.

Toby stared absentmindedly at Milson cautiously circling the body in the chair, his thin face intent, sharp nose pushed forward as though to smell out the tiny signs—the revealing hairs, threads, grains of powder, flakes of skin, specks of dust—almost certainly deposited there by Margot Bell's last, deadly visitor. As he watched, Milson bent forward eagerly and stared, like a gun dog pointing. Toby felt a sharp, unreasoning stab of irritation. "Any idea when we can expect the others, Constable?" he asked, turning sharply to the young man behind him and completely ignoring Dr. Thoms. "Thought they'd be here by now. A few prints'd be handy at this point, eh?"

"They should be here any minute, sir," the boy said eagerly. "I rang when we got here, before—"

"Fine. Well, off you go, then. You heard Dr. Thoms. He's got more important things to attend to than our little project." Toby turned deliberately back to the spotlighted corpse. The doctor gave a sort of huff of disgust, and Toby caught Milson pausing in his bloodhound activities to exchange understanding, professional glances with him. Milson quickly rearranged his face and returned to his personal patrol of the floor.

"Drive carefully," called Toby airily, without turning around. "We'll be in touch."

"I wish you luck in that," snapped Dr. Thoms, and trotted off at speed down the corridor, leaving the young constable to lope distractedly in his wake.

Toby wondered briefly about that parting remark, then dismissed it from his mind to concentrate on more important matters.

"What have you found, Milson?" he inquired of Milson's narrow, crouching back. "Anything useful?"

Milson pointed under the chair. Toby bent over and peered till his eyes located two small, round, white things lying on the floor. Pills, or sweets, maybe.

"Got an envelope?" he inquired. Foolish question, he thought.

Milson nodded and crouched to harvest his find. Toby heard a sharp intake of breath. Aha, Milson had got a surprise. He watched with interest as his assistant slowly straightened up and held out his hand. Toby squinted at the objects inside the plastic square. He prodded them with a blunt finger. They weren't pills at all. They were . . . His eyes met Milson's in shocked disbelief.

"Buttons! Bloody hell!"

They both turned to look at the body on the chair. Then they looked again at each other. Toby licked his lips. "Cup of tea, I think, Milson," he said firmly. "Cup of tea, and some chat with the inmates coming up, wouldn't you say? Find our housekeeper friend and get a room organized, will you? I'll stay here and have a look around. Come and get me when you're ready."

"Yes, sir. Who would you like to see first?" Milson waited, a pained expression already beginning to form on his face in anticipation of the answer. He was not disappointed.

10

"I thought Miss Bell's office would be the best, sir," said Mrs. Hinder, ushering Toby into the magnificent room. "Your tea will be ready shortly."

"Excellent. Fine. Thank you," rumbled Toby, his attention momentarily diverted by his surroundings. God, call this an office? he thought, taking in the soaring molded ceiling, the warm cedar woodwork, the stained glass, the soft, padded armchairs, bowls of flowers and huge antique desk gleaming in the lamplight. As if to complete the picture, a slim, elegant woman in black and gold sat at a side table reading from a pale pink folder and taking notes with a gold pen. She stirred and rose to her feet with a whisper of silk as they entered. Toby straightened his shoulders and stepped forward, smiling formally. Trust the owner of this room to have a secretary to match.

"About time!" snapped the vision, in an all-too-familiar voice.

Toby's jaw dropped. "Birdie!"

She stuck her jaw out belligerently. "Well, who were you expecting? Cleopatra?"

"You look . . . I didn't recognize you!"

Her expression didn't change, but color rose in her face, betraying her extreme discomfort. "Told you to lay off or you'd go blind," she said coarsely. "Now look . . ."

"What've you done to yourself? You look gorgeous!" Toby was genuinely fascinated.

"Dan, cut the crap, will you? It's not the time. I'm here on a story. They did everyone over today. I had to be in it too, didn't I?" Birdie clenched her hands together. "But for God's sake, we've got to talk sensibly. I thought you'd never get here. I nearly went bonkers, waiting. Being stuck in this place gives me the creeps, if you want to know. It was bad enough before, but now —Margot Bell—God, have you seen her?"

"Very nasty," Toby observed cautiously. He wondered how much he should tell her. He moved to the desk and sat down behind it, trying to adjust himself to dealing with this new Birdie. Not only did she look different, she was different in herself. She'd always been so cool, so infuriatingly confident. And murder had always been a game with her, a puzzle, a battle of wits. Normally she'd be reveling in this situation—a nice, juicy murder with her right on the spot, with every excuse in the world to stick her beak in. But she was badly rattled. He wondered wildly whether a new hairdo, a slather of makeup, and a set of new clothes could change someone's personality. Women's magazines always said they were a tonic. But in Birdie's case the effect seemed to have been the reverse.

"Nasty? I'll say! And you don't know the half of it!"

"Well, why don't you tell me about it?" Toby found himself speaking in the rumbling, comforting tone he usually used for damsels, children, and elderly ladies in distress. How odd to be using it with Birdie.

She glanced at him quickly. She too had registered the tone. A mixture of expressions chased each other across her face. She clenched her hands together again and made an obvious effort to pull herself together. "Milson had better be here," she said. "There's a lot to tell. He'll need to take notes."

"Sure," he said gently, nodding. "He'll be in in a minute." He tapped the desk in front of him with a pencil and waited, trying not to look at her as she struggled to regain her normal manner. He listened to the rain pounding steadily on outside. Usually he found rain a comforting sort of sound. Providing he was warm and dry somewhere, just listening to it, of course. But there was something about the relentlessness of this that was unnerving. And there was another sound, too, in the background. A rushing, roaring sound. At last, he thought. The scene of the crime blokes from Windsor. None too soon. But the sound went on and on, and finally he realized his mistake.

"Is that the creek we can hear?"

Birdie nodded, twisting abruptly in her chair to face the window. "It's flooding," she said quietly. She turned huge amber eyes back to Toby and swallowed. "The housekeeper says we'll be flooded in by morning. We won't be able to get out."

Toby snorted. "It couldn't happen that quickly," he pronounced confidently. "Takes days."

"Not here. Betty Hinder says—"

"Birdie, don't let that old bat get under your skin, for God's sake. We've got a four-wheel drive. We'll get you out in relays if necessary. Or ring Windsor for more cars. We'll fix it. Just relax, will you?"

As Birdie opened her mouth to reply the door swung open and Milson appeared with a tea tray. He eyed Birdie with startled suspicion as he brought it to the desk and set it down. She returned the look defiantly.

"All the people in the house are in the sitting room, as the housekeeper said, sir," he remarked to

Toby, his eyes sending a clear message beyond that of the flat words. "They've been told to stay together. I believe everything's quite in control at the moment. The staff searched the house with the PC from Windsor and say they're sure that no intruder's hiding anywhere. Now, anyway." He began to pour the tea, his long, bony fingers incongruous against Deepdene's fine, floral china. "Some of the ladies are quite restless," he added. "And one of the men."

"If you mean William," said Birdie dryly, "the word would be hysterical, wouldn't you say?"

Milson passed her a cup of tea. His eyes flicked up and down, taking in the soft cap of chestnut curls, the beautifully made-up face, the black and gold tunic dress and black silk trousers. He said nothing, but the corners of his mouth turned down.

"They'll have to wait," rumbled Toby. He glanced at Birdie's tense face and took a noisy sip of tea. "Ah, that hits the spot," he said appreciatively. "Pass us a biscuit, Birdwood. Don't hog the lot."

Birdie smiled uncertainly and pushed the plate toward him. And suddenly the tension in the room evaporated. Bizarrely, Milson's appearance had made all the difference. The old alliance of the other two against him had been almost instantly reestablished, and with it their ease, elegant clothes, fancy hairstyles, and unaccustomed nerves notwithstanding. With a sigh of satisfaction Toby dunked his cookie in his tea, swallowed it in one gulp, and took another. "All right," he said. "No more farting around, Birdwood. Milson's here to do the honors; I'm all ears. You tell us—what's been going on round here?

In the sitting room across the hall Alistair was finding it more and more difficult to keep control of the situation. He and Betty Hinder had done their best. Sandwiches, cake, hot soup, tea and coffee, brandy, whiskey, wine, a roaring fire, magazines, and, in desperation, the television set and videos from the library. But as the minutes ticked on, the soft, pink walls closed in. You could feel the tension rising. It had eased for a while when the police arrived, but now it had become palpable again.

He wondered what Verity Birdwood was saying in the office across the hallway. About the place, the guests, the anonymous letter he'd destroyed; the other letter he now knew Josie had found and given to Margot at lunchtime . . . lunchtime . . . aeons ago. He wondered that it was Verity who'd told him about it, murmuring, white-lipped, as she went to call the police. That Josie or Edwina hadn't blurted it out, as they stared at the sight of Margot, dead.

He wondered how many of the people in the room really believed the comforting fiction of the marauding intruder now, no doubt, kilometers away. When he'd put it to them, firmly, slowly, holding his hands together to stop them shaking, speaking overloudly to disguise the trembling in his voice, William, rocking, crying, had stared at him wildly with swimming, terrified eyes and moaned aloud. And no one who had seen the body could fail to remember his terror of the night before, the picture painted then of violent death so like this one. No one, surely, could really believe in a stranger who penetrated this isolated spot unseen and unheard, entered the house through locked and bolted doors, killed so savagely in the one possible half-hour available, and disappeared into the streaming dark through the same bolted doors, leaving no trace behind? Yet no one had argued with him. For the alternative, the obvious alternative, was too terrifying to allow into the open. Far better to pretend to believe a lie, to hold back and down the knowledge that would engulf them all in waves of fear and panic.

Alistair felt himself shudder, and gripped his hands together, digging the nails into his palms. But

they all knew it. You could see it in their faces. Rain
splashed into pools on the sodden grass outside and
thunder rumbled and cracked in the night sky, but for
them Deepdene was no refuge. Somewhere in this
house Margot Bell lay dead under a spotlight, mouth
gaping, blood pooling beside her on the floor. And they
all knew that someone in this room was not what he or
she seemed. Someone here had tightened that knot,
had plunged in those scissors, and watched the blood
flow, and rejoiced in the death. Someone was a killer
behind a mask.

He glanced at the beautician Angela, huddled
white-faced on the couch. She was staring at the TV
screen while a romantic comedy flickered on its merry
way to inevitable confusion, resolution, and happy
ending, but her eyes were glazed. He doubted she was
seeing anything. No wonder. It was she who had discovered the body; her screams, ripping through the
corridors as she ran, that had shattered the convivial
mood of the evening, and opened the door on horror
for them all.

Big Josie sat beside her, solid, motherly, and reassuring. For some reason she'd been the only one able to
calm the girl down, and since then Angela had panicked when she wasn't nearby. Bizarre events created
strange alliances. Josie, fine sandy hair now shaped and
feathered into her cheeks, discreet makeup lifting and
defining her features, was wearing a long, shapeless
garment bought, by the look of the intricately patterned
fabric, on some trip to Indonesia or Malaysia. Margot
would have turned up her nose at it, Alistair caught
himself thinking. But somehow it suited Josie, in a way
that a more Margot-approved garment would not. It
didn't suit her figure. It didn't suit her complexion. But
it suited—what?—her essence, or something. She
looked very womanly in it, Alistair thought. Not
pretty, not feminine, not smart—definitely not smart—

but strong and capable, fertile and enduring. Formidable, in fact. Maybe that was what had calmed Angela, made her stop screaming at last, close her eyes, and sob quietly on Josie's broad shoulder. Maybe that need to protect had sealed Josie's garrulous mouth.

Belinda sat with William in a corner. She was white-faced under her makeup and her pretty dark curls were tangled, but her small hand patted his arm, and she talked to him in a low voice, leaning toward him, screening out the rest of the room. She'd managed to keep him quiet for the last half-hour like this. Such a nervy, anxious little person herself, but able, apparently, to rise to the occasion when necessary. Please God her nerve and her luck would hold.

So far William's hysterics had remained inarticulate. He'd kept his promise to say nothing about Laurel Moon coming to Deepdene, even after the discovery of Margot's body, when Alistair's hand gripping his arm was the only thing keeping him upright, Alistair's fierce whispering in his ear the only thing holding back his screams. He'd still said nothing, even to Belinda, it seemed, because she showed no sign of turning her attention to anyone else in the room. It was a miracle. Maybe he was too frightened. If he knew about the second letter . . . if Josie had talked, or Edwina. Or even Conrad. Alistair fidgeted. He wished the police would hurry up with Verity Birdwood so he could talk to them. Then maybe the whole thing could be sorted out quickly. If William snapped beforehand, made wild accusations, for example . . .

He saw William look up at his companion and give a half smile. Good for you, Belinda, he cheered silently. Belinda's vulnerable face flushed slightly with pleasure as she returned the smile. She looked extremely pretty, Alistair thought. That was probably helping. William was by no means unsusceptible to female charm. Look how he'd fallen for Margot—like a ton of bricks. But

Margot ate him alive. Belinda would be a different story.

Alistair felt a hand on his shoulder and turned with a jerk to see Conrad's tanned face bent toward him. The man moved absolutely silently. He'd been slouched against the wall at the other end of the room only seconds before. Alistair frowned.

"I've got to get out of here, man," murmured Conrad, and yawned, showing healthy pink gums and gleaming white teeth. "I can't handle this."

"It can't be helped," said Alistair coldly, moving slightly away from him. "None of us likes it, but the police told us to stay together, and that's what we're going to do." What was it about this man, he thought, that made him draw himself up, and stiffen inside? It was as though Conrad was an alien species from which his own flesh recoiled instinctively. Well, in a way he was. He was cold as a lizard, despite the overt sensuality of his face and manner. For God's sake, he had been poor Margot's lover, and yet he'd shown no emotion, even when he saw her body. Just looked, pale blue eyes unreadable, turned, and melted away through the shrieks and hysteria, intact and apparently unmoved, interested only in removing himself from a situation he found uncomfortable.

He was doing the same thing now.

Conrad let his eyes drift around the room. "You'd better watch it, or there'll be trouble."

"It's my responsibility," said Alistair stiffly. "Just leave it to me, will you? I'll handle the guests."

The other man shrugged. He jerked his head slightly toward the fireplace. "You'd better start handling over there, then, man," he muttered. "Before she goes right off the deep end. I don't want to be around to see it if she does."

Alistair glanced at him in dismay, then cautiously turned his head to look. Edwina, sleek and handsome, was reading in an armchair, a drink at her elbow. She was the one person he had trusted to keep her cool in this situation, and he hadn't been disappointed. What was Conrad on about? Then his eyes reluctantly moved beyond Edwina to the shadows of the corner.

Helen had risen from her chair and was staring out into the room. Her big hands hung loosely by her sides. Her expression was fixed. Her whole body quivered with tension. Alistair felt a chill. Helen had been, as expected, the most successful makeover by far. He remembered the feeling of satisfaction as he worked on her hair earlier in the day, and saw its magnificent potential realized. He remembered, too, the feeling of vague disquiet he'd felt as he handled it while she sat disengaged and unresisting in the chair. Shining honey-colored wings now brushed her perfect jawline. Her heavy-lidded eyes under perfectly arched brows were huge and gleaming. As Alistair watched, her mouth opened slightly. A drop of moisture began to form on the bottom lip. She made no attempt to wipe it away. Just stood, staring, while the quivering in her body strengthened to a shudder. A moaning sound began, deep in her throat.

Alistair stood frozen to the spot.

"God, do something, man," muttered Conrad in his ear. "*Do* something."

But it was too late. Alistair just had time to register the shocked, white faces of the other people in the room, snapping upward from magazines, turning abruptly from TV and conversation to stare, before the moaning became a growling shriek, the shriek a frightful, singing wail, and Helen fell jerking and shaking to the floor, and all hell broke loose.

11

"Christ almighty!" Toby wiped his streaming forehead. "This is a bloody madhouse!" He looked at Helen lying quiet at last on the bed. "What in hell's the matter with her? An epileptic, is she?"

"She didn't say so on her form," Alistair panted. "We ask them about illnesses and conditions—heart and diabetes and epilepsy and so on, just in case, you know, and she didn't tick anything at all." He looked exhausted, and so he might, Toby thought. It had been quite an evening, all things considered. And this Helen was no lightweight, skinny as she was. Getting her upstairs, still occasionally struggling and flailing, had been a nightmare, even for three of them.

Milson smoothed back the glossy black hair that Toby had just seen in disarray for the first time ever. "It didn't appear to be an epileptic seizure, sir. More likely it was simply a hysterical turn of some kind. Probably to be expected."

Alistair eyed the figure on the bed nervously, and took a step back. "You mean—oh, God! William said . . . I should have listened . . ."

"No point in going into that now, Mr. Swanson,"

said Toby crisply. "She'll be able to answer questions in due course. When do you think, Milson?"

Milson had removed his jacket and in crisp white shirt had somehow managed to acquire a vaguely medical air. Milson made a point of regularly attending the refresher courses in first aid that Toby eschewed. Toby found the demonstrations of heart massage and mouth-to-mouth resuscitation unnerving, haunted as he was by the conviction that he was more likely to require these services himself at some point in the not too distant future, than need to use them on someone else. Most of his customers, after all, were cold before he got to them, whereas with his diet and exercise habits, he was a textbook case of a heart attack waiting to happen. He pulled at his tie. It was very warm in here.

"Impossible to say at this stage," said Milson, still in paramedical mode. "We'll just have to wait and see. Anyway, she's just resting now. All the vital signs are normal. I'll stay with her until the doctor gets here."

Alistair looked agitated. "But look, shouldn't we . . . ?" he fluttered.

Toby took his arm and guided him firmly from the room. "Call me in the office if she starts talking, Milson," he called back over his shoulder, and shut the door firmly. He looked at his watch. Ten o'clock!

"Getting late," he muttered, moving the reluctant Alistair toward the stairway. He thought furiously, his brow furrowed. With a bit of luck the team from Windsor would have arrived by now. They must have been held up on the way. Conditions were appalling. Still, they hadn't exactly rushed it. Put out, maybe, because a team from Sydney had come to take over the investigation. Well, he'd soon put a flea in their collective ear. This wasn't the time for playing games.

They reached the stairs and stood looking down at the deserted vestibule below. The sitting room door was closed, the people inside waiting—for their return, for news, for anything to break the tension that gripped them. "Anyone else likely to give us trouble?" he asked, to break the heavy silence.

"Angela Fellowes, our beautician, who found Margot . . . Margot's body . . . is very upset. And William Dean, Margot's secretary, is in a bad way," said Alistair slowly. "He was close to Margot. And, well, you've probably heard about his history from Verity Birdwood. She tells me you know each other. For William, this is . . ." He looked sideways at Toby, as if wondering how much he knew.

"Nightmare stuff. Yes." And no wonder he's got the wind up, Toby thought. He winced, reliving the lurch in the pit of his stomach as he stood in a blood-stained back room of this warm, closed house, his growing sickness as Birdie had leaned forward later, talking fast and urgently, not, as he'd expected, about that day and the day before, but about a time ten years before, about other deaths, deaths he remembered, deaths exactly like the one he had just seen.

He'd cursed himself then, for his blindness, and her for her panic. He should have seen the parallel from her description of the murder on the phone. She should have told him. Not just gabbled on about rain, and needing help, bustling him into blundering up here without grabbing the Laurel Moon file, without preparation of any kind, expecting only a straightfor-ward investigation. But he had felt a flutter of memory, hadn't he? A vague feeling, a something tapping on the edge of his mind? If he'd listened to that, he would have made the connection, wondered about it, consid-ered the possibility of a coincidence, or alternatively a bizarrely delayed copycat killing. Then he would have dug out the file anyway, just out of interest, or to be on the safe side, and he'd have it here now. But he'd bro-ken his own first rule and ignored it, in his delight at having something to take him away from the office and the dreariness of routine, in his pleasure at discomforting Milson. Silly, childish bloody fool!

He cleared his throat and hitched at his belt, aware that Alistair Swanson was watching him. He began walking down the stairs. "I'll have a word with Angela and William Dean presently, Mr. Swanson. Then we can let them get off to bed. One thing you could confirm for me: Verity Birdwood, who as you've obviously gathered has worked with the police before, tells me most of the people in the house now were present last night when William talked about the Gray Lady murderer being freed. Except for the girl Angela and . . . the massage man, is it?"

"Angela and Conrad. Yes, that's right, they weren't there. They live in, but they don't usually attend the late evening drinks. Betty Hinder, the housekeeper, wasn't there either. She'd gone home by then."

"Did you notice any particular reaction—from anyone at all?"

Alistair frowned. "Not really. Most people were upset by it, naturally. They talked about it. Josie said she thought it was a disgrace the killer—Laurel Moon —had been let out at all. In fact, she said she should have hanged. Edwina—she's a sensible lady—argued with her on that. Little Belinda just put her hands over her ears and tried not to listen. And Helen . . . Helen . . ." His voice trailed off.

"Yes, Mr. Swanson?"

"Helen said that ten years in a place like Laurel Moon had been in should be enough punishment for anyone, or something like that. We all sat up and took notice, because she'd hardly said anything at all up till then." He gripped Toby's arm. "She really sounded as if she knew what she was talking about," he whispered. "But I never thought . . . Oh, my God!"

"Is it likely the three staff who weren't present at

drinks would have heard about the conversation later? That night, or today?"

Alistair shrugged. "Quite likely. People talk, don't they? Well, I told Betty Hinder myself, I remember, this morning. She already knew about William's past, of course. I just mentioned he'd been talking about it the night before."

"What about the other bit—that William had heard Laurel Moon was coming here?"

"No, I didn't tell her that."

"And the beautician? Would she have heard about the fracas at drinks?"

"I didn't say anything to Angela—she hasn't been here long, and I don't know her all that well—but Conrad could have told her. They work quite closely together. The massage room's next to the beauty therapy room. They have interconnecting doors."

"How would he have known?"

"Oh, I should think Margot told him last night that William had been performing . . ." Alistair's voice trailed off and he looked uncomfortable. "Well, I don't know, really. I'm just guessing."

"Sure."

The two men paced each other down the stairs, watching their feet.

"I gather Margot Bell *was* on particularly intimate terms with this Conrad, then," Toby observed casually.

Alistair flushed and nibbled at his lip. "Why do you say that?"

"Well, plainly because you indicate she could have talked to him last night. After, presumably, she'd excused herself to go to bed and gone upstairs. Since Conrad's room is, I gather, downstairs in the annex, the only way they could have met was by design. Up in her room, for example. Would this be likely, Mr. Swanson?"

"I don't . . ."

Toby stopped and hitched at his belt again, belligerently this time. "Listen, Mr. Swanson," he growled, "there's a woman dead out the back there. And someone here killed her. We might have a theory about who that was, but we haven't got an earthly as to why. And anyhow, theory's not fact, and not proof. Understand? Just answer my questions. There's no time for pussyfooting around."

Alistair shuddered. "No." His voice cracked and he cleared his throat. "But why do you need to know about Conrad and Margot and all that?" he asked, almost peevishly.

"I need to know everything, Mr. Swanson. Now, how did Margot Bell react when she heard Laurel Moon might be coming here—or was here already?"

"Margot didn't know."

"What? Didn't you tell her?"

Alistair showed the whites of his eyes. He ducked his head away to one side. "Actually, no. No, I didn't tell Margot. I told William and Verity Birdwood to say nothing, and I decided to keep it completely quiet myself."

"Why, Mr. Swanson?"

Alistair hesitated. "I couldn't see the point of telling," he said finally. "For one thing, it wasn't necessarily true. For another, if the poor woman was coming here, or if she was here already"—Alistair swallowed and went on—"she was coming for help. We advertise discretion. That goes for everyone, as far as I'm concerned."

"Very commendable. But surely your partner should have been told. Presumably she would have felt the same way, and played along?"

"Not necessarily," mumbled Alistair. "Margot and I . . . sometimes had different ideas about that sort of thing." He glanced at Toby and quickly looked away again.

Toby thoughtfully scratched at his roughening chin. "I see. So you didn't tell Miss Bell immediately. Fair enough. But then, as I understand it, you started getting nasty mail. One note that you destroyed, according to Birdie—Verity Birdwood—and one Margot Bell herself opened, which, with a bit of luck, we might still be able to lay our hands on. Didn't that change your mind?"

"I thought about telling her about the note—I did!" The other man shook his head desperately. "But I wasn't going to interrupt her last night . . . um . . . and this morning she—well, she was a bit out of sorts this morning, and then we got very busy, and the opportunity never arose, if you see what I mean, and I just decided—to let it drop."

"I see." And the longer the wretched man waited, for sure, Toby thought, the more appalling the prospect of breaking the belated news to the blissfully (or not so blissfully) ignorant Margot Bell became. "Wasn't Miss Bell curious about the note she opened?" he asked mildly.

"I didn't even know about that till—till after we found her dead. Verity told me." Alistair gripped the banister, his knuckles showing white. "Apparently Margot opened it at lunchtime and I—wasn't there. I was working. Look, obviously it would've upset her. But there are lots of nutters in the world, Mr. Toby. Margot would have had no reason to associate the note she opened with Laurel Moon. As far as she was concerned it would have just been a nasty letter—could have been from anyone, guests or staff. She'd have had no reason to think . . ."

"Think anyone's life was in danger? I see, yes." Toby left that one in the air for a moment, watching the blood drain from Alistair's cheeks. Then he began placidly walking down the stairs again. He waited at the bottom till Alistair caught up before going on. "So, getting back to the point," he said in a low voice, glancing at the sitting room door, "if we leave Verity Birdwood out of it for the moment, only you and William knew that Laurel Moon was coming to Deepdene. That she could be already here. That if she was here she wasn't too happy, going by those threatening notes."

"I suppose so, Mr. Toby." Alistair's voice was barely audible, and Toby had to lean closer to hear. "Except . . ."

"Except what? Who else knew?"

"Well, Laurel Moon knew, didn't she? She knew. And only she knew what she was going to do."

Only she knew. The whispered phrase hung between them as they stood in the magnificent marble-floored foyer, the stairs rising up behind them to the silent bedroom floor above. In both their minds rose the image of Milson, white shirt gleaming, narrow dark face concentrated and intent, sitting up there by a bed in the room called "Eve." Through Milson's eyes they saw the gaunt woman lying there, shining honey-colored hair tumbled on the pillow, dark, dead eyes mercifully closed now in deep sleep. The chest rose and fell almost imperceptibly, the big, bony hands twitched now and then against the clean, white sheet on which they lay. Alistair shivered.

Toby straightened his shoulders deliberately. He felt like shaking them, to shrug off the dull weight that had been settling there ever since he came into this house. "I'll ring Windsor now, Mr. Swanson," he said. "Come with me, please. I just have one or two more questions for you before I talk to anyone else." He began to cross the vestibule to the office.

Alistair stood where he was, staring stupidly. "You can't," he said, in dull surprise.

Toby turned on his heel and scowled. He'd had enough. "Can't. Can't? Of course I can, Mr. Swanson! Look, I thought I'd made it clear that—"

"No! No, I don't mean that!" Alistair stumbled after him. "I thought you knew. You can't ring. No one can ring. The lines are down. Have been for a couple of hours. Didn't Betty tell you? Or Dr. Thoms?"

"No they bloody didn't!" Toby remembered the little doctor's final malicious parting shot. So that's what he'd meant. He thought quickly. "Right, then, I'll send someone. The Windsor team—they'll be here by now, surely. Or Verity Birdwood, maybe." It was a bugger, because he'd wanted Birdie to take notes for him while Milson stayed upstairs.

"You can't," Alistair repeated, still staring at him as if he were crazy. "Didn't you see? Don't you know . . . ? The rain . . . they let the dam spill last night . . . the creek's in flood. The police from Windsor can't get here now. They'll have turned back long ago. They won't try to get in by boat till it's light. Verity can't go for help. It'd be suicide. There's no way in—or out."

"That's impossible, Mr. Swanson," said Toby stiffly. He felt his palms beginning to sweat. "My constable and I drove in here only a little over an hour ago. Our vehicle is four-wheel drive. We'll simply—"

Alistair grabbed his arm and began dragging him toward the office. "Look," he gabbled. "You just look, if you don't believe me." He threw open the door and pulled Toby inside.

Birdie was sitting on the window seat, looking out through the curtains. She looked up as they entered, her pointed face pale under the skillful makeup. Toby strode to the window and pulled the curtain aside. Rain beat on the veranda roof, and splashed on the stone paving beneath. The light from the room streamed out, catching the pale lines of their car parked by the front door and the sheen of puddles that dotted the gravel on which it stood. But beyond the car, where the ground sloped down to the gateway and the creek beyond, Toby's straining eyes caught movement where no movement should be. The earth was rippling, catching the light. It was alive, creeping and swirling around the trunks of the poplar trees. It wasn't earth. It was water. Toby looked left and right in disbelief and everywhere he looked it was the same. In the space of an hour, the house had become an island.

"I told you," said Birdie accusingly. She turned back to the window.

Dan Toby stared helplessly at the back of her neat, cropped head, the slim nape of her neck. He glanced at Alistair, and saw the gleam of sweat on his high forehead. He looked out again at the streaming rain.

"Bloody hell," he whispered.

When Alistair had gone back to his charges in the sitting room, Birdie and Toby sat together self-consciously for a moment. Toby's stomach gurgled. Bloody hamburger, he thought.

"Nervous tummy, huh?" Birdie said, and sniggered.

"Indigestion," he retorted, sniffing. "You've cheered up. Funny sort of time to do it, isn't it? Stuck here in the teeming rain, no phone, no way out, hysterics every bloody way you look, and a murderer on the loose. What kind of nut case are you anyway, Birdwood?"

Birdie sniggered again. "It's so bad it's good," she said. Not for the world would she have admitted how reassuring she found his presence. Her tone changed abruptly. "Look, while we're by ourselves . . . Did Helen say anything?"

He nodded. "On the way upstairs she did. I'm surprised you didn't hear her, even with the door shut."

"We could hear shouts, but no words. What did she say?"

"All sorts of stuff about blood and being locked

up. She was raving. Kicking and screaming. Fell and twisted her ankle and we had to carry her the rest of the way. She's asleep now, Milson says. He'll be there when she wakes up, though, and then we'll see what else we can get."

"Poor woman." Birdie's voice was thoughtful.

"I don't know about poor woman. I'd be saving my sympathy for Margot Bell, myself." Toby hesitated. "You're assuming it's her, I gather? Laurel Moon?"

"Aren't you?"

"Oh yes. She answered to the name, though that could've just been hysteria. But she's about the right age, by the look of her, she's got the scars on her wrists and stomach, and from what you say she's the obvious candidate. Still, till we question her—by God, Birdie, I wish you'd said on the bloody phone Moon was involved. I could've got the file—pictures—everything. Then we'd be home and hosed."

"I know. I just . . . I don't know . . . Shit!" Birdie moved restlessly beside him. The silk of her tunic rustled, and he could smell the unfamiliar cosmetic scent of her hair as she shook her head. "We were just so full of it here, I just sort of assumed it. I thought I said it. And the line was so bad, I could hardly hear you. Stupid!"

"Ah well . . ." Toby let it pass. He settled back. His stomach gurgled again, monstrously loud in the silence, and he punched at it absentmindedly. "Has anyone else said anything? About Margot Bell being killed that way? They've made the connection, presumably."

"Of course they have. They don't know about the evidence that Laurel Moon's actually here incognito, but everyone heard William say Laurel Moon had been let out. Everyone remembered the Gray Lady murders. Josie actually reminded the whole room about how Moon went about the killings."

"So what do they make of it?"

"Before you got here Alistair was running this line about someone breaking in. Well, if you accepted that, ignoring bolted doors and all that sort of complication, you'd have to assume, wouldn't you, given the way Margot died, that the intruder was Laurel Moon herself, who'd somehow tracked William down or ended up here by some bizarre chance? Unless you were willing to accept the even more unlikely coincidence that a perfect stranger chose a method of killing that matched a conversation he knew nothing about. Anyway, Angela the beautician and Mrs. Hinder the housekeeper still claim to hold the break-in theory. Out of loyalty to Alistair, I'd say. One of the guests, Belinda, is on their side. To try to calm William down, in her case. She's got the fancies for him."

"What about the others?"

"Once you and the others got Helen out of the room, Josie and Edwina and our spivvy friend Conrad started saying out loud what the others probably actually think. That Margot must have been done in by someone already in the house, copying the method described at drinks last night. And Josie at least made no bones about who she thought that was."

"Helen?"

"Of course. She said she saw Helen was funny in the head, as she put it, as soon as she laid eyes on her. Then Conrad spilled the beans about the threatening letter Margot got at lunchtime. William nearly jumped out of his skin when he heard about that. But he still didn't say anything about Laurel Moon—or the first letter. I think he was sort of paralyzed with shock and fear."

"The thing is," Toby said, almost to himself, "why go for Margot Bell? Why not William, like he thought she would? There'd be good reason for it, from memory. Why kill someone else entirely? Unless it was by accident."

"Hardly that. Margot was laid out under a spotlight waiting for Angela to give her a neck massage. Everyone knew where she was. Whoever killed her knew exactly what they were doing." Birdie hesitated, then rushed on. "And I don't think you can just assume it was Helen, Dan, whether she's Laurel Moon or not."

"Don't you?" Toby pressed his lips together, and considered. He could have argued with her rationally. He could have carefully gone over the whole thing with her. For a moment he considered doing just that—listening to her arguments, then putting forward his own. If he had, as it happened, the nightmare that was to follow might have been averted. But it was late, people were waiting, she was nervy and uncertain, and he was sure. So he decided to bully instead. "Look, just leave that to me, will you? You're just a witness here. I don't want any of your crackpot theories taking up valuable time. All right?"

Birdie shrugged. He looked at her sharply and continued, pulling out his notebook. "All right. Now, Helen had the opportunity, from what you said before the kerfuffle. Just go through that for me, will you? Tonight's drinks party, from the top."

He waited, pen poised, and finally, reluctantly, she began to speak.

"And that's it. We came back here and started ringing the cops. Or I did. I told Alistair I could handle it. Left him free to deal with the general hysterics. I couldn't get on to the locals, so I rang you. You know the rest." Birdie fell silent. Again, they could hear the sound of the rain.

Toby grunted. "So," he began slowly, "this Helen —we'll call her that for now—could've got to Margot

Bell and killed her quite easily in the time she was away from the sitting room."

"Yes. But we shouldn't forget, Dan, that just about everyone else could've paid Margot a visit too."

Before Toby could answer, the phone rang on the desk. He picked it up. "Good," he said, listening. "Good. All right. Just stay put. I'll be back to you. Looks like the Windsor team won't be here. Can't get through. Phone lines are down too. Yes. Yeah. Quite so. Bye." He put the receiver carefully down in its cradle and turned back to Birdie. "Milson," he said briefly. "She's still out of it. He's searched the room. Nothing. Just a few clothes, a toothbrush, and some money, and the key to her own room in her pocket. No identification. Nothing. He'll stay on up there. You'll have to help me with the interviews. I'll explain you've had experience so you've been co-opted."

"They won't like that, Dan."

"They'll have to lump it. Now look, Birdie, with Milson out of commission I need your help to tie up the loose ends. But I haven't got time to argue with you. I take your point that people other than the Helen woman left the room between when Edwina what's-her-name left Margot Bell at about ten past six and when she was found by Angela at half past. So theoretically they could've got to Bell then. But we can rule some out, can't we? Josie was under your eye in the sitting room the whole time. So was Edwina. William and Belinda were together. Conrad wasn't out of the room long enough to do anything. That leaves our campy mate Alistair, the supposedly swimming Angela, Helen, and of course Mrs. Hinder, who you seem to have left out of your reckoning altogether. And we'll get all their stories down. But look, Birdwood, take it from me. All that's irrelevant. What's relevant is Helen's movements, what her relationship with Bell was. That's what it's going to come down to in the end."

Birdie stood up and stretched. "I wish I was as sure as you." She turned back to him and caught him looking at her appraisingly, with a slight smile. "What're you staring at?" she demanded crossly.

He shook his head, still smiling. "You look so different! I can't get used to it. You should have your hair done like that all the time, Birdwood. It really suits you."

"Oh, dry up, will you?" Birdie turned away, pushing her hand roughly through the new haircut. But the gleaming curls fell neatly and charmingly back into place, Toby noted. This Alistair was good at his job, it seemed.

"Well, I'd better go over and make myself known to the mob." He hitched at his belt. "I'll start the interviews now. They'll be keen to get to bed. With a bit of luck I'll get a clear picture of where everyone was, and when, without too much farting round."

"I wouldn't count on it."

"Oh yes. Think about it. Whatever they're saying out loud, your mate Josie couldn't be alone. All of them must have put two and two together about our friend upstairs by now, even without knowing she's actually the Gray Lady murderer. From what you say she was acting very oddly before the murder. Then she leaves the room during the critical period. Then she throws a violent conniption while she's waiting to be questioned. Pretty damning, wouldn't you say? So they know we've got a prime suspect upstairs, under guard. They've got nothing to be scared of, have they? No reason to hide anything. Come on. Let's get the show on the road."

He ushered her out the door, and caught her quizzical glance as she brushed past him. "Don't do your usual act, Birdwood. This is all pretty clear-cut. You know that in your gut, don't you? It's just routine now."

She shrugged. "Whatever you say, Dan," she murmured demurely. And led the way to the sitting room.

12

"So if you'll please bear with me a bit longer, I'd be most grateful." Toby finished his spiel with what was supposed to be a reassuring smile. Belinda, clutching William's arm in a shadowy corner of the room, gave a smothered little shriek. Toby adjusted his expression rapidly. The smile had obviously been a mistake. "Once you've had your chat with me—just routine, as I've said—you can get off to bed. In the morning, no doubt, reinforcements from Windsor will be here, and the whole matter will be cleared up. In the meantime . . ."

"Excuse me, Mr. Toby." The woman Toby knew to be Edwina spoke politely but authoritatively from her armchair. "You're saying that we have to stay here tonight? Surely, under the circumstances, that's a bit much to expect?"

He eyed her thoughtfully. She was obviously a lady used to getting her own way. He noted the firm line of her jaw, and steady, determined eyes, and rose to the occasion.

"I'm afraid there's no alternative, madam."

"But there must be an alternative!" The strong

voice trembled very slightly and he saw that the big, neatly manicured hands were gripping the arms of the chair with unnecessary force.

"We're flooded in, Edwina," said Alistair softly. "I did tell you. It's unfortunate, but . . ."

"Unfortunate! Un-bloody fortunate!" exploded Josie, leaping to her feet and looking furiously around the room. Her cheeks were flushed scarlet. "Locked up here with a corpse and a murderer all night! I should think it is unfortunate. What if she gets out in the night and goes for someone else? You've only got one bloke with her, haven't you?" She rubbed her nose violently with the already sodden handkerchief she was clutching in her hand and rounded on Toby, who winced. "Tall, skinny streak, too. He couldn't handle her on his own, if she was determined. Mad people have superhuman strength. Don't you know that?"

"Josie . . ." Angela held out a pleading hand. "Please don't . . ."

"This poor girl's at the end of her tether!" Josie raged on, ignoring her completely. "And he's not much better!" She stabbed her finger in the shrinking William's general direction. "And the rest of us have had it! Do you hear? I'm not going to stand here and—"

"That's enough!" Toby's voice was icy. He stepped forward and narrowed his eyes. Josie faced up to him defiantly. Her broad chest was heaving. The smell of eucalyptus hung around her like some primitive perfume. It flashed across his mind, bizarrely, that she was just about as big as he was. If she wanted to make a fight of it he wouldn't like to make a bet on the outcome, in his condition. He felt Birdie move closer to him. Which one of them did she think needed protection, he wondered. Herself, or him? The thought amused and calmed him.

"I don't like this any more than you do, madam," he said sternly. "But what we can't change we must endure. What's more, we don't have a shred of proof that any one person is responsible for what's happened here tonight, and wild accusations serve no purpose at all. Now, the best thing that you can do for your friends is calm down, cooperate like a sensible woman, and let me get my job done so we can all get some sleep. Is that clear?"

The fire died in Josie's face, and the energy drained away, leaving her flabby and tired-looking. No longer an Amazon. Just a big, flushed woman with a bad cold. She turned away and self-consciously plumped herself back onto the couch.

"Now then!" Toby maintained his firm demeanor. Obviously it was called for. He bowed slightly in Edwina's direction. "I understand the unpleasantness of this, and believe me it won't be prolonged a minute longer than necessary. I'll see Miss . . . Angela first, and then the rest of you one by one." He nodded formally to Angela, sheltering in Josie's shadow, and then turned to Alistair. "Perhaps some tea might be in order," he said calmly. "Could Mrs. Hinder provide that, do you think?"

"Oh sure, yes," Alistair babbled. "Betty, will you . . ."

"Right." The thin woman in black moved from her place by the wall and threw Toby an unfriendly look. "You'll be wanting some too, will you?"

"Yes, please, Mrs. Hinder, if you don't mind. In the office. You could bring Miss Birdwood's in there too." Toby turned to go. He wasn't giving an inch, but his neck was prickling. He could feel their eyes on him, following his every move. Thunder growled outside the windows. He paused. "Might be as well for someone to give Mrs. Hinder a hand," he said casually to Alistair.

Alistair stared at him, his hazel eyes almost black, so dilated were the pupils. His mouth fell slightly open.

Then he pulled himself together, glanced rapidly around, very obviously dismissed the distraught Angela and haggard William, and focused on Conrad. He cleared his throat. "Conrad, you could help Betty, could you?"

Mrs. Hinder curled her lip as Conrad pushed himself languidly from the fireplace. "I don't need . . ." she began, but Alistair waved away her objections.

"Conrad will help you," he said firmly. "Which will make it all the quicker. All right?"

She sniffed with disgust and turned her back on him, pushing her way through the door to the dining room. Conrad, grinning, slouched behind her. Toby felt Alistair move slightly and turned to look at him. He was staring after Conrad fixedly, his soft mouth set in a hard line, his brow furrowed. No love lost there, Toby mentally noted, and flicked his eyes in Birdie's direction.

But Birdie wasn't watching Alistair. Her gaze was directed at the other end of the room, where Josie sat with Angela in front of the TV set, her eyes closed, one hand pressing the handkerchief to her nose, the other patting the girl's arm in a soft, regular beat of reassurance. Angela's eyes were wide open, staring straight at the flickering screen where Humphrey Bogart and Katharine Hepburn played out their unlikely love affair amid the leeches and reeds of *African Queen.* But the stare was glassy and fixed. Whatever thoughts were struggling behind those vacant eyes, it was certain that neither love nor the rigors of river navigation was playing any part in them.

"In your own words, Angela. Just what happened." Toby attempted to conceal his impatience. No good pushing the girl further off her tree than she was already.

Angela blinked her pretty, vacant eyes and licked her lips. "I was swimming," she began, and stopped.

"Yes?"

"I went swimming like I do every night, from six to six-thirty."

"You don't go to the little drinks party, then?"

The girl shook her head, fair ponytail swinging. "No. I don't have to. Thank *goodness*. William has to go. But Conrad and I don't. I go swimming."

"Yes." Toby exchanged glances with Birdie. This girl was simpleminded to the point of being just plain simple. "So tonight you went swimming as usual," he prompted gently. "You forgot you had an appointment with Margot Bell, and—"

"Oh *no!*" Angela shook her head again, violently this time, and her cheeks burned scarlet. "Oh no, I'd *never* forget a thing like that. Heavens! Miss Bell *didn't* ask me to do her neck. She never said a *word* about it. Well, actually, I barely *saw* her all day. And not to speak to."

Birdie leaned forward. "It was a busy day," she said sympathetically. "And you haven't been here all that long, have you? Easy for things to slip your mind. Are you sure . . . ?"

Angela's eyes filled with tears of frustration. "That's what Alistair said! But honestly, Miss Bell never said *anything* to me. Heavens!" She appealed to Birdie. "Don't you think I'd *remember* if she had? I'd have been scared to *death*—you saw how cranky she was this morning. And anyway, *Conrad* always did her massages on Monday nights. He *always* did. Things here run like clockwork. Nothing changes. Of *course* I'd have remembered! I'd have thought of nothing else all *day!*"

Toby cleared his throat. Interesting. He studied the young, healthy face before him. Seemed transparent enough. "Well, all right then, Angela. You were swimming, and Mr. Swanson came to remind . . . ah, to tell you, that Miss Bell was waiting for her massage. What was the timing of all that, would you know?"

She stared at him vacantly. "The time? Well, no, I don't know *exactly*. I don't pay that much attention to time, when I'm off duty."

"Just do your best," droned Toby patiently.

Angela's smooth brow wrinkled with effort. "I went along to the changing room like always, just after I heard William go up to the house," she began slowly. "His room's next to mine. Conrad's on the other side. I went through the massage room to the pool—it's empty by then and I'm allowed to do that, you know." She paused. Toby felt himself swaying forward, eyebrows raised, urging her on to greater things—or at least to get on, period.

Angela's face cleared and brightened. "It was *exactly* six when I finished in the changing room and went out to swim!" she announced triumphantly. "I remember now. I looked at the clock, then I walked out to the pool and just went straight in. Let the water just *take* me. I don't wear my watch in the pool. I know some people do, but I like to feel *free* of time, you know, when I'm swimming."

"Yes. But what I'd really like to know, Angela, is just when Alistair called you. To tell you about Miss Bell."

She looked at him limpidly. "Oh, I wouldn't know about that."

"You can't even make a guess?"

She shook her head stubbornly. "I just forget all *about* that sort of thing, when I'm swimming. I warm up really, *really* well, so then once I get in the water I can just, you know, *live* in my body. It's so *important* to be aware of the *blood*, and the *breath*, and the *water* and nothing else. Just—"

"When Alistair called you, how many lengths had you swum?" Birdie interrupted casually.

"Oh. Well, by the time he made me hear—you know, he said he'd been trying for a while, because I really *am* in a world of my *own* in the water—I was just turning to do the twenty-first," Angela answered promptly.

"And how fast do you swim a length?"

"Forty-seven seconds, usually. I can go *faster*, of course, but . . ."

"Right." Birdie made a note, and grinned at Toby. "So . . ." She scribbled on the pad in front of her. "Forty-seven times twenty is nine forty, um . . . divided by sixty is fifteen and a bit—add a couple of minutes as a margin for error . . . you'd been swimming about seventeen and a half minutes."

Angela gazed at her admiringly. "I didn't think of working it out that way," she said.

Toby ran his hand over his thinning hair. For a mad moment he wished Milson was with him. Milson was a pain in the arse, but there were times when a smart-arse was ten times worse. "So," he rumbled. "Mr. Swanson called you . . ."

"Yes. He called me and I finally heard and got out of the pool, and he told me about Miss Bell waiting, and I said she hadn't said *anything* to me, and he said better get changed quickly and go down to see her anyway, so I did. I was so *flustered*, you can *imagine*. I couldn't *think* what had happened, or why she wanted me."

"And how long did it take you to change into your clothes, do you think? Five minutes?"

"About five minutes."

"That would have got you to the beauty therapy room well before twenty-five past six," Toby rumbled, scratching with the stub of a pencil on the back of an envelope he'd found in his pocket. He looked up at her.

"But you didn't give the alarm till just after half-past six."

"Didn't I?" Angela looked confused and frightened. "Does that *matter?*"

"Hold on, hold on," Birdie chipped in, ignoring Toby's cross look. She thought she could see what was happening here. Angela was really the most literal-minded person she'd ever dealt with. She took it slowly. "It took five minutes to change your clothes, Angela. Are you including a shower in that?"

"No—oh, *sorry*, did you mean me to? The shower took about three or four minutes. I mean"—Angela appealed to them with big, baffled eyes—"I *had* to get the chlorine off, didn't I? It's so bad for your hair and skin . . . and then I suppose it took about two minutes to do my hair . . . I couldn't really dry it *properly*, just make it fit to be seen . . . and then I *ran* to the beauty therapy room. Oh, I was in a real panic. And then . . ."

She broke off, and the color drained from her face. Birdie raised her eyebrows at Toby and got up. She crossed the room and put her hand on Angela's arm. "Go on, Angela," she murmured. "You got to the beauty therapy room at about six twenty-nine. What happened then? Just get it over."

Angela stared straight ahead. "I opened the door and went into the room," she said through stiff lips. "Miss Bell was lying in the chair, under the light. She had witch-hazel pads on her eyes. I could smell it. And the blood. Like a butcher's shop. Her face . . ." She shuddered, and Birdie tightened her grip. "Her face was so *horrible*. Her tongue was sticking out. And the blood was all over her chest and neck, and dripping on the floor. She was dead. I could see she was quite dead. One of the gowns was lying on the floor, in a puddle of blood, the strings trailing out and I thought, that's what the murderer must have worn. I thought, he might still *be* here. Next door, in the massage room, waiting. Somebody said afterward that the connecting door was locked, but I didn't know that then. I screamed. I couldn't do anything. I couldn't move. I just screamed and screamed, but no one came. And after a while I made myself move. I backed out of the room and ran down toward the main house. I must have been still screaming, because they all came running into the hall, and I took them back, and showed them . . . oh!" She buried her face in her hands.

"Did you touch anything at all in the room, Angela? Or see anyone else touch anything, or pick up anything?" asked Birdie.

The girl shook her head, her face still hidden.

"Did you see anything, anything at all, that seemed odd, or out of place, or different, in the room?"

Angela raised a tearstained face. "There was nothing, except what I've said. Nothing at all. Everything was exactly as I left it, ready for tomorrow."

"Could you really be sure of that?"

"Oh yes!" Angela nodded vehemently. "I've got a *very* good memory for things like that. I'd have noticed."

Toby sat back in his chair. "Well, I think we'll leave it there, then, Angela," he said gently. "You can get off to bed now and get some sleep."

"*Sleep!* I'll *never* sleep!" The girl's lips trembled. "Every time I close my eyes I see . . . it—that picture. I can't go back out to that annex. I *can't!*"

"You'll be quite safe. It's quite safe now." Toby cast his eyes eloquently toward the door and Birdie, taking the hint, urged Angela out of her chair and began to move her gently on her way. "I'll see Alistair Swanson again now, thanks," he added casually. Birdie turned to look at him. He seemed to be taking this assistance business a bit far. He yawned and stretched, then folded his arms and returned her stare blandly.

She sniffed audibly and ushered Angela out into the hall.

"I'll get William and Conrad to walk you to your room after you've had your tea," she said quietly, as they crossed the marble floor toward the sitting room. "Don't worry. You'll be all right."

The girl nodded, staring at her feet. She rubbed the back of her hand childishly over her eyes. "I'll be all right," she repeated in a low voice. She stopped. "He must think I'm an idiot," she said, jerking her head back to the office and biting her lip. "I wasn't any help at all, was I? But I really *don't* notice times and things when I'm not working, and there really *wasn't* anything to notice in—in that room. Except for . . . what I told you." Her lip trembled.

"Oh well," Birdie interrupted rapidly. "Don't worry about it now. But in the morning, when you feel better, have another think. Get the picture in your mind. There might be some funny little thing you noticed without realizing it at the time. Something a bit out of place, something where it shouldn't be. Anything like that could help. O.K.?"

"O.K." Angela paused. Her smooth forehead wrinkled slightly. "You know, now that you say that . . . I *do* think there was something. Isn't that *strange?* Like you say, something small. Something . . . Oh, I don't know!" She pressed her fingers to her brow and closed her eyes.

"Sleep on it," advised Birdie. Angela was obviously very suggestible—and overexcited. If she wasn't careful she'd have her on her hands for half an hour, and Toby would have a fit. She put her hand on Angela's arm and pulled gently.

The girl nodded doubtfully, and they entered the sitting room together.

.   .   .

Alistair's account of the evening tallied with Birdie's and Angela's exactly, though Birdie noted he skillfully avoided any mention of tension or difficulty and concentrated on the bare facts. He was a natural peace lover—her exact opposite, in that respect, she thought. Which must have made his life here at Deepdene rather stressful, given Margot's propensities. She decided to remark on this. He hesitated, then gave a rueful smile.

"Oh, Margot was difficult sometimes. She was temperamental. Of course she was. But—look, we'd known each other for a long, long time. And there was a mutual respect there that kept us going. We rubbed along all right."

"This office"—Toby spread out a broad hand to indicate the luxurious fittings around them—"this was hers, I gather. Rather different from yours out back, isn't it?"

"This is the showplace office, yes. Just like Margot was the showplace partner, Mr. Toby," said Alistair gravely. "In a place like this, appearances are very important. Sad that it has to be like that, but there you are. Margot did our PR. She also handled our accounts and tradespeople, with William's help. The basic running of the place was my affair."

"Must be a lot in that, Mr. Swanson."

"There is." Alistair's eyes were tired, but a light burned deep below the fatigue. "It's worth it, though." He leaned forward. "It's very worthwhile work. It's the fulfillment of a dream I had for years. In our way—I know it probably seems a small thing to you, Mr. Toby, but in our own way we've made a lot of people very happy. Made them find out about themselves. In some cases, helped them find out how to live, for the first time in their lives."

"As long as they've got the money to pay, of course." Toby regretted the words as soon as they slipped out.

Alistair flinched as though he'd been struck. "I wished it wasn't like that," he muttered, "but how could we do it otherwise? I always hoped that eventually we'd be able to afford . . . you know, to lower the fees, or maybe take one guest at a reduced rate every fortnight—someone who really needed the help, that sort of thing. For a while I really thought we were getting there. But . . ." He sighed. "Everything's so bloody expensive! And the last year—the last six months, especially—we've been really feeling the pinch."

Toby looked thoughtfully at him. Was he serious? Nothing in this place looked as though anyone connected with it was feeling the pinch. He decided to get the interview back on track. "What will happen to this place without Margot Bell, do you think, Mr. Swanson?"

Alistair stared at him, the lines on his face suddenly very visible, dragging down from mouth to jaw. "I don't know," he said heavily. "I . . . haven't had a chance to think. I get Margot's share of the business. We both made wills that way when we started. But we need more cash to keep the place running. Margot was going to try to get it. I'm no good at that sort of thing. But now . . ." He made a hopeless gesture. Tears began to well up in his eyes but he made no attempt to brush them away.

Toby cleared his throat. "Ah—could I just ask you, finally, Mr. Swanson, who was responsible for accepting the ladies who came here? I gather you have more applications than you can accept?"

"Oh yes." Alistair blinked rapidly. "Lots more than we can handle. I choose them—I try to take people who really can be helped. Who need the help. Then they send photographs, you know, and I try to choose a good variety of types for every fortnight—and group them according to age, if possible, so they'll have something in common."

"Helen. The lady calling herself Helen. You've got her application there, with the others?"

Alistair looked at the pile of pink folders on Margot's gleaming desk. He nodded, and bit his lip. "I thought she'd be great," he whispered. "Wonderful bones. Wonderful eyes. She said in her letter she'd been ill. She said her doctor had suggested she put herself in our hands. I thought we'd really be able to do something for her. I thought, I remember, 'Margot will be pleased with this one.' And Margot was, too. Oh, God help me!" He buried his face in trembling hands.

13

Toby moved uncomfortably. "Well, ah—look, don't upset yourself, Mr. Swanson," he said, eyeing Alistair's shaking shoulders. "You've had a shock. A big shock. You've done everything you can, and I don't need any more from you tonight. Why don't you get off to bed, now? I'm sure Mrs. Hinder can handle things from here on in, can't she?"

Alistair shook his head. He rubbed his hands roughly over his face and stumbled to his feet. "I have to stay with the guests," he muttered. "Don't worry, I'll be O.K. Just lost it for a minute. Who do you want next?"

"The secretary. William."

Alistair nodded and bolted out of the room. Toby slumped back in his chair and pulled at his tie. "Get all that?" he asked Birdie.

She nodded. "Can I see the files?"

"Later. We've got to get these people to bed. I've nearly had it myself. They must be run ragged. Oh, while I think of it . . ." He picked up the phone and dialed. "It's me. Everything all right? Nothing? God! You're sure she's not faking? All right. Stay put. I'll be up soon." He put the receiver back in its cradle and frowned. "Milson swears she's still out of it," he said. "It's getting a bit bloody convenient, isn't it?"

"What would she gain by pretending?"

"Time."

"For what?"

"God, I don't know, Birdwood. Time to think of a way to get out of here, maybe. Maybe she wasn't counting on being flooded in. The Lord knows I wasn't. Or maybe she's getting her defense ready. Or thinking who to kill next. Or maybe she really is asleep because killing always makes her tired. Who knows how a nutter's mind works?"

"She's supposed to be cured, Dan."

Toby snorted. "We've heard that tale before. Bleeding heart psychiatrists wouldn't know if their arses were on fire half the time."

There was a muffled sound from the door. They turned to see William Dean drooping against the architrave, his hand pressed to his mouth, dark eyes huge in his fine-boned face. How long had he been standing there?

Toby beckoned impatiently, irritated at having been caught out. William sidled into the room and crouched, rather than sat, on the chair facing the desk. Toby tapped his blunt fingers on the desk top, glanced at Birdie, and concentrated on settling himself down. He didn't want this chap to go off the deep end. A gentle touch was required. He tried to repair any damage by nodding reassuringly at William, who shrank visibly. What a wimp, thought Toby in disgust. And according to Birdie he'd been Margot Bell's lover. What on earth had she seen in him? Maybe she was a bit kinky—liked to . . . but no, she'd gone on to have it off with Conrad, and he didn't look like the masochistic type, whatever else he might be. And Birdie had said one of the other women here was taking an interest in

William now. Incredible! Must be the looks. He was certainly good-looking, if you liked that sort of thing. He eyed William's tall, willowy body, the high-cheek-boned face, long neck, and silky black hair, the thick black eyelashes cast down to brush the smooth cheeks. Camp as a row of tents, he would have said, if he'd seen him in the street.

"I won't keep you long—ah—William," he began, in as friendly a voice as he could muster. "Just need a few details from you. All right?"

The young man nodded wordlessly, without raising his head. Toby grimaced at Birdie, who returned his look with an amused one of her own. He pressed on. "You heard about the possibility of Laurel Moon coming here yesterday evening, didn't you? How was that, exactly?"

"It was Joyce." William's lips barely moved. "An old friend . . . of my . . . my fiancée's. The one who —died. She rang. At about ten to six."

"Name and address?"

"Mrs. Joyce Tremayne, 3 Winslow Crescent, Darling Point."

"What did you do when you heard?"

"I was very worried. I tried to tell Margot."

"You tried, but . . ."

"She wouldn't listen. She wouldn't talk to me at all. We'd had—a disagreement. She thought I was just annoying her. Wanting to make it up. But it wasn't that at all!" Suddenly William lifted his head, and looked straight at Toby. The long, black lashes were wet. "I'm not stupid," he said, with pathetic dignity. "I could see there was no point."

Toby trod carefully. "You had no way of knowing when Laurel Moon might come here, from what Joyce said?"

"Not exactly. Except Joyce thought it would be soon. Her friend had heard a week ago that it was about to happen. So I thought this batch of guests, or the next . . . one of them . . . I wouldn't know which one, I thought. I didn't ever see the woman. I was sick—in hospital—by the time she was caught. They wouldn't let me see the papers." William's slender fingers fumbled with each other in his lap. He was growing increasingly agitated. "I wouldn't be able to protect myself. I had to tell Margot. She'd have fixed it. She wouldn't have that woman here. She'd have looked after me." The sensitive mouth trembled.

Little boy, thought Toby. But this time a trace of sympathy was mixed with the contempt. He chose his next words carefully.

"But Margot wouldn't have known Laurel Moon if she saw her either, would she?"

"She'd have found out." William spoke with complete assurance now. "She knew people. Important people. She'd have known who to ring. She'd have found out."

"When you first met the guests yesterday evening, did you think one of them might be Laurel Moon?"

William hesitated. "I didn't really know. I wasn't thinking very clearly. After Margot came down to cocktails and I could get away I slipped out and looked at their files in Alistair's office. They didn't tell me much. All the guests are about the same age. People often don't give their right names here, and she wouldn't anyway, would she? I knew Belinda was O.K. She's Margot's friend's sister. And the ABC lady, Verity, was O.K. And we'd seen stuff about Edwina in the paper, and her picture. She's some important businesswoman, or something, and Margot knows—knew—some people who know her, so it wasn't her. So that left Josie and—Helen." He flashed a quick look at Toby, who preserved an interested, noncommittal expression.

William coughed nervously and went on. "I looked at them but I couldn't tell. It could have been either of them. Or neither of them. I'd had a few drinks —a few too many drinks. I decided to forget about Margot, and do something myself. I started to talk about Lois, to see what happened. I sort of worked it into the conversation."

"And what did happen?"

"Nothing. No one did anything much. Except Margot got angry, and left. And Belinda . . . was very sweet and kind. She made me a cup of tea and tried to calm me down. Of course, she didn't know I was scared. She just thought I was upset, because of Lois. She's so gentle. She said she'd been unhappy too." William shook his head. "She's got no self-confidence. I think her family—her sister especially—bullies her a bit. She married very young, but it didn't last long. Her husband treated her badly," he added, almost in surprise. "You wouldn't think he could, would you?"

Toby said nothing. He'd pigeonholed Belinda as a loser at first sight. In his experience the meek rarely inherited anything but a kick in the pants from the first bully they encountered. And there were plenty of bullies about. To cover his silence he tugged at the knot of his tie, already hanging well below the second button of his shirt but still, somehow, giving him that strangled feeling. "What happened then?" he asked after a minute.

William bent over the desk, his eyes on his hands. "Then Belinda and the others went to bed, and I went into the library with Alistair and talked to him. I told him. He said not to worry. He said if she was coming here, she was coming to get help, not cause trouble. He said she'd have no way of knowing I was here. He said ten years was a long time, and she'd been disturbed and now she was better. And he said not to tell Margot or anyone. Even when Verity brought the letter in. He said we had no way of knowing it was really from her —Laurel Moon. He said I was overwrought—all that stuff. Alistair's always like that. He's nice, and he works hard, but he just likes everything to be calm and peaceful, and for everyone to keep quiet." Amazingly, a slight smile trembled on his lips. "Poor Alistair," he murmured.

"Yes." Toby could see his point. "So after that you just went on to bed, did you? Had Alistair reassured you at all?"

"Not really. I kept thinking about Josie and Helen, and wondering. And I thought about the letter, too. But I knew I couldn't do anything. I took a couple of my pills and went to bed. And I did sleep. I didn't think I would, but I did. And then in the morning . . . I don't know—everything seemed so ordinary. The night before seemed like some sort of bad dream. They were all there at breakfast, just looking like the guests always look on the first day. A bit strained, and excited. Some of them were nervous, about the appointments and so on. Belinda was, I know. Margot lost her temper with one of the maids. Alistair was running around. Josie rang up her children. It was all just—ordinary. And the day went on like that. We're always very busy, the first Monday of a fortnight." He looked up, and shook his head. "It wasn't that I forgot about what Joyce had said. I just got busy, and nothing had happened, and I just let it drift."

"Did you see Margot Bell during the day?"

William winced. "Oh yes. Like always. She keeps —kept—herself free Mondays ten till eleven and twelve till one. Those were my times for checking the accounts with her and so on. And I saw her at lunch, up the other end of the table. But after that I didn't see her again. She had consultations all afternoon."

"You didn't go out to the annex at all?"

"Oh well, yes." William looked startled. "I always pop down to my room to, you know, tidy up, at the end of the day. But I don't have much time. And I don't see Margot. She always has—had—her massage straight after her last appointment. She needed it to relax. And I always get back to the office for half an hour before drinks. To get things ready for her . . . in the morning." His voice had begun to tremble slightly.

"Right. Well, when you saw her earlier, then, she didn't mention any change to the usual arrangements for her massage, William?"

"No. She didn't say a word about it."

"And how did she seem? Worried at all? Upset? Anything out of the ordinary?"

William shook his head. "Nothing really out of the ordinary. She was in a bad mood in the morning, but she often was." He realized what he'd said, broke off, and flushed. "I mean, some people aren't morning people, are they? Margot got very tired. She had a lot to think about."

"Sure," said Toby soothingly. He heard Birdie flip over a page of her notebook and glanced over to where she was sitting. God, she looked different! She looked up and gave him a hard stare, pen poised meaningfully. He sighed and turned back to William.

"She was much better when I saw her at midday," William volunteered eagerly. "She was quite happy. She'd just—" He broke off.

"Just . . . ?"

"Just done Helen's makeup," said William slowly. "She was thrilled with it. She said Helen would be magnificent. One of our best makeovers ever. She said she was sorry she wouldn't see her till dinner. She couldn't wait to see what Alistair would do with the hair." He stopped speaking, but his mouth stayed slightly open. Tears began to gather in his eyes again.

Toby cleared his throat. "Just one more thing, William," he said, rather loudly. "It's important." He watched with relief as William closed his mouth, hastily brushed at his eyes with the back of his hand, and paid attention. "The drinks party, earlier tonight. I'm trying to establish everyone's movements—just as a matter of routine, of course," he added hastily as William's eyes widened. "When did you get there?"

"Six o'clock exactly, like always. I have to be there on time to greet the guests and pour drinks."

"So you were the first person to arrive?"

William shook his head. "No. Conrad was there," he said in a tight voice. "He'd helped himself to a drink. It's like his cheek. I couldn't understand why he was there. He was supposed to be with Margot by six."

"Did you ask him?"

William shook his head. "I wouldn't give him that satisfaction," he said. "He wouldn't have told me, anyway. He's like that."

"All right. Now, what happened then?"

"Well, then Belinda came in. Then Helen and Josie, almost together. Then Alistair and Verity. Then Edwina."

"You went out of the room with Belinda at one point, I gather?" Toby asked mildly. "Where did you go?"

William flushed. "Oh—just to the library. To try to find a book."

"Did you find it?"

The flush deepened. "Um—well, no, actually, we didn't. We just talked a bit, then went back to the others."

"Were you together the whole time?"

"Yes . . . oh . . ." William paused and pressed his lips together. He looked hunted.

"Detail's important, William," Birdie prompted encouragingly, looking up from her notebook.

"Oh, of course," said William, reverting to type. "Yes. Well, Belinda did go to the ladies' room. Obviously we weren't together then, were we? I waited in the library till she came back." He smiled uncomfortably.

"How long would you say?"

"Oh, I don't know." William stuck his hands in his pockets. "How long does it take?" he added, with a rather sad effort in the direction of ribaldry. "About five minutes, I suppose. Then we went back to the sitting room together."

"Right," rumbled Toby. "Well, thank you, William. You've been very helpful. Now, last thing—could you give me an account of Margot's movements for today?"

William blinked at him in obvious surprise. "Of course I could."

"Could you scribble me some notes about it, do you think?"

"It's written down already," said William. "Where Margot was. Where everyone was. It's all on the timetable." From the way he said the word, he could have been talking about holy writ.

"But presumably people run late and so on. I meant . . ."

"Oh no!" William was very earnest now. "Oh no, we never run late here, Mr. Toby. And especially on the first Monday. Margot and Alistair always say how important it is for every guest to have had her facial and massage, and her hair and makeup done in time for the drinks at six. It's part of the treatment, you see. They have to see a big change on the first day. But to do that with the staff we've got we've got to stick to the timetable exactly. Staff and guests are always told." He paused. "Margot, Conrad, and Angela each have one-hour appointments, and they always stick to that—leaving a bit of time to clean up and so on before the next person. Alistair has two-hour appointments—for perms and coloring and so on you need that. He's usually pretty good. Sometimes he runs a tiny bit late. But only a minute or two."

"Ah." Toby sat back. "Well, could I have a copy of that timetable, do you think? Could you get me one, William?" God, he thought, I'm talking to him like a kid, now.

"There should be a copy in Margot's desk," said William anxiously, leaning forward. "It's there, isn't it? In the top right-hand drawer?"

Toby slid out the drawer. It moved, he noted, as smoothly and noiselessly as a well-oiled joint. A beautiful piece of furniture, this desk. He'd never owned or used anything like it. Every drawer he'd ever come in contact with rattled, grated, or stuck. And was full to the brim. This one wasn't. A pink folder lay there, pristine, with only a slim gold pen and a gold ring with two keys on it to keep it company. He took it out and opened it. An impeccably neat timetable lay before him. He glanced at it appreciatively, and looked up at William. "Ah, yes. This will help," he said. That was the understatement of the day.

William rose unsteadily to his feet. "Can I go now?" He held on to the desk, as though he needed the support.

"Yes. That's all for now. Thank you. You've been very helpful."

"Can I . . . can I ask something?"

"What do you want to know?" As if I need to ask, thought Toby.

William took a deep breath. "Helen—upstairs. Is she Laurel Moon? Did she kill Margot?"

Toby hesitated. "I can't really tell you that, William. Helen is still unconscious—or asleep, really. We have no proof of anything yet." He looked up into William's haunted eyes and weakened. Why not tell the poor bugger? Put him out of his misery, about his own fears at least. "But my assistant is with her, keeping guard. Strictly between the walls of this room, I don't think you have any more to fear, put it that way."

A look of inexpressible relief flowed across William's drawn face. And then a sort of guilty horror took its place. He gripped the edge of the desk more firmly, and wet his lips. "Do you think she killed Margot because of me?" he whispered. "Because Margot was close to me?"

"I don't know," said Toby simply. "Could be. Or it could just have been that Margot Bell was there, alone and helpless, at the right time. The Gray Lady murders seemed to be quite random, remember, except the last one—the aunt. Or maybe something happened between the two of them that we don't know about. That's one of the reasons I wanted the timetable."

Birdie stirred in her chair and Toby was recalled to duty. He shouldn't be talking to a witness like this. "I'd go to bed and get some sleep if I were you, son," he said firmly. "Put this out of your mind. You're quite safe. It'll all be over in the morning. All right?"

William nodded. "Thank you," he said. He smiled uncertainly, hovered for a moment, and then walked quickly out of the room.

"He'll sleep easier for that," said Toby. Not that he had to explain his actions to Birdie, he thought, a trifle crossly.

"Whatever you say," Birdie replied. She stood up and stretched. "You realize he'll rush right over there and tell everyone else, don't you?"

"I told him not to."

"Dan, get real!" Birdie stood up and stretched. "It's your funeral, anyhow."

"Birdie, there's not a doubt in my mind that that's Laurel Moon up there in that bed. She more or less convicted herself out of her own mouth, while we were carrying her upstairs."

Birdie shrugged. "I'm not arguing with you, am I? I'm just saying that because someone was a killer ten years ago, that doesn't mean they're necessarily a killer now."

"The method was exactly the same. You saw that with your own eyes. Exactly the same, Birdie."

Birdie shrugged and looked away. "Everyone here heard how the Gray Lady murders were done, Dan. Only last night."

Toby glared at her. When he spoke his voice was hard. "You know your problem, Birdwood? You're dead stubborn. You'll never be a detective's bootlace if you can't listen to the experts. Milson and I both saw pictures of the Gray Lady victims ten years ago. Not pretty. And exactly like Margot Bell, lying out there now. We know. You don't. Just take my word for it, will you?"

"Oh, dry up!" snapped Birdie. She'd never known Toby to be this unreasonable. Why wouldn't he listen to her? For God's sake, she'd been proved right so often in the past. Half his reputation was thanks to her. Just because she'd been done up like a mindless dolly bird he seemed to think she'd turned into one. "Just dry up," she repeated bitterly.

The angry silence hung between them in the still, warm air. Outside, thunder growled and relentlessly the rain fell. They looked at each other helplessly.

"Why don't you tell that to the bloody weather?" Toby offered. It was feeble, but enough. Birdie smiled wanly.

"It'd probably have about as much effect," she said. "All right, you old bastard. Give us a look at the timetable. I only vaguely remember where I was at any given moment today, let alone anyone else."

They pored over the timetable together in silence. A few interesting features there, Birdie thought. But she had no intention of risking another snub by mentioning them. She said nothing, but covertly watched Dan Toby nodding and pulling at his lip as he digested names and times. Seeing her own name with all the others reminded her of the change he had seen in her. She squirmed inwardly. Squirmed even more remembering how it felt, lying there helpless, Velcroed snugly into a slippery pink smock while perfect strangers touched, stroked, and questioned her.

She winced, and looked around to find Toby staring at her. "Well! Are you ready?" she snapped, discomforted. "Who's the next victim? Edwina?"

Toby blinked, rubbed his chin, looked at his watch and considered. "No, look, let's have the massage bloke. He'll be quick. That'll be the staff disposed of except Mrs. Housekeeper, and if I know her she'll hang round till the death whenever we talk to her. Will you get him? And see how the others are holding out, while you're at it."

"O.K." Birdie stood up. "You'll love Conrad, Dan."

"Is he as bad as he looks?"

"Infinitely worse. Ah, but he gives a great massage." She stretched, sighed, and left the room, leaving Toby staring thoughtfully after her.

TIMETABLE DAY ONE

Time	Margot	Alistair	Conrad	Angela	Josie	Helen	Edwina	Verity	Belinda
8–9	Free	Edwina	Free	Free	Free	Free	Hair (Alistair)	Free	Free
9–10	Verity	Edwina	Free	Josie	Facial (Angela)	Free	Hair (Alistair)	Tour (Margot)	Free
10–11	William	Josie	Belinda	Helen	Hair (Alistair)	Facial (Angela)	Free	Free	Massage (Conrad)
11–12	Helen	Josie	Edwina	Belinda	Hair (Alistair)	Makeup (Margot)	Massage (Conrad)	Free	Facial (Angela)
12–1	William	Helen	Free	Verity	Free	Hair (Alistair)	Free	Facial (Angela)	Free
1–2	Lunch	Helen	Lunch	Lunch	Lunch	Hair (Alistair)	Lunch	Lunch	Lunch
2–3	Josie	Belinda	Verity	Free	Makeup (Margot)	Lunch	Free	Massage (Conrad)	Hair (Alistair)
3–4	Verity	Belinda	Helen	Edwina	Free	Massage (Conrad)	Facial (Angela)	Makeup (Margot)	Hair (Alistair)
4–5	Belinda	Verity	Josie	Free	Massage (Conrad)	Free	Free	Hair (Alistair)	Makeup (Margot)
5–6	Edwina	Verity	Free	Free	Free	Free	Makeup (Margot)	Hair (Alistair)	Free

14

Toby could tell instantly that Conrad Hunter had dealt with police before. Many times. Almost certainly he didn't have a record. He was the kind who somehow always slipped away from you. Admit nothing, volunteer nothing. He'd learned that from the cradle. He sprawled in the chair facing Toby, every line of his body expressing insolent relaxation, and Toby effortlessly saw in that pose, and in that sensual face with its veiled, heavy-lidded eyes, the reckless schoolboy, the sulky adolescent, the ruthless young adult this man had been as he fenced with other authorities, behind other desks in other places.

He pushed the timetable forward. "Did you stick to this, today?" he asked brusquely. "Any changes at all?"

Conrad shrugged. "No chance," he drawled. "That thing's the bible round here. Nothing changes."

"Something changed today, though, didn't it? Margot Bell canceled her appointment with you. Or so you said."

Conrad smiled slowly, showing straight, white teeth with prominent canines. "She canceled, yes."

"When was that?"

"First thing this morning. Before breakfast."

"Had she ever canceled before?"

Conrad looked at the backs of his strong, golden brown hands. He seemed to be simply admiring them. "Not that I remember."

"Well, why this time?"

He shrugged again. "She didn't say."

"Did she say she was going to have Angela instead?"

"No. She just canceled."

"Didn't you wonder why? Didn't you ask her?"

"No. I just assumed she had something else to do. Not my business."

Toby tried another tack. "How long have you been working here?"

"About a month."

"And what were you doing before that?"

"I was at Right-Moves, in the city."

Toby knew that place. Whip-slim girls in leotards cut up to the armpits, businessmen with paunches and mid-life crises, machines that looked like instruments of torture in a glass-walled room, and mirrors everywhere. "Bit of a change here for you, then," he observed.

Conrad shrugged. "I like a change."

"How long had you and Margot Bell been lovers?"

A slow, insolent grin. "Who's counting? About two weeks, I guess."

"Didn't take you long."

"I never knock it back, man. She knew what she wanted. I was happy to oblige. Put it that way."

"And now she's dead," Toby snapped, goaded beyond endurance. "How do you feel about that?"

Got you, said Conrad's veiled eyes. But he said nothing.

There was a flash of lightning, and a crack of thunder. The lights flickered. A quickly stifled exclamation came from Birdie's corner. Toby hunched his shoulders, but Conrad didn't move. Outside, behind the snugly drawn curtains, the rain fell.

"You saw Margot last night, late," said Toby levelly. It was a statement, not a question. Conrad made no reaction, and Toby went on: "Did she tell you about William's little drama at the late night drinks?"

"Yeah. William's a fruit cake. He drove her crazy."

"You were up in her room?"

"Of course I was. You can't imagine her coming down to mine, can you?" For the first time Conrad's face showed the edge of some feeling, a twist of bitterness. "The little room in the annex, with Whingeing Willy and Angela the pure in the neighborhood? Not likely." His eyes flickered with what could have been malice. "Mind you, she didn't mind the odd quickie in the massage room. That turned her on."

"Did she say anything about the guests last night?"

"A bit. She was fed up. She said none of them was worth the effort, except Helen. She was right there. Alistair's a fool. She'd never have got anywhere sticking with him."

"She said that?"

"More or less."

Toby took his time. "She said nothing else about any one particular person?"

"Only that Alistair and William had gone soppy over Belinda, and she wished she'd never agreed to take her. Hadn't even seen Belinda's sister, the one who put the hard word on her to do it, for twenty years, she said, because she's been living in Italy, or something. And she didn't really owe her any favors. You know the sort of thing." Conrad yawned and stretched. The buttons of his white shirt strained over his chest. Toby saw that the golden skin of his neck was marked with two reddish-blue bruises. *She knew what she wanted.*

"So her basic mood was just irritable and fed up?"

"Well, yeah. But she didn't stay pissed off for long, man. That's what I was there for." Conrad blinked lazily. "I could always calm her down. Then stoke her up again, the way she liked it, if you know what I mean."

Wink wink, nudge nudge. Toby maintained his professional expression with an effort. He found himself loathing this man, but he realized, with a shock of distaste, that the loathing was spiked with envy. And Conrad knew it. Toby pushed the thought down.

"She was laughing when I left," Conrad went on, watching him. "Looking in the mirror. Making plans. Laughing." He looked at the backs of his hands again.

"You didn't stay all night?"

"Oh no. I always went back to my room. She liked her own space. So do I, if it comes to that."

"Did you see her in the morning? How was she then?"

"Pretty black. I don't know why. She rang and canceled her massage at about seven. Short and sweet. I didn't ask questions. I saw her later, just before breakfast, raving at one of the girls. I knew her in that mood. I kept out of it. Nothing to do with me."

"And after that?"

"I didn't see her at all."

Toby glanced at the timetable in front of him. "You finished work at five, I see."

"About that."

"What did you do then?"

"The usual. Cleaned up. Went out and sat in the spa for ten minutes or so. Got out. Got dry. Went back to the massage room to change."

"Time?"

"Didn't look."

Toby almost snarled. "Have a guess."

"Maybe twenty to six, quarter to six, ten to six. Something like that."

"Did you see Angela swimming?"

"No. She wouldn't have started by then. She swims—"

"From six to six-thirty, I know." Toby repressed a sigh. "All right. What did you do then?"

Conrad raised one eyebrow. "Got dressed again and went up to the house," he drawled. "Since I didn't have a date with Margot I thought I may as well get in on the drinks and the girls for once. Don't see why Willy should corner the market."

"By girls you mean the guests, I presume," snapped Toby.

The man in front of him shrugged. "Whatever you like."

"So you went straight to the sitting room from the massage room, did you? No detours?"

"Nowhere to go, was there?"

"Who was there when you arrived?"

"No one. I was the first. Look, man, take it in, will you? I didn't see Margot after work. I saw her last night, and then I didn't see her again."

"Till you saw her dead." Toby couldn't resist it.

Conrad stared at him, expressionless. "That's right."

"When you left the sitting room during the cock-tail party, where did you go?"

"Went looking for Helen. She'd gone out before."

"And?"

"I found her—in the annex sitting area, looking out the windows. I chatted her up a bit, then took her back to the party."

"Why?"

"Why not?"

Silence.

"Anything else to tell me? Anything you want to know?"

"No."

Toby sighed heavily. "All right, you can go." Back under the rock you came from, he added viciously to himself.

Conrad lifted his superb body unhurriedly from the chair, and left the room, smiling.

Toby slumped back. He ran a hand over his forehead, over his thinning hair. He felt angry, righteous, heavy, gray, and old. He didn't look at Birdie.

"What plans, do you think?" Her voice took him by surprise.

"What?"

"He said she was making plans when he left her. What plans?"

"Does it matter? Birdwood, could you get Mrs. Whatever-her-name-is to make some more tea? No, coffee this time. And have some sent up to Milson? He doesn't like it, but he'll need it by now. Can't afford to have him nodding off." Toby straightened himself up, slowly started to pull his tie back into place. The show must go on. "We'll see the finance hotshot—Edwina—now. All right?"

"O.K." Birdie left him alone without another word. Toby watched her go. He picked up the phone to check on Milson, then put it down again, staring thoughtfully at the door she'd closed behind her.

What plans?

When Birdie opened the sitting room door she found its remaining occupants all in various stages of sleep. Not surprising, considering the time, and the day they'd spent. The lights had been dimmed, and the fire allowed to die down to a glowing mass of coals. Edwina was dozing in her armchair, heavy legs stretched out in front of her, hands folded on her stomach. Josie was slumped in one corner of the big couch, and Belinda was curled in the other, her cheek pillowed on her arm. In front of them the TV screen still flickered, but the sound had been turned down. As Birdie moved into the room Belinda's dark eyes opened. She peered over the back of the couch, and smiled tentatively. Birdie smiled back but said nothing and went silently on to the sliding double doors on the other side of the room. They were open a crack, and light streamed through from the dining room beyond.

As she'd expected, Alistair and Betty Hinder were there, sitting at the table together, empty teacups and a tray between them. They weren't talking, just sitting quietly in companionable silence. They turned to look at the intruder, their faces pale in the bright light. She walked toward them, feeling self-conscious, aware she was not welcome.

"Could Mr. Toby and I have some coffee, Mrs. Hinder?" She tried to be matter-of-fact. "And an extra cup for the policeman upstairs? We're feeling a bit weary."

"Join the club," said Betty Hinder sharply. "He'll be awash, that Toby. Done nothing but drink hot water since he got here." She got wearily to her feet. "Oh well, yes, I'll get it."

"I'll come with you, Betty," said Alistair soothingly. "Better not to go alone—remember . . ."

"Oh, give it a rest," she retorted roughly. "That's all bull, and you know it. We're safe as houses. That William told us when he came back. I know he said not to say, but I'm not playing his silly games, if you are." She jabbed her chin severely in Birdie's direction. "So—what's your Mr. Toby doing keeping those poor women out of their beds like this? I've never heard anything like it! What he's doing letting the staff go off to sleep while the guests hang around having to sleep in chairs, I don't know. And what's the point? He knows who did it, you know who did it, and we know who did it! She's upstairs under lock and key, isn't she? And a cop with her. With a gun, most probably. Right? Why can't we all go to bed?"

"Betty . . ." pleaded Alistair. "Come on . . ."

"Oh well, someone has to say it!" retorted Mrs. Hinder. "Anyhow, you stay there and don't move. You look like death warmed up. First Mondays are hard enough on you without all this extra. And you're not looking much better," she added to Birdie, shaking a bony finger in front of her nose. "Don't forget you had a shock only yesterday, and nearly came to grief. Now this today. You watch yourself or you'll be packing up!" She looked severely at both of them, then turned on her heel and strode off, very upright, to the kitchen.

Alistair shook his head and laughed ruefully. He looked exhausted. "She's right, though. I'll be glad when morning comes," he said wearily. "When this is —all over. Though what'll happen to this place . . ." He looked around the dining room; the empty tables, the clean fireplace, the luxurious folds of the curtains drawn over streaming windows, as though he could already see the prospective buyers pacing it out, gesturing, talking in low voices.

"It'll be all right, surely," said Birdie. She wished she could offer more than trite reassurance. It was easy to feel sorry for this kind, hard-working man. And it was easy to see that he was right. Through no fault of his own, his world was crumbling.

He smiled sadly, the fine skin around his eyes creasing in familiar lines. "That's what Betty says. She doesn't understand money—she's worse than I am—or PR. She thinks the place'll boom with Margot gone. She always was a bit one-eyed about Margot. Had it in for her, since the day we came here. Thought she hogged the limelight and overspent on herself. And she's always thought she cheated George on the bits of maintenance he did. But Margot didn't, you know." He looked earnestly at Birdie, willing her to understand. "Margot always paid well—extremely well, sometimes, to get things done fast. I know she did. And she always paid George and the others in cash, to help them out." He glanced at Birdie with a tinge of guilt. "The black economy. I know it's not right, but these guys live from hand to mouth, half of them. They like the cash. And I can't believe the government misses their few dollars. Like Margot always said, it's the big boys that the taxman should be after."

Birdie made no comment. Alistair was obviously an innocent in matters of business. Margot could have told him anything about what was a fair price for a workman's time. She couldn't believe Margot paid anyone lavishly if she could get away with it, and had no doubt that Betty Hinder's version of events was the more likely one. Betty mightn't be a financial whiz, but she had a lot of common sense. Margot was certainly paying cash to get the lowest possible quote, not to help anyone out. And she thought that, in his heart, Alistair knew it. All this defense of Margot smacked of protesting too much. He just couldn't face the thought of how absolutely his opposite Margot had been. He'd never faced it.

The double doors rattled and they both looked around, startled. Belinda stood there, looking drowsy and ruffled, like a small, plump bird. Alistair stood up and held a hand out to her. "Like some coffee, Belinda?"

She nodded and came forward shyly. "I didn't mean to disturb you," she said, lisping slightly. "But I was wondering if it was my turn yet. To talk. I really . . ." She swallowed and flushed. "I mean, I know we know—what happened. It's all right to say that much, isn't it? But he is keeping us up, isn't he? And William said he asked him what he saw and did and so on. And when she came back Angela said he'd told her to think carefully and try to remember everything. She said she was going to try. But . . ." A note of petulance crept into her voice and her brow creased. "I actually *have* something to tell him, but he keeps putting me off and seeing other people."

Birdie thought quickly. It didn't really matter who Toby saw next. She herself thought his order of interview was odd. "Why don't you come in to him now? All the others are asleep anyway, I think."

"Oh. Well, are you sure?" Now Belinda had what she'd said she wanted she'd grown diffident and uncertain again. "If he's asked for someone else . . ."

"It doesn't matter," said Birdie, more brusquely than she'd intended. This girl and William . . . what had Conrad called him?—Whingeing Willy—had a lot in common. They were made for each other. And gave her the screaming heebies.

But not Alistair, it seemed. He put out a proprietorial hand and ran expert fingers through Belinda's shining, ruffled hair, creating casual order out of chaos. "That's better." He smiled into her eyes, and pulled a straying curl back into place over her forehead. She giggled appreciatively. "I'm hopeless," she sighed. "All your hard work . . ."

"You're not hopeless, you're lovely," he said. "And don't forget it."

Mrs. Hinder appeared from the kitchen carrying a tray loaded with three cups, cream, sugar, and a huge silver coffeepot, plus two foaming mugs of chocolate. She crossed the room, nodding benignly at Belinda. "Heard you from the kitchen, love," she said in a low voice as she reached them. "I made a hot chocolate for you. Feeling all right?"

"Yes, thanks. Thanks very much." Belinda took the offered mug, and began sipping at it quickly, as if to show her gratitude.

"Chocolate for you, too, Alistair," Mrs. Hinder said firmly, "or you'll never sleep. You know how you are." She put the other mug on the table. "Now. Will I take this into the office, or what? Does he want me to take a cup upstairs?" She cocked her head at Birdie. Her look gave away nothing.

"I'll take it, Mrs. Hinder, don't worry. Toby can organize upstairs." Birdie held out her hands and took the tray. It was heavier than it looked. The silver pot gleamed, reflecting the room in miniature. "Are you ready, Belinda?"

Belinda nodded, gulped at her chocolate, turned and scuttled back to the sitting room, holding the mug with both hands against her chest.

"She's a sad little piece of work, eh?" muttered Betty Hinder, watching her unsteady progress. "Dear oh dear. A bully of a husband, and now she's taken up with that poor apology of a William. Some girls are fools where men are concerned. Just go from one rotter to another."

"Sh!" warned Alistair. "She'll hear you. Actually, I think she and William'll be good for each other. Don't you, Verity?"

"Oh yes. A marriage made in heaven," said Birdie, deadpan. Mrs. Hinder snorted with approving laughter.

Birdie followed Belinda into the sitting room, balancing the heavy tray carefully. As they reached the door to the hallway, Edwina stirred and Josie grunted. Damn, thought Birdie. I should have gone out the dining room door so as not to disturb them. I didn't think.

"Birdie!" boomed Toby's voice from across the darkened vestibule. "Ah, there you are. Took your time, didn't you?" His broad shape loomed in the office doorway. "Got the coffee for Milson? I need it, and a lot more."

"Sh!" hissed Birdie. "People are asleep! Oh, shit!"

Her ankle twisted a little and she lost balance, tilting the tray. Belinda, hovering at her shoulder, squeaked.

"Put it down or you'll lose the lot." Toby strode toward them and took the tray. He looked around, then marched over and plumped it down on one of the tables that flanked the foot of the stairs. He darted a sharp look at Belinda.

"I thought you could see Belinda next," Birdie said. "Edwina's asleep."

"Well, sorry, but I can't see anyone just at this minute," retorted Toby briskly. He came back to them and stood tall, ostentatiously looking down on them. "Sorry, Belinda, but you'll have a bit longer to wait. I'm needed upstairs." He bared his teeth at her in an insincere smile. She smiled worriedly back, and bit her lip. "And you, Miss Birdwood, if you can spare me a moment in the office?"

"Can I pour a coffee first? I'm dying for one."

"No time for that. And I need the whole pot. Get your mate to make you another one." Offensively energetic, Toby was hustling her across the hallway. Birdie looked over her shoulder at Belinda, standing forlornly by the sitting room door. Oh well. As she was turning back she caught a movement out of the corner of her eye. A flicker of movement, a shadow, near the stairs. Was someone there? Or was it just a trick of the light? She hesitated, to get a proper look, but Toby pulled her on impatiently. Oh, what did it matter, anyway? And she wanted to hear what Toby had to say. She followed him into the room, and watched him close the door, decisively shutting out the hallway, Belinda's drooping little figure, and the creeping shadows.

"She's awake," Toby said without preamble. He rubbed his hands. His eyes were alive. "And talking. Milson says there's no doubt. Now, I want you to hold the fort here while I go up. It's"—he looked at his watch—"eleven forty-five now." Birdie glanced instinctively at her own wrist, remembering belatedly that her watch was lying sodden, battered, and useless up in her room. "I'll ring within, say, half an hour," Toby went on. "If we can get a confession the others can get off to bed without being bothered. All right? But don't tell them anything yet. Understand?"

"William's already *told* them most of it, Dan. As I said he would, if you'll remember. But, Dan, Belinda says she knows something . . ."

He waved her away impatiently. "I'm sure she does. I'm sure she knows lots of things. She's the type who listens at doors. Whether what she knows is any use to us, I doubt." He leered at her. "Look, you're the detective. Get her to tell you. Say I said."

"Dan . . ."

He grabbed her arm and walked her out into the vestibule again, leaving the office door wide open. "Don't hassle me, Birdwood. Just do as you're told. I've got to go," he said rapidly. "Get back over there. Leave this door open, and listen for the phone. All right?"

"All *right!*"

He ruffled her hair and strode away. She stood, fuming, while he picked up the tray and made off with it up the stairs. She hoped he'd trip, but he didn't. He even managed a cocksure wave as he reached the top. He turned to the right and disappeared, on his way to "Eve," where Milson, and Helen, awaited him.

So it was all over. Birdie walked slowly toward the sitting room. Already things had started seeming more normal, the shadows less sinister, the walls less enclosing. A relief. But there was no joy in it. Birdie was aware of a flat, sick feeling. She knew she hadn't wanted it to be Helen. She hadn't wanted it to be that simple, that savage, that sad. But it was. It was as obvious and clear as Toby had said from the first. Helen, the woman who used to be called Laurel Moon, had killed Margot Bell. Maybe because of William, but probably for no reason at all that would make sense to a sane person.

Ten years ago she'd killed six women. Now she'd killed again. What had reactivated that madness? The place? The people? Last night's chilling conversation, that must have brought the whole thing back? All three, probably, plus the personality of Margot Bell herself. The aunt, the last Gray Lady killing, had been a very strong woman, it seemed. She'd kept her niece, who'd always been the family scapegoat, under her thumb, repressed and frustrated, till neurosis grew and flourished and bore violent rage as its fruit. At first the rage was deflected onto other women of about the same age and type, and then turned on its real, original object. At least, that's what the paragraphs on the Gray Lady murders concluded in a learned article Birdie had read about serial killings.

Apparently serial murderers often followed that sort of pattern. All the crimes described in that article were sickeningly alike, despite their surface differences. Serial murderers from Jack the Ripper to the Boston Strangler seemed to share obsessive qualities, compulsively following certain rituals in their methods of killing, however bizarre. But just because they were so bizarre, serial killings sometimes spawned their own grotesque subculture of copycat murders. The police usually tried to combat the confusion by keeping some aspect of the genuine killer's distinctive *modus operandi* secret. But the press as a rule made much of serial killings, and very often they led to violence and horror over and beyond their natural limits—for years after, if the murderer was not apprehended—as others, often simply cold, calculating beings with a wish to dispose of someone and pay no penalty, leaped on to the killer's bandwagon, and joined the bloodfest.

Surely it had not been unreasonable to think that the murder of Margot Bell could have been just such a case. She had been a woman who roused strong emotions in the people with whom she dealt. It had seemed to Birdie that there were several very strong motives for murder lying under the smooth surface of life in this place. But murder wasn't the inevitable result of motive, she reminded herself soberly, or there'd be continuing wholesale slaughter in every family, office, institution, and traffic jam in the country. It was as Toby said. She'd just been stubborn. She hadn't wanted it to end this way. Murder was one thing. Murder for no reason but madness was, to her at least, another.

Laurel Moon remembered little of her crimes—or so the psychiatrists who examined her had said. She suffered from blackouts. She couldn't be held responsible for what she had done. That was the best her doctors could do for her. They couldn't argue her innocence. A neighbor had actually seen her strangling her aunt. Had watched, horrified and screaming through a plate-glass window, as the woman she knew only as "poor Laurel" turned once to stare blankly at her, then plunged the dressmaking scissors into her unconscious victim's neck. Had beaten on the window, breaking it and gashing her hands, then run, terrified, for help.

The police had found Laurel Moon bleeding to death beside her aunt's corpse, her wrists, chest, and stomach slashed with the scissors ripped from her victim's neck, her own neck torn by her victim's desperate fingers. They'd saved her. Pumped blood back into her body and saved her. For justice. An asylum for the criminally insane.

Birdie paused at the sitting room doorway, her hand on the gleaming brass knob. She thought of Helen, last night, entering this room on Conrad's arm, transfigured, taking a glass of champagne from Alistair and laughing. Then, it had seemed like a rebirth. But it had been a rebaptism, in blood, that had flushed her cheeks and fired her dead eyes. Birdie shivered. She needed a coffee. And company.

They all drank hot chocolate in the end. Alistair added logs to the fire and coaxed it back to life and they sat in a tight circle around it, holding their hands around warm china mugs, breathing in the rich, milky smell, licking sweet froth from their lips. Betty Hinder sat on an upright chair behind them, as though on guard. They listened to the fire crackle, and to the rain.

"It's easing," said Alistair, cocking his head. "Hear it, Betty?"

"Yes. It'll have stopped by dawn, I'd say. George'll be over in the boat."

Belinda looked around. "But we still can't get out. Last night we were all here," she lisped softly. "Now there's just the six of us left. It's like *Ten Little Indians*."

Josie snorted, and felt for her handkerchief. "Hardly. With three of the Indians tucked up safely in bed. Wish I was, don't you, Edwina?"

"Yes." Edwina's thick, perfect skin was dull with fatigue. Mascara had smudged under her deep-set eyes, giving them a haunted look. "I need a cigarette," she said abruptly to Alistair. "Would you have any?"

He hesitated. "Margot keeps—kept . . . There are some in the office, across the hall. I'll get one for you."

She shook her head and stood up. "I'll go. It's my vice. I'll walk for it. I'd like to stretch my legs anyway. Where are they?"

"In a box on the desk. Are you sure . . . ?"

But Edwina was halfway to the door.

Birdie scrambled to her feet and followed. "I want one too," she muttered, as Edwina turned to look at her in surprise and little welcome. Birdie closed the sitting room door behind them. It had been a good thirty-five minutes since Toby went upstairs. He should be ringing any moment now, and Murphy's Law dictated that it would be the moment Edwina walked through the office door. If she answered that phone Birdie would never hear the end of it.

"It's twelve-thirty," remarked Edwina as they crossed the hall. "How much longer are they going to keep us here, Verity? I presume you know. You seem to be in their confidence for some reason." She looked impassively at Birdie. *I knew you were trouble somehow,* her eyes said. *You're not one of us. You lied to me.*

"I don't know," said Birdie defensively. Twelve-thirty? It had been longer than she'd thought. Dan should have rung by now. She walked into Margot Bell's office with Edwina. They crossed to the desk. Birdie surreptitiously checked to be sure the internal phone was on its hook. Yes. So what was Toby playing at? "You know, Edwina," she said honestly, "I'm as much in the dark as you are."

And as she said the words, the lights went out.

15

Thick blackness blanketed them, closing them in. There was a second's absolute silence, then an eruption of sound from the sitting room—a confused babbling and wailing, and a couple of ominous thuds.

Birdie instinctively stretched out her arms and stepped forward, her fingers tangling in the heavy folds of the curtains, her elbow bumping something solid that grunted and swore.

"Take it easy!" Edwina's voice was gruff but gloriously familiar in the enveloping dark.

"Sorry. What the hell's . . . ?"

"I'd say the power lines have come down. A falling tree, probably. Not surprising in this weather." Birdie heard a rustling sound as Edwina calmly felt her way to the window seat and sat down. She was a cool customer.

The door across the hall clicked open. "Edwina! Verity!" Alistair's voice echoed across the vast space. "Are you O.K.?"

"Yes!" they chorused plaintively in unison, and laughed.

"Stay there," he called unnecessarily. "I'll go out and start the generator. Won't be long."

"Hold on." Betty Hinder's reedy voice carried as well as Alistair's shout. "I'm coming with you." There was a scrape and a bump.

"Betty, stay where you are!"

"Don't be more of a fool than you can help! You can't go wandering around out there in the pitch black by yourself. What if you fall over and break a leg? What if the thing doesn't start? Then we're all in a fine mess."

"I'll go out and get William, then." Alistair was weakening. Birdie grinned to herself in the darkness.

Betty's snort was eloquent. By now she'd obviously reached him. "He'd be as much use as a pocket in a singlet. Here, hold on to me. I can find my way round this place blindfolded. And as for generators . . . well, since George'd rather sit in the dark twiddling his thumbs any day than get his feet wet, I can handle them too. Now, let's go."

Alistair gave in. "All right, now, everyone just sit tight. It'll be ten minutes or so."

"No!" Another voice rose through the blackness, high and whimpering. "I can't stay here! I've got to get out! Stop it! Let me . . ." There was a scuffling sound, and a clatter as something hit the floor. The voice squeaked in panic.

"Belinda!" thundered Alistair. "Sit down! Have another biscuit! Josie—the candles on the sideboard!"

"O.K.! Go on, Alistair. We'll be all right!" called Josie. She sounded quite cheerful.

"Famous last words," grunted Birdie. She felt cautiously around, located the window seat somewhere down near her knees, and lowered herself gingerly onto it beside Edwina, who hastily moved along to accommodate her. They perched together uncomfortably for a moment.

The darkness was complete, in the room and out-side the window. The valley walls rose up, enclosing them. No light, not the faintest glow in the sky, re-lieved the blackness. Birdie hadn't been aware of the hum of the air-conditioning, but now that it had died its absence created an eerie sense of absolute stillness in the house. Outside, the rushing water of the swollen creek, the splashing of the rain on the rippling ground, were the only sounds.

She held her hand in front of her face and squinted, trying to make out its shape. But the darkness was total. It was like being blind. With a shock, she remembered Dan Toby. He hadn't called. Why not? And now he couldn't call. The internal phones needed electricity to work. Involuntarily she caught her breath.

"There's nothing to worry about," said Edwina be-side her.

Birdie shook her head, realized her companion couldn't see her, and spoke aloud.

"It's not the dark. It's Toby—and Milson. I think I should go up there. Try to take them a light."

"The proper lights'll be back on in ten minutes," said Edwina reasonably. "They're big boys, aren't they? They can look after themselves."

Of course. Why then did Birdie feel this sense of foreboding? The picture of Toby, waving so cockily at her from the head of the stairs kept coming into her mind. And it was dark, so dark that she could see noth-ing else.

She pushed herself to her feet and felt for the desk. Maybe . . .

"What *are* you doing?" Edwina's voice was amused.

"If there are cigarettes," said Birdie, "there might be a lighter."

"If there are cigarettes," Edwina replied, "please give me one and *pray* there's a lighter."

Birdie felt around the polished surface, trying to remember what had been on it when she'd been in the room last. Her fingers brushed paper—the timetable—and a small pile of cardboard—the guests' files—nearly upset a vase of flowers . . . yes, there'd been an ash-tray and an enameled box near the vase. Her hand brushed a corner. That was it! She grasped at the box and opened the lid. Cigarettes . . . and tucked into one corner, a small, slim lighter. She flicked it, and the tiny flame appeared, bright in the darkness.

Edwina exclaimed and stumbled over to join her. They both lit cigarettes. "I've given up," Edwina remarked seriously, after a moment. She exhaled a plume of smoke, and watched it dissolve into the darkness with satisfaction. "So have I," said Birdie. She took one last, long drag, sighed, and stubbed the cigarette out. "Poison," she said. Edwina murmured muffled agreement.

Birdie flicked the lighter again, and dimly the room's shapes appeared. The doorway was directly in front of her. "I'm going upstairs," she announced. "I think there's something wrong."

"You're crazy. With that pathetic little light? You'll break your neck."

"I'm going. You stay where you are."

"Not bloody likely." Edwina leaned over, felt for the ashtray and crushed her cigarette into it. "If you go, I go. I'm not sitting here twiddling my thumbs in the dark. There are limits."

They edged cautiously toward the doorway and out into the hall. Flickering light from the sitting room cast a dull glow on the marble tiles. More than enough to see by, now that their eyes had adjusted to the dark. But the stairway rose in front of them, disappearing into pitch black about halfway up.

They moved silently, by unspoken agreement. Neither wanted Josie's and Belinda's company. They reached the stairs and began to climb, one behind the other.

Soon they were in darkness. They moved stair by stair, feeling their way, holding tightly to the banister, as if to a lifeline. The silence and the dark were thick around them. "This is madness," whispered Edwina. She was so close that Birdie could feel her breath on the back of her neck.

Birdie flicked the lighter and held its tiny flame out in front of her till it got too hot to hold, straining her eyes to see. "We're nearly there," she said. "Four or five more steps." Her heart was beating hard, somewhere up near the top of her chest. It was as if she could feel it in the base of her throat. She felt like choking. Something was wrong, she could feel it. The blackness at the top of the stairs was infinitely menacing. But she dragged her feet on over the thick carpet, grateful for the sound and warmth of Edwina behind her.

She almost stumbled when she reached the top, though she'd been waiting for the moment when her raised foot met empty air. She heard Edwina's exclamation as she faltered. "It's all right. We're at the top," Birdie murmured, edging around the balustrade to give her companion room.

They looked down at the vestibule below. From here they could see the faint glow from the sitting room. "We'll edge around the gallery, facing this way," whispered Birdie. "So we'll be able to see the light from Josie's candles." The thought cheered her.

"Oh!" Edwina grabbed her arm. "I've just remembered. I think there's a candle on a table just here. You know, by the couch? A candle in a silver candlestick. I saw it yesterday."

"Yes!" Birdie flicked the lighter and they edged away from the safety of the balustrade, holding on to each other, free hands outstretched, bodies tensed against unexpected bumps. Birdie found the side chair

and sank into it while Edwina stood clutching the arm.
She reached across to the corner table. Here she'd
found the pink envelope, the anonymous letter. It
seemed weeks ago. The lighter cast a tiny pool of light
on the polished wood, and at the back of the table a
silver candlestick gleamed. Birdie grabbed it with a hiss
of satisfaction. It was heavy. She pulled it toward her
and lit the candle. The wick caught, and a big, yellow
flame rose up, pushing away the darkness, lighting up
the little sitting area, the stained-glass window in
shades of gray, the door to the staff stairway.

"Ah! That's better!" Edwina gave a long sigh.

Birdie looked up at her and grinned. "Lucky you
remembered it," she said. "Let's go."

They walked slowly along the gallery, toward
"Eve"'s door. No need now to feel their way, or turn to
the secondhand light from the vestibule for reassurance. With the candlelight, Birdie's panic had eased.
Now she wondered what Toby would say when he saw
her—with Edwina in tow, too. Ten to one she'd just get
to him and the lights would go on. Damn! She should
have waited, like Edwina said. But she knew she
couldn't have waited.

It was very quiet, except for the rain pattering on
the roof above them. They reached the corner of the
gallery. Helen's door was ahead. Birdie's arm was aching with the weight of the candlestick. She lowered it
slightly as they reached the door marked "Eve." There
was no sound from inside. She glanced at Edwina,
standing tall by her shoulder, lifted her free hand, and
knocked.

The door swung open under her hand. Inside it
was black as pitch, and in the blackness, someone was
breathing.

"Dan!" Birdie thrust the candlestick high in the air
before her. The flame blew back, faltered, recovered,
and flared up once more. Edwina gripped her arm.

"Dan! Are you in there?"

Nothing. Just breathing, hoarse and deep, in the dark. Birdie pushed the door wide and stepped forward.

"No, Verity!" Edwina was trying to hold her back, but Birdie pulled away, holding up the light.

Toby lay sprawled on the couch like a bulky bundle of old clothes. His arm was thrown over his face, as if to protect it. Birdie crept toward him. The candlelight threw shadows around the room, picked out something white lying on the floor beside the desk. Milson's shirt. Milson, lying crumpled, long legs sticking out under the desk chair.

"Verity!" Edwina's voice penetrated the paralyzed silence of Birdie's mind. Edwina's urgent hand plucked at her sleeve. She made herself turn around.

Helen was sitting on the side of the bed. Very upright, very still, her hands in her lap. As they looked, she turned her head. Her eyes gleamed. "They're asleep," she said softly. "Just asleep."

Birdie's scalp prickled. She backed away till she reached the couch. She held the candlestick high, like a weapon. She felt for Toby with her left hand. He was warm. Breathing. Breathing heavily. It was Toby's breathing she had heard from the door. She pushed at him, shook him, but he wouldn't wake. Wouldn't stir.

"He's been drugged," she said. Her voice sounded loud in her own head. Birdie saw the tray on the low table by the couch, its silver coffeepot winking in the candlelight. She saw one cup still on the tray, unused, one still a quarter full on the table where Toby had put it down. Where was the other? Of course. On the desk, where Milson had been taking notes. She could see it now.

She skirted the coffee table and sidled over to the desk, without taking her eyes off Helen. Crouching down, she touched Milson's cheek, felt for the pulse of

his neck. She could hear him breathing too, now. He
was deeply asleep. She called his name, and pulled at
his sleeve, but there was no response. She stared, fascinated, at his unconscious face in profile. One cheek was
buried in the carpet. He looked as though he'd been
carved in relief.

"Are they all right?" Edwina's voice again pulled
her back to the need for action. She got slowly to her
feet. The candlestick was a dead weight on her arm.
She put it down on the coffee table.

"I think so," she said. "Depends what they've had,
and how much. But they don't feel clammy or anything, and their pulses are all right. They're just out of
it. Whatever it was, it was strong." She forced herself to
look at the watching figure on the bed. "Did you give
them some pills, Helen?"

Helen stared, but didn't answer.

"How many pills did you give them, Helen?"
Birdie persisted. "How many?" She heard her voice
crack, and gripped her hands together. She had to keep
calm. As cold as ice.

Helen shook her head, as if to clear it. Her brow
was furrowed with concentration. "I didn't give them
any pills," she said finally. Her voice strengthened. "I
didn't give them anything. They tried to give me coffee, but I wouldn't have it. They drank the coffee. And
after a while they just said they were feeling tired, then
they both went to sleep. That's all. Then the lights went
out."

"Helen, have you been out of the room?" asked
Edwina. The question was firm, authoritative.

"No."

"The door was open, though."

Helen shrugged. "It might have been. I don't
know. I didn't go out." Her brow furrowed again. "I
don't think I did."

Birdie's stomach leaped sickeningly. She crossed to

Edwina's side. "We've got to get help," she muttered to her. "My room's next door. We'll put her in there and deadlock her in."

Edwina nodded, and turned to Helen. "You need a rest," she said, in a friendly, businesslike way. "You'd better come and lie down next door. We can't move these men. They're too heavy. All right?" She held out a capable hand.

Helen stood up obediently, and staggered. In two strides Edwina had reached her and taken her arm. "I forgot," Helen gasped, leaning on her shoulder. "My ankle." Even in the candlelight they could see the bruise, dark blue-gray, staining the white skin. Edwina and Birdie looked at each other for a moment, thoughts racing. Then Edwina put her arm around Helen's narrow waist. "I'll help you," she said matter-of-factly. "Easy now. We'll take it steady."

They made slow and painful progress out of the room. As they moved out to the gallery the lights flickered and came on. Birdie blinked, her eyes watering. Glorious light! Even in the midst of it, Birdie hadn't quite realized how oppressive the dark had been. The hum of the air-conditioning reached her ears, filling the silence. Thank God! Warmth and life seemed to have begun flowing around them again. Around them and into them. She could feel it. She ran ahead and opened the door of "Juliet," standing aside to let Edwina and Helen through.

Edwina half carried Helen to the bed and pushed her shoulders gently till she sat. "We'll be back soon, Helen," she said, and turned to go. But Birdie stood behind her, the candlestick still in her hand. She stared at the woman on the bed. "Your real name's Laurel, isn't it?" she said quietly. She hadn't come this far not to be sure.

The woman stared at her, opened dry lips like a bird wanting water. She swayed.

"Leave it," muttered Edwina. But Birdie had to know.

"You're Laurel Moon," she insisted. "Aren't you?"

Helen bowed her head. She began to sob; great, racking sobs that shook her whole body. She covered her face with her big hands.

They backed out of the room, and left her, locking her in.

"You mean she was loose?" Josie's big face was pale. "We could have all been killed!" Belinda made an inarticulate sound and Alistair patted her arm.

"Well we weren't!" snapped Betty Hinder. She wiped her hands, smeared with grease, on the skirt of her black dress, realized what she was doing, and snorted in disgust. "That Teddy Silver. I'll give him a piece of my mind when I see him next. He's paid good money to service that generator, not just pay it a visit."

"Maybe he hasn't been yet this quarter, Betty," Alistair soothed absentmindedly. He continued patting Belinda, but his forehead was wrinkled in thought.

"Oh, he's been all right. That William told me only yesterday. I asked specially, because of the rain. Been and taken his money, too, and now look! We're nearly left in the dark. What would you have done if I hadn't been here, eh?"

"I don't know, Betty." The wrinkles on Alistair's forehead deepened.

She snorted again and then grimaced, kicking out with one leg. "And those gum boots leak," she complained. "My toes are wet on this foot. I didn't notice when I put me shoes back on."

"Mrs. Hinder, could you go up and see how Dan and Constable Milson are?" asked Birdie, in a fever of impatience. "You said you might be able to . . ."

"Oh yes." Mrs. Hinder started to climb the stairs.

"Do a pot of coffee, Alistair, will you? They'll need it. The sleeping beauties, I mean."

"Watch it! It was your coffee put them out in the first place, Betty," hooted Josie raucously.

There was a frozen silence. Mrs. Hinder turned and looked back down at her. Her eyes were steely. "Mrs. Hinder to you, thanks," she said with quiet venom. She came back down the stairs, lips pursed. Startled, Josie backed away.

"Betty . . ." began Alistair, but she brushed past him. "Got to put my spare shoes on," she said brusquely. "I've wet all the inside of this one. My stocking's sopped." She pulled off her right shoe defiantly and held out her foot. Her chin dropped comically. The people closest to her gasped. The stocking toe gleamed wet and scarlet.

"Oh, Betty, look, you've hurt yourself!" Alistair bent to see, pulled at the draggled nylon. "You've cut yourself! What have you done? How . . . ?" His voice trailed off. He held up his hand, stained with red. His mouth fell open.

Mrs. Hinder crouched down and felt her toes. Her hands, too, came away red. "Nothing wrong with me," she snapped. "Well?" She waited, as if for an explanation. Birdie thought she knew it. She felt sick.

"Where are the gum boots?" she asked Alistair.

"By the back door. The kitchen door, where they always are," he said stupidly, staring at his hand.

"Let's go and look," she said, and let him lead the way into the back of the house, through the storeroom and into the big, gleaming kitchen with its scrubbed pine table. The others followed, trailing behind them silently.

Two pairs of wet and muddy gum boots stood forlornly by the door that led out to the courtyard and herb garden beyond. Birdie picked up the right boot of the smaller pair. She turned it upside down and shook it. Nothing happened.

"What's she doing?" she heard Josie ask the world in general, but no one answered. She considered her options, then determinedly pushed her hand down inside the boot, reaching out with her fingers till they found what she'd been looking for, crushed into the toe.

She withdrew her hand carefully, trying to keep her find from dragging against the inside of the boot. She kept her back to them.

"What's she got?" asked Josie avidly.

"Mrs. Hinder, have you got a clean plastic bag or something?" Birdie called. There was no answer, but within moments a thin brown hand was holding out what she needed. She slid her find into the bag, and folded it over. Then she turned to face them. Belinda whimpered. Alistair stepped forward expectantly.

"Latex gloves," said Birdie briefly, showing him. "Like the ones you use when you're coloring hair."

But this time the stains on the gloves weren't hair dye. They were blood. And it was shining, scarlet, and fresh.

"Mrs. Hinder," said Birdie calmly, "please get your spare shoes on, make the coffee, and go upstairs. Do everything you can think of to wake Dan Toby or Mr. Milson or both. We need them. Don't worry about Helen," she added, anticipating the response. "She's locked in my room. I deadlocked it. She can't get out. Please. Hurry!"

"Yes, Betty, do as she says," said Alistair. His face was very pale. The housekeeper turned immediately to the sink and began filling the kettle.

"The rest of you should go back to the sitting room and wait. Alistair and I are going to wake up William, Conrad, and Angela." Birdie tightened her grip on the grisly evidence in her hands. "We'll join you as soon as we have."

"No!" Belinda was shaking her head. "No! I'm not going back there. I think we should all stay together. I do! Alistair, we should all stay together." She clung to his arm.

"I think so too," said Edwina heavily.

"And so do I!" Josie added, folding her arms over her broad bosom. "I'm not taking a step without everyone else."

Birdie hesitated. It was madness, but she couldn't afford to waste time arguing. "All right!" she snapped, turning on her heel. "Come on! Keep together and hurry!"

They almost ran back through the kitchen storeroom and out to the annex. Déjà vu. This was the way they'd come, together like this, to meet Angela, screaming that Margot was dead. Dead! Rain still frosted the multipaned windows and pattered on the tin roof. Outside the windows the paving was awash, and the herb garden sodden. They passed the entrance to the changing rooms and pool, turned down the therapy room corridor. Windows on the left, closed doors to the right. Hair, massage, beauty therapy . . . makeup . . . Margot dead. Belinda was whimpering, Josie panting. Alistair was moving with a strange crablike motion, his back turned away from the doors, his eyes fixed on the streaming windows.

They reached the storeroom at the end and turned left into the staff quarters corridor. Birdie stopped at the first door. She felt fear rising in her and fought it down.

"Which is which?" she murmured to Alistair.

"Spare at the end, then Conrad, then Angela. This is William," gabbled Alistair. He was very rattled. He banged violently on the door in front of them. The watchers drew back. "William," yelled Alistair. He strode on without waiting for a reply, banging on Angela's and Conrad's doors in turn and calling their names, his voice shockingly loud, echoing against the glass of the windows, bouncing from the walls.

Conrad threw open his door. He was bare-chested but had pulled on a pair of jeans. His long golden brown hair fell tousled to his shoulders. His eyes were heavy with sleep and he looked surprisingly young and vulnerable. He began walking toward the tongue-tied group before him. "What's up?" he asked, almost plaintively. "What's happened?"

Now William had staggered into the corridor, slim in elegant dark blue silk pajamas, his fine, black hair disheveled. He stared, blushed, muttered something, and went back into his room, reemerging a moment later with a shabby tartan dressing gown. He stood there blinking like a tall, bony owl, trying ineffectually to pull the gown on without looking what he was doing. Josie watched his efforts with interest. Everyone else tried not to look.

"Angela!" Alistair pounded on her door again. "It's Alistair. Get up!"

But there was silence behind Angela's door. Alistair turned back to Birdie. His eyes were filled with fear. "Will I get a master key?" he asked through stiff lips.

"Yes. You'd better."

Alistair turned and ran.

"What's happening?" William turned from one stricken face to another.

"Is there more than one master key, William?" asked Birdie.

He blinked at her. "There's one in Margot's desk, with other keys. Alistair's got one. And I think there's one in the safe. Yes, there is. Why?"

Birdie didn't answer.

Alistair's thudding footfalls came down the corridor. He rounded the corner, catching his breath. Birdie held out her hand and he gave her the key. She approached the door, knocked sharply again, and slid the key into the lock. It turned smoothly, and the door swung wide. Birdie switched on the light.

Angela lay on her back on the floor, her head facing the door. Her fair hair was tied into a loose plait. Her day clothes hung over the back of a chair nearby. White dress, white slip, cotton bra and panties. She was wearing pale blue pajamas. The jacket had been ripped open, the buttons scattered, to reveal small, perfect breasts. Her legs and arms were flung out at awkward angles, as if she'd been dropped onto the carpet from above. Birdie saw all this as though from a great distance. She saw the rolled-back eyes, the blue-tinged face, the dark pool of blood that soaked the carpet around the shoulders. She saw the nail scissors, buried deep in the torn, tortured neck, where a leg of a pair of white panty hose still trailed away, draggled with scarlet. Behind her, Alistair staggered. She put her hand back, pushed him out of the doorway. That was a mistake, because then everyone saw, and the screaming started.

16

"He said we were safe!" William beat his fists on his knees. His dark eyes were red-rimmed with fatigue and tears. Birdie glanced at Alistair, throwing great logs on the fire in front of them, poking and blowing at it roughly, lost in his own thoughts.

"He thought we were, William. Now, again, are you sure you didn't hear anything from Angela's room? Anything at all?"

He shook his head. "I didn't hear a thing! It was all completely quiet, except for the rain. I thought she was asleep! We'd told her to go to sleep, and not worry, Conrad and me, when we took her to her room. Didn't we, Conrad? And I thought she had! I thought she had!"

"I nearly checked on her, you know." Conrad was sitting forward in his chair. He'd pulled a sweater on over his jeans but his hair was still wild and stubble prickled his jaw. "I nearly did. But it was past eleven-thirty. She'd had a good half-hour to settle down, and she'd been a bit het-up before, talking about trying to remember details for the cops and so on. I thought if she had got off to sleep I'd just disturb her and the whole thing'd start again." Abruptly he dropped his face into his hands. "Poor little bitch," he muttered. He took a deep breath and straightened up, running his hands back through his hair self-consciously.

"I thought I heard a phone ring," said William suddenly. "I was asleep—almost asleep. But I thought I heard a phone. In Angela's room. Or Conrad's. Or even one of the therapy rooms. Just a couple of rings. But a phone." He looked from Birdie to Conrad expectantly.

Conrad's brow creased. "I didn't hear any phone. You must have dreamed it."

William shook his head. "I didn't," he said positively. "I'm sure I didn't, the more I think about it."

"When would this have been, William?" asked Birdie.

"I don't know. I got into bed at about half-past eleven. It could have been half an hour after that. Maybe an hour. I don't know."

"It must have been before the power went off. We know that much, anyway."

He stared at her, obviously bewildered. "I didn't know the power *had* gone off. Are we using the generator? Oh yes, of course we are. The noise. I didn't even think about it." He shivered.

Birdie bit her lip. She needed help. Betty Hinder hadn't yet succeeded in rousing the men upstairs. She needed to talk to someone she could trust. If she was right, there was no time to waste. She twisted around to survey the room. There was only one possible candidate. She left William, and walked over to where Edwina stood looking out the window at blackness and rain. "Could you give me a moment outside?" she murmured.

Edwina nodded without showing any surprise, and followed Birdie out of the room and into the hall. The others watched them go wearily, without comment.

"We've got to talk," Birdie said rapidly. "Out the back, where no one can hear. All right?"

"All right."

They began walking toward the back of the house in silence. The annex was dark, and Birdie flicked all the switches on the wall beside the door, flooding the area with light. They walked to the sitting area near the pool entrance and sat, facing one another over a low table scattered with fashion and home decorating magazines.

"Well," said Edwina. "What's up?"

"Toby's still out of it," Birdie began, leaning forward, "and it's too risky for me to keep this to myself." Despite the urgency she felt awkward. Edwina was looking at her a little quizzically. Probably thought she was exaggerating, being melodramatic. She fought the feeling down and pressed on, speaking as clearly and logically as she could. Edwina would respond to that.

"If Helen killed Angela," she said flatly, "she did it while Toby and Milson were asleep. Toby went up to her room at eleven forty-five, taking the tray of coffee with him. Until then *she'd* been asleep, guarded by Milson. It would have taken at least fifteen minutes for Toby and Milson to drink enough drugged coffee to knock them out. Probably we're actually talking about twelve-fifteen or so. Right?"

Edwina nodded. She was paying close attention now.

"The lights went off just after twelve-thirty."

"Right." Edwina was waiting for her to get to the point.

Birdie took a deep breath and clasped her hands together. They felt icy. "Milson searched Helen's room. He's a very thorough man, Milson. He didn't find any latex gloves, or any scissors there. He found only clothes, a toothbrush, and some money. The key to her own room was in her pocket. So we're postulating the theory that Helen got downstairs, found a master key, got hold of some gloves and a pair of scissors, found Angela's room, overpowered and killed her, returned the key, stuffed a pair of bloody gloves into the toe of a gum boot in the kitchen, and started back upstairs, all in the space of, at the absolute most, half an hour, more likely fifteen or twenty minutes, the last five minutes of it in the pitch dark, with a sprained ankle so painful she could hardly walk on it."

"She could have hurt her ankle later."

"No. Toby told me she'd hurt it while they were trying to get her upstairs."

Edwina stared at her. "I didn't realize," she said slowly. "But listen, you're wrong about the time. She had an hour—maybe three-quarters, as you say—but still . . . I didn't look at my watch but we couldn't have got up to that room before about one o'clock."

Birdie leaned forward urgently. "You're forgetting, Edwina. Betty Hinder and Alistair went out to the generator just after the lights went off. Betty was wearing the gum boots, and the gloves had been put in the toe by then. Angela was dead by then, and her killer well away."

Edwina rubbed her hand over her mouth. "You're saying . . ."

"I'm saying that she couldn't have done it. Helen couldn't have killed Angela. But someone wanted us to think she did. Someone put a drug in the coffee to knock out Toby and Milson, so Helen would have no alibi. Someone who didn't know about her ankle. Who didn't know I was expecting a call from Toby so I would go up and check on him if he didn't ring."

"That's everyone. No one knew those things."

"That's right." Birdie let it sink in. She watched Edwina's face as she thought.

"But why kill Angela? If it wasn't—just madness? Who'd have any reason to kill Angela?"

"Whoever killed Margot Bell. Because Angela saw something, or noticed something in the beauty therapy room, and they were scared she'd tell. Angela was first on the scene, it was her workroom. If anyone was going to notice anything, she was. And the killer knew it."

"The killer . . ." Edwina stared across the low table at Birdie. She rubbed her mouth again distractedly. "But . . . the method. The Gray Lady murders . . . Helen said . . ."

"Helen—Laurel Moon—was set up. Someone used her method to kill Margot Bell after they heard William's story that first night. It was a copycat murder, and we jumped at it. We played right into the real killer's hands. Or at least Toby did. I tried to warn him, but he wouldn't listen. I don't know why he was so stubborn. We've worked together before, quite a few times, and usually he listens to me—in the end. But this time he was convinced he knew the answer, and he wouldn't even look at any other possibility. Then, to dispose of Angela, who posed some sort of danger, the killer tried the Gray Lady method again. Safe as houses. Once Helen's real identity was established, she'd never be able to get out of it."

"What an evil thing!" Edwina beat her hands together softly, her face grim and intent. "What an *evil* thing!"

"Yes."

They sat in silence for a moment. Then Edwina stirred. "Who?" she asked simply.

"We've got to find out. Quickly. Before anyone else . . . anything else happens. We have to go back there and talk. See what we can find out. The killer won't be worried."

"What do we say? What do we ask?"

"We'll talk about Margot, and Angela, and the last couple of days. Get them to remember, and gossip. Get some idea about motive, especially in Margot's case. Then work on opportunity. Get a picture of what everyone was doing when, try to pick up inconsistencies and blank spots. Then we'll compare notes. All right?"

"O.K." But Edwina looked doubtful. She turned away.

"Anything wrong?"

"Oh no." The tall woman smiled ruefully. "Oh no. It's absurd. Selfish and absurd. It's just that in my business, this sort of thing . . . can be really dangerous."

"It is a bit dangerous," Birdie said quietly. "I didn't spell it out. I assumed you'd realize . . ."

Edwina waved her hand. "Oh, not that sort of dangerous. Dangerous to my career." That rueful smile again. "The precious career, you know? Being mixed up in a murder case is not well thought of in banking circles. And now . . ."

"Look, there's no reason why you should get any publicity at all," said Birdie firmly. "You just help me out. I'll talk to Toby about it, and we'll keep your involvement completely quiet. I really have worked with him before. It'll be all right, I promise."

This time Edwina's smile was grateful. "Thanks. I'll hold you to that. Now, who'll do who?"

"Well, I've been thinking. In Angela's case, everyone more or less could have slipped out to the annex at some point, before the lights went out. William and Conrad went out there to their rooms one after another, and straight after she did. Betty and Alistair were pottering around the kitchen and dining room making coffee and tea and so on, separately as well as together. And you, Belinda, and Josie were supposedly asleep in the sitting room. Any one of you could have sneaked out while Toby and I were busy in the office without the others knowing."

Edwina laughed. "Thanks a lot! What if it was me?"

"That's a risk I'll have to take. But I haven't drummed up a motive for you, yet, mate, so I think I'm safe." Birdie grinned at her.

"You mean you've got motives for the others?"

Birdie shrugged. "Well, obviously the staff are the best bets. They're the ones most likely to have urgent, personal reasons for killing Margot. There are at least three good motives there. I don't know about the fourth. As far as Josie and Belinda are concerned, we need to dig deeper. There are things about both of them that don't add up."

"Great."

"Anyway, getting back to the dope in the coffee: Toby put the coffee by the stairs and left it while he talked to me in the office. William or Conrad could have crept back into the main house and doped the pot then. You in the sitting room ditto. Alistair could have done it by coming through the dining room door. Betty could have done it at her leisure in the kitchen. Not much joy there. That's why I think we should put Angela's murder on the back-burner, and concentrate on Margot Bell." She paused. Edwina was staring at her with that quizzical look again. "What?"

"You're a cool customer, aren't you?" drawled Edwina. "Talking about putting murders on the back-burner? How many times have you done this before, anyway?"

"Quite a few," muttered Birdie. She pushed impatiently at her glasses. "Now, look. Margot Bell's case is easier. The people who left the room during the critical time, between ten-past and half-past six, were Alistair, Betty Hinder, Helen, Conrad, and William and Belinda. Conrad was last, and I don't know if he would have had time to do anything, but you never know. He did meet Helen in the annex, so he was in the right general area. William and Belinda were supposed to have been together for the whole time in the library, except for quick trip to the loo, but . . . oh!''

"What is it?"

"I've just remembered something Belinda said. She said she had something to tell Toby. Something she thought was important. Look, I'll talk to her, and to Alistair. I've got to know him reasonably well. You do Conrad and William. And Josie."

Edwina groaned. "Thanks a lot, Verity. What about the housekeeper?"

"Call me Birdie. I'll do Betty. She'll talk more freely to me. I think she's adopted me—orphan of the storm, you know. All right, let's go." Birdie stood up. She felt energized. Her body was tingling with excitement.

"Wait!" Edwina got to her feet and put her hand on Birdie's shoulder. She towered over her. "You said the critical time was six-ten to six-thirty. Why?"

"That's the critical time. The time in which Margot Bell could have been murdered," said Birdie patiently. Edwina was being a bit slow.

"But why then?"

"Because that was the only time Margot was alone. You were with her till about ten past six, when you came to drinks, and Angela found her dead at about half-past six! Right? Can we go now?" Birdie started for the door.

"No, wait!" Edwina's hand tightened on her shoulder. "Verity—Birdie—I didn't realize you thought . . . but, I see, why wouldn't you? You don't understand. I didn't leave Margot Bell at ten past six. She'd finished my face by a quarter *to six*, and I left her straightaway. I hadn't enjoyed our conversation, and I didn't want any more of it."

"But you didn't come into the sitting room till at least ten past six!" Birdie was flabbergasted.

"No I didn't." Edwina spread her hands and

shrugged. "I went up to my room and fiddled around for a good twenty minutes before I came down again. Sheer bloody-mindedness really. I didn't feel like being her messenger girl, and I couldn't give a bugger about the place's social life. I was just here for the treatment, God help me."

"Why didn't you say so before?" Birdie was aghast. This changed everything. Of course, how stupid of her not to see that Edwina, at least, wouldn't let Margot bully her.

"No one asked me," said Edwina reasonably.

"So!" Birdie tried to run her hands through her hair, forgetting that the usual bush of curls had gone. She tugged disgustedly at the soft wisps curling round her ears. "Dear, oh dear, never *assume!* When will I learn?" She jerked her head in the direction of the door. "Let's go, then," she said. "It's wide open. Everyone's in it. Oh, Lord!" She bolted through the door to the house proper. A slight smile playing on her lips, Edwina strode heavily behind her.

17

Birdie went into the sitting room first. She'd decided it was better if she and Edwina weren't seen as a team. Belinda was sitting with William by the fire, holding his hand. It was an oddly domestic picture. He sat passive and invalidlike, overwarm in his thick dressing gown. She murmured sympathetically, nodding a cozily disheveled head. They might have been a married couple coping with late night indigestion. Birdie made her way over to them, smiled, and made much of warming her hands at the fire. They watched her with polite suspicion.

"I suppose the Windsor police will be coming to take us out of here, in the morning, as soon as it's light," she remarked chattily.

"Not me," said William restlessly. "I live here, remember. This is my job and my home. Where else would I go?"

"But you don't want to stay here, William, do you?" said Belinda. They'd obviously talked about this before.

"I can't leave Alistair in the lurch," said William, and drooped. Belinda squeezed his hand.

Birdie noticed Edwina wander casually into the room and drop down beside Josie, with a show of weariness. Josie's eyes were puffy, but her nap had obviously done her good, for she smiled quite cheerily, dug out the inevitable handkerchief from her sleeve, and blew her nose heartily, in preparation for conversation. So far so good. Birdie turned her attention back to Darby and Joan.

"Belinda," she began in a diffident voice. "Remember what you were telling me before—about something you had to tell Dan Toby? You never got a chance to carry on with that, did you?"

Belinda and William exchanged glances. They had obviously talked about this, too. Belinda tossed her head slightly. "No, I never did. He put me off. Again. He's not very good at his job, I don't think."

"I've been so curious ever since you mentioned it. What was it?"

"Oh . . ." Belinda tossed her head again resentfully. "It's probably not important at all. Especially now." She pursed her little rosebud mouth, as if to keep the secret in.

"We don't know that," pressed Birdie. "They say every little detail helps." That's what I said to Angela, she thought. Oh God, she said there was something. I thought she was imagining things. Why did I rush her off to bed? Why didn't I help her remember? Then she would have told me. Then she wouldn't have died.

"It's not a little detail," William was saying loudly. "Tell her, Belinda."

"Oh . . ." Belinda wriggled, making the most of her moment. "Well, it's just that I heard Margot Bell shouting at someone. Really shouting. I heard every word. Early yesterday morning."

"Yes." Birdie tried not to let the disappointment show on her face. "That would be the maid who got the sack, wouldn't it? You heard it all, did you? How embarrassing."

"No!" exclaimed Belinda petulantly. "Oh no, lots of people heard *that*. I mean before. Half an hour before. Up in her room."

"In her room?" Birdie stared at her.

"Yes." Belinda flushed slightly. "I was going down to breakfast, and I was early, for once, it was only a quarter past seven, and I thought I'd just sit down near the top of the stairs there for a minute. And then the door—you know that door there?"

"To the staff stairs?"

"Yes." Belinda's flush deepened. "Well, it was open a bit, and I heard this shouting . . . and I thought, I'd better close it, because I didn't want to overhear anything private . . ."

Not much, thought Birdie in grim amusement. Toby was right. Belinda is the type who listens at doors. She nodded vigorously. "Oh, of course," she said.

". . . and while I was shutting it, I just couldn't help hearing what she was saying," Belinda went on. She leaned forward and lowered her voice. "The *language*," she whispered. "I could hardly believe it!" She turned to William, wide-eyed, and he nodded in a sad, knowing way. Birdie felt a sudden, sharp burst of something like pity for Margot Bell. Life was going on without her, and the power she'd wielded over so many lives had died with her. Now the weak, soft beings she had terrorized could creep in safety to her memory, to dissect and patronize her faults and foolishnesses with impunity.

"What did she say?" she asked in hushed tones.

"Oh—I couldn't repeat all of it," simpered Belinda, "but she said, screamed, really, 'You're f . . . ing disgusting! At the end of this f . . . ing fortnight you can just f . . . ing get out!' And then the other person must have said something quietly, because there was a space, and then she screamed out again, 'F . . . that! You're not getting a brass razoo out of me! And you won't say a f . . . ing word or you'll be sorry! You'll stay the f . . . ing fortnight and say f . . . ing nothing! And keep away from me!' " Belinda leaned forward, wide-eyed. "And then I heard someone coming down the stairs—and I took off!"

"I'll bet!" said Birdie with feeling. She could just imagine. "So, you never saw who it was Margot was talking to?"

Belinda shook her head regretfully. "No I didn't. William and I have been trying to think who it could have been. I thought it might have been Alistair. He'd seemed a bit upset with Margot Bell a few times. But William says it couldn't be."

"Alistair's a partner," said William knowledgeably. "Margot couldn't have told him to get out."

"No," said Birdie thoughtfully. "And obviously it wasn't you, William."

He went brick red. "Of course not!" he spluttered indignantly. "I didn't even see Margot till breakfast."

"Oh, of course. Sorry." Birdie smiled soothingly. "Silly of me. But didn't she say anything to you about —whoever it was, when you met later, to talk about the accounts? You were obviously close to her."

"No." He still looked ruffled. "She didn't say anything. I can't understand it. She usually told me everything." He paused. "I've been thinking . . ." he began.

"What?" Birdie saw that Belinda was looking at him expectantly. This was something they'd discussed, too.

"Well," William said coyly, "I was thinking that if she'd had a falling-out with Conrad Hunter, she mightn't tell me about that. She mightn't tell Alistair either."

"Why not?"

He shrugged. "Oh," he said indulgently. "Poor Margot always found it really hard to admit when she was wrong. And Alistair and I—we always told her that guy was a spiv. She should never have hired him, let alone . . . well, you know." He looked uncomfortable.

"Women of that age get taken in so easily," lisped Belinda complacently. She wriggled a little deeper into the couch. "It's sad, really."

"Yes," agreed William. "Poor Margot."

Birdie left them to it.

"Get anything?" Birdie murmured to Edwina as they stood together at the drinks cabinet, their backs to the room. From where the others were sitting it should look like a casual conversation.

"Nothing much except a million cold germs," said Edwina briefly, pouring herself a sizable brandy. "Medicinal purposes," she explained, straight-faced, shaking the last golden drops from the bottle. She added a very small slurp of ginger ale to her glass and took a sip. "Ah, at last, a decent drink. They make them too weak round here." She looked at her watch. "You realize it's two-thirty, don't you? How come we're still all on our feet?"

"Most people have had a bit of sleep. Enough to keep them going." Not me, though, thought Birdie. And I'm getting a bit fuzzy. She gulped at her own drink. The Scotch burned her throat, spread its warmth through her chest. Would this make her better or worse? Too late to worry about that now.

Someone put a hand on her shoulder. She spun round in shock, nearly spilling her drink, and looked into the apologetic face of Alistair.

"Sorry," he murmured. "Didn't mean to startle you. I was just going to say, don't you think I should try to get everyone off to bed? There's not much point in them staying up, is there?"

Birdie thought quickly. The last thing she needed was for the group to split up again. "I wouldn't try it," she advised. "I think they're better off together at this point. And William and Conrad can hardly go back to the annex now."

"No." Alistair's eyes wrinkled with strain. Deep shadows hollowed his pleasant face. Birdie remembered that he, like her, had not slept. "I was thinking they could bunk down in my room. I wouldn't be going up."

"I'd leave everyone be." Edwina spoke decisively beside him. "We've got the police and Helen upstairs. I don't fancy going back to my room, and I shouldn't think anyone else does either. They'll drop off to sleep where they sit if they feel like it."

He nodded, obviously grateful for firm direction. "Anything you ladies want?" he murmured, with a rather sad stab in the direction of hostly geniality.

"We're out of brandy," Edwina noted innocently.

"Actually, I'm starving," said Birdie quickly. "Edwina and I were wondering if we could make ourselves a sandwich or something." A few minutes' consultation in the kitchen with Edwina would be very useful at this point. And in fact she was very hungry, she realized. It had been a long, long day.

"Oh sure!" Delighted by the opportunity for action, Alistair took their arms and hustled them toward the doors to the dining room. "I'll show you where everything is."

"Oh, we'll be right," protested Birdie. But Alistair had the bit between his teeth.

"I'll do some cheese and biscuits for the others and get some more brandy while I'm at it," he whispered. "Come on!"

Edwina winked at Birdie over his head. Accepting the inevitable, Birdie allowed herself to be led away.

"Betty said you designed the kitchen," Birdie remarked, watching Alistair raiding the huge refrigerator. She shivered. The kitchen was rather chilly after the warmth of the sitting room. The air-conditioning wasn't quite as efficient here. Everywhere else in the house her thin silk tunic was more than adequate. Here she could have done with a jacket.

"Oh yes." Alistair put ham, cheese, butter, pickles, and chutney onto the big table beside the bread. He closed the refrigerator and opened a pine door beside it to reveal an enormous pantry stocked with every kind of canned and packaged food. "Salmon?" he asked. "Asparagus?"

"Oh no, this is great, really." Birdie's mouth had actually started to water. She began to saw away at the bread.

"The Brie will be too cold," worried Alistair. He fluttered around finding plates and knives, opening and closing cupboards. "Brandy . . . brandy. I'm sure Margot got it. Where's she put it? God knows what it'll be like. She got it cheap, William said. I suspect it fell off the back of a truck." He disappeared into the storeroom, clattered around, and reemerged empty-handed. He threw himself down at the kitchen table. "Can't find it. It's nowhere. God! Surely William couldn't have worked his way through two dozen bottles in a week," he mumbled indiscreetly. He was obviously at the end of his tether.

Edwina was leaning heavily on the sink, gazing out the window at the herb garden dripping in the dark. "You know, this really is a great place," she remarked. "You and Margot were lucky to get it, Alistair."

"It was cheaper because of the flooding," Alistair

said frankly. "Though I must say it hasn't been much of a problem, really. It's usually only a matter of a few days—and not every year." He looked around the gleaming kitchen. "It is nice, isn't it? I just wish . . ."

Edwina turned around. "You know," she said abruptly, "when Margot asked me to intercede with the bank for you I couldn't really see—"

"*What!*" Alistair almost shouted the word. Birdie looked up from her sandwich-making with interest. He had gone very pale. Edwina regarded him with obvious surprise. He put a trembling hand to his mouth. "Sorry. Sorry," he stammered. "It's just—I had no idea Margot had spoken to you. I can't believe she'd have . . . troubled you with our . . . our private matters of business." It became clear that he was trembling not just with nerves, but with anger.

"Oh." For once Edwina seemed at a loss, but she collected herself quickly. "I am sorry," she said formally. "I naturally thought Margot was speaking for you too, Alistair. She certainly gave me that impression."

Alistair smiled bitterly. "Yes. She would. She seemed to have decided this place was hers to do with as she liked. But she certainly was not speaking for me. She knew very well that I wouldn't have had anything to do with it. You're here as a guest, not our financial adviser, for heaven's sake."

"As I told her, actually." Edwina was cool and uncompromising. "Well, I am relieved, Alistair, if you don't mind my saying so, that you weren't involved. I did feel it was rather—unprofessional. Not what I'd have expected from this place."

"No, of course not." Alistair began to clatter biscuits onto a silver tray, his head turned away from her. The tips of his ears were pink. He was obviously very upset. "Did she say anything, by the way," he asked, with a casual air that deceived neither of the women, "about cutting the makeover times to a week?"

"She mentioned it," Edwina replied lightly. "I said I thought it would be a pity."

Alistair picked up the tray, his mouth set in a thin line. "If I told Margot once," he said grimly, "I told her a hundred times. There was no way I was going to let that happen to Deepdene. This place was my idea. My dream. She had no business . . ." His voice trailed off and his shoulders sagged.

"Alistair, look," said Edwina impulsively. "I'm sorry you're upset, and this mightn't be the time, but I may as well finish what I started to say. I've been thinking about what Margot told me—the facts and figures and so on—and frankly I can't see why on earth this place shouldn't pay. And pay very well too."

"It used to," said Alistair dully, clutching the tray against his chest. "But everything's gone up—the place needs a lot of upkeep. And the last six months . . ." He took a breath and straightened his shoulders. "Look, thanks, Edwina, but it's not your problem."

"I know. It's your problem. Your business. In both senses." Edwina put her hands on her hips and smiled at him. It was a very attractive smile. "And I could say to you my looks were my problem and my business, couldn't I? But you don't see it that way. While you were doing my hair you told me you enjoyed your work because you're good at it, and the problems fascinated you. Well, I'm like that about money problems. I enjoy them. See? So why don't you let me have a go at yours. I don't promise anything, but I might be able to make a few suggestions that'll help."

Alistair looked bewildered, but grateful. "Well, if you like—if you can see a way . . . sure, of course," he murmured. "But what—"

"Just tell me it's O.K. to have a rummage through

your accounts. Oh—and get William to help me if I need to."

"Be my guest!" Alistair was blinking with pleasure. "Thank you," he added belatedly.

"Good. Well, I'll start on that in a minute. I'll never sleep tonight, now. Your office, or Margot's?"

"The books for the current tax year are in Margot's, the historical stuff in mine."

"All right, then."

Birdie was nearly dancing with impatience. If Edwina wanted to help Alistair out, surely she could wait till more urgent things were settled. Like who did in Alistair's partner, for example. What a bizarre sense of priorities! "Do you want your sandwich now, Edwina?" she demanded with some asperity.

"I'll leave you to it," said Alistair hastily. "Better take this in to the others." He smiled warmly. "Thanks again, Edwina. I really appreciate it."

"That's fine. Remember, though—no guarantees!"

"Sure!" But Alistair looked more lighthearted as he left the kitchen, carefully balancing his tray.

Edwina grinned at Birdie's sour expression as the door swung closed. "You think I was wasting time, don't you?" She grabbed a ham sandwich and bit into it. "Mmm—that's good," she mumbled, chewing with relish. She looked very pleased with herself.

"I would have thought murder was more important than money at this stage, that's all," said Birdie coolly. "Still . . ."

"Money's a great motive for murder, Birdie. One of the best. Isn't it?"

Birdie stared at her. She reached for a sandwich of her own and began to eat it. It was good. "You mean all that was just so you could get a look at the files?" God, and Edwina had called *her* a cool customer!

Edwina shrugged. "Well, look, it's half and half. First, I really don't see why this place should be having a cash-flow problem, when you consider what they charge and the fact they're fully booked. And that sort of problem really does fascinate me. Then—when I realized Alistair hadn't known Margot was going to talk to me . . . more ludicrous nonsense I've never heard, Birdie, than that woman talked. She obviously lived her life thinking 'contacts,' as no doubt she called them, could make her way for her. Maybe they have, till now. Male contacts, anyway." A slightly malicious look crossed her face.

"Anyway . . ." Birdie prompted, with her mouth full.

"Anyway," Edwina continued, "when I discovered Alistair didn't know, I realized it was fairly likely he didn't know quite a lot of things about the way Margot Bell operated. Obviously she kept things close to her chest where she felt she needed to. She had a word with me on Monday morning, just before I went for my massage, when she knew Alistair was safely out of the way. She raised it again when she was doing my makeup and again she was safe from interruption from him, because he was doing your hair at the same time. All very deliberate, I see now. And Josie said something . . ."

"Josie—I thought you said you didn't get much out of her?"

"I thought I hadn't, but thinking about it just then . . . she did say a few things. She was gossiping about Margot, among other things, with my encouragement, and that of several glasses of wine, and she obviously didn't like her at all."

"It was mutual, too, obviously. Dislike at first sight."

"Yes. Anyway, mixed up with all this stuff about how good eucalyptus was for colds, and how she wished she'd brought her humidifier with her, and her youngest child's shocking croup attacks, and how

she'd finally got her teeth capped seven years ago after
having to go round for a year and a half looking like a
fright with a broken front tooth because they didn't
have a penny to spare, there was all this other stuff.
Dark hints, you might say, about Margot being an ex-
travagant, spoiled snob who was in fact no better than
she should be, if people only knew it. And she raised
again the question of the anonymous letter she found."

Birdie started. Bizarrely, she had actually forgotten
about the letters. How could she? If Helen hadn't done
the murders, it was highly likely she hadn't written
those letters either. Her eyes widened. If . . .

"If Margot was being blackmailed—" Edwina
voiced her thoughts.

"She could have been taking money out of this
place, to pay!"

"Hence the sudden cash-flow problem. Alistair
wouldn't know . . ."

"My God! Edwina!" Birdie gripped Edwina's arm.
The two women stared at one another. "And if she
stopped paying, because the place couldn't take it, and
the blackmailer turned up here, incognito, to put pressure on . . . Look, this might be it! Can you start on
the account books now?"

"Why not? Nothing better to do." Edwina grinned
at her.

"I'll help." Enthusiastically, Birdie picked up two
more sandwiches and looked round for a plate to put
them on.

"Oh no!" The exclamation was involuntary, but
Edwina looked immediately apologetic as she registered Birdie's reaction. "It's simply," she explained
gently, "that I'll really work much faster alone. It's my
thing. I know what I'm looking for. You don't, and it
would take me too long to explain it to you. You'd be
much better off concentrating on other things. I'll get

back to you as soon as I find anything. Promise. All right?"

"Sure. No problem," said Birdie, forcing a smile. Patronizing bloody loner, she thought bitterly, oblivious to the pot and kettle ironies that would have been blatant to any observer who knew her.

With a wave, Edwina strode energetically off through the storeroom, obviously, metaphorically anyway, rubbing her hands with glee at the labors that awaited her. Birdie stood in the cold kitchen, the plate of sandwiches still in her hand, feeling let down and not a little irritated. Not a word at any stage had Edwina said to her about Margot Bell's asking her for help with the bank. Professional reticence; discretion, Edwina would probably have claimed. What bull. She just liked keeping things close to her chest till she needed them. Poker-faced politician!

She slowly realized that she'd underestimated Edwina. She'd forgotten that Edwina, as naive as she was in the ways of the beauty business, was a very successful businesswoman in her own cutthroat field. Now the initiative in this investigation had been quietly removed from her own hands and transferred to Edwina's. What "other things" were there for her to concentrate on? What was there for her to do until Edwina found the evidence of blackmail she was looking for? If only Alistair hadn't destroyed that letter! The library fire had been cleaned out and reset on Monday. No hope of any ashes surviving intact. And the second letter . . .

Birdie put down the plate, picked up a sandwich, and absentmindedly bit into it. Margot had taken the second letter. She had taken it from Josie as she'd walked out of the dining room after lunch. Straight after lunch she was . . . Birdie dug into her pocket and pulled out the timetable, shaking it impatiently out of its folds. She spread it out on the table, and her heart thudded. Straight after lunch, at two, Margot was due to make up Josie. And Margot had appointments every hour after that, all afternoon.

So she wouldn't have had a chance to destroy the letter in one of the front room fires. Josie had said she folded it up and stuck it in her pocket. What if it was still there?

There was only one way to find out.

18

Alistair's office was small, friendly, and cluttered, and
smelled of paper, apples, and the leather of the old
desk chair. Photographs, letters, cartoons, a copy of the
timetable, scrawled reminder notes, postcards, a bunch
of dried lavender, and several feathers were pinned
randomly on the noticeboard above the solid old oak
desk that had surely been inherited with the establishment. Some of the photographs, Birdie saw, were of
Deepdene and its staff. In one, Betty Hinder, eyes wrinkled against the sun, stood primly on the front veranda
with several other women and a couple of men, including a serious-faced William. Margot, in designer over-
alls with a scarf over her head and clutching a very
new-looking straw broom, waved, smiling, in another.
That must have been in the very early days. Birdie
hunched her shoulders and shivered, despite the
warmth of the still air.

She pulled open the top drawer of the desk. It was
filled with pens and chewed pencils, ink-stained eras-
ers, and boxes of paper clips. At the back was a small
round tin that had once held barley sugar. Birdie
pulled it out and opened it. Bingo! A bunch of keys,

one bearing a worn piece of sticking plaster marked
with the faded legend M. How easy could it get? And it
would have been just as easy, she reminded herself, for
anyone else to find.

Carefully returning the tin to its place, she stuck
the keys in her pocket with the timetable and crept out
of the room. She turned off the light and stole toward
the annex. The keys jingled as she walked, and she
stuffed her hand into her pocket to hold them still, feeling like a thief.

She let herself through the annex door and closed
it behind her. Her hand hovered over the light switch.
She had intended to make her way to the beauty therapy room in the dark, to lessen the chances that she'd
be disturbed. But now, confronted by the thick darkness, her resolution weakened. She compromised by
flicking only one of the switches, the one that lit the
corridors. Someone might see the light from the kitchen
window, but she'd have to take that risk. It would be
madness to attempt to make her way in the pitch dark.

But as she moved on silently, she became conscious that even with light, ghosts walked the annex
corridors. The old section of the house was bad
enough, but at least it still retained, in its old furniture,
old books, spacious rooms, and high ceilings, the memories of other times, other functions, other people.
These watertight, airtight, carpeted passages with their
low ceilings and matching doors behind which hy-
gienic cells of rooms lay hidden, held no echoes of the
past to humanize them or reduce her growing sense of
oppression. Down this corridor, behind two of these
doors, two women, who had lived and breathed,
dreamed and planned only yesterday, lay cold in the
dark, soaked in their own blood.

Birdie's feet slowed as she reached the beauty therapy room. She had no wish to enter it again, but her
fingers pulled the keys from her pocket as though by

their own volition, and felt for the sticking-plaster label that marked the master.

She slipped the key into the lock and turned it. She felt resistance and, for a split second of disappointment mixed equally with relief, thought she was going to be thwarted—or spared. But with a click the lock released, and the door swung open under her sweating hand. She switched on the light.

The scene was the same. The ghastly blind face, the shocking pool of red in the bare white neck, the shining scissors buried deep, the naked white shoulders and trailing arms, the tacky trail of red pooling on the ground. But this time Birdie could face the figure on the chair without shuddering. Was that because life had now departed so far from it that looking at it was like viewing a waxwork in some tawdry chamber of horrors? Or was it that the more often you were exposed to violent death, the less it moved and terrified you? Was this why doctors, nurses, soldiers, police, undertakers could go about their often grisly business professionally, calmly, without breakdown and nightmare? And why murderers found each death easier, and needed less and less reason to kill again?

Birdie bit hard on her lip, looked quickly over her shoulder, and made herself walk into the room, shutting the door behind her. It clicked efficiently, locking her in. She approached the chair, fastidiously skirting the sticky scarlet mass on the floor beside it, kicking aside the ragged ties of the cape that lay tangled and puddled where the murderer had dropped it once the need for it had passed. She stared at the body, wondering, now she was finally here, whether she could dare to touch it. It would be interfering with the scene of a crime. Toby would be furious. But Toby's not the one facing this problem, she reasoned desperately. He's upstairs unconscious. He's upstairs unconscious because he made a mistake. Because someone's a killer, here, in this house, on the loose. And I can't wait till he wakes up to do something about it. He'll just have to understand.

She looked at the body lying in front of her. Bare shoulders. Of course! Margot had been prepared for a neck massage. She had taken off her jacket, and the protective cape was tucked into the top of her bra. Birdie spun around. On open shelves on the wall behind her piles of pink capes lay primly folded, each one with its Velcro tabs neatly fastened at the back and its hem discreetly hidden. Beside the shelves there was a cupboard. Birdie pulled the end of her sleeve over her hand and, using the thin silk as a shield, carefully pulled one of the doors open. Margot's cream jacket hung there on a pink plastic hanger. It was, as Birdie remembered, long—to mid-thigh length—and of the finest wool crepe, exquisitely cut. A very faint, delicious trace of some French perfume still clung to it and Birdie, slipping her fingers into its deep pockets, found herself muttering curses, as though to ward off the evil eye.

The pockets were empty. Not a handkerchief, a safety pin, an old receipt, or even a loose thread, let alone a folded sheet of paper, met her eager hands. Nothing marred the perfect fall of the creamy wool. She groaned under her breath, pushed the cupboard door shut with her shoulder, and turned back to face the moment she'd thought she might be spared.

She crouched beside the chair and with the tips of her fingers lifted the side of the pink fabric that covered Margot from chest to knee. A white silk camisole, tangled and skewed over bare white skin. Cream wool trousers, twisted round on the hips with holes where the waistband buttons had been. So Margot Bell had fought her death in the end, but the struggle had ended quickly. The attack had been utterly unexpected, and ferociously sudden.

Birdie slipped her hand gingerly into the pocket of the trousers, eyes closed. Her fingers slipped on silk lining, probed deeper, pushing against the dead weight of hip and thigh, pressing down the cushion of the chair. She felt something. A folded corner. Heart thumping, hardly breathing, she grasped the object and slid it out into the light.

It was a pink envelope, folded several times to make a small square. Birdie backed away from the chair, and unfolded it as carefully as she could.

She blinked, and held the envelope close to her face, focusing with difficulty on the familiar printed capitals that seemed to swim under a mist in front of her eyes. "DEEPDENE—URGENT." She wrinkled her nose. What . . . ? She pulled out the note inside.

" 'You bitch,' " she read. " 'You'll be sorry. You can't escape me. You'll pay, Margot bloody Bell.' "

Birdie's eyes widened behind the thick glasses. She backed toward the door, clutching the note. Margot Bell, blind, sprawled on her chair. Birdie shook out her sleeve again and pulled open the door, slamming it behind her. The noise seemed deafening, despite the rumble of the generator and the drumming of the rain on the roof. She could see that lights were on in the kitchen across the courtyard. Someone might be in there. Someone might be watching her now. She fled panting back up the corridor, toward the front of the house. In her hand she grasped the note, careless now of fingerprints, knowing only one thing. When she'd held the note to her face, she'd been conscious of an oddness—something that didn't quite fit. Then she'd realized what it was. A familiar smell clung to it. Just a faint scent. But it had no place around Margot Bell. It wasn't French perfume. It was eucalyptus.

·   ·   ·

Edwina sat at Margot's desk absolutely at her ease, methodically dealing with piles of check stubs, invoices, and account books, the mere sight of which made Birdie feel slightly sick. She looked up severely as Birdie slipped into the room.

"Edwina—have you found anything?" Birdie heard herself panting, and swallowed, trying to catch her breath.

Edwina pointedly marked her place with a sharpened pencil. "There are a few interesting things here in the more recent accounts, but nothing I can identify yet. It's all a bit of a mess. It'll take time—and peace and quiet—to see a pattern." She frowned slightly and leaned forward as she noticed the pink paper in Birdie's hand. "What's that you've got? God—it's one of those . . . But I thought they were all got rid of!"

"Margot held on to hers," said Birdie quietly. "I just went and got it."

"You what?" Edwina stared at her openmouthed. The pencil slipped away from the line it was marking, but she took no notice.

Birdie stepped forward. "Does it smell of anything to you?" She held the paper out.

Edwina jerked her head back in horror, but Birdie walked toward her, beckoning impatiently. Reluctantly Edwina leaned forward and cautiously sniffed at the proffered letter. Birdie watched as the expression of distaste changed gradually to one of dawning recognition.

"Eucalyptus, isn't it?" said Edwina slowly, and sniffed again. "That's what it is, isn't it?"

"It smelled like it to me," said Birdie.

They looked at each other.

"Josie," Edwina whispered. "You're saying *Josie* wrote the letters."

"I'm saying that this letter, which looks to me just like the one I saw, though it's addressed directly to

Margot Bell, at least spent some time in Josie's handbag. How else could it have picked up that eucalyptus
smell? No one else has their handkerchiefs soaked in
the stuff. Josie came out of the ladies' room with the
letter in her hand, remember? She said she'd just found
it, and she gave it to Margot. No chance, if she really
had just found it, that it could have picked up the smell
then. I'm betting she had the letter in her bag all
through lunch—maybe all morning. And in fact, yes,
I'm betting she was the threatening letter writer. I think
she'd got tired of leaving her scare tactics to chance.
If she'd planted one letter already, and seen no reaction
from Margot, she might have realized it'd been
kept from her, and decided to make absolutely sure the
second one got to its mark without interference from
Alistair or William or anyone else."

"Josie!" Edwina rubbed her hand over her mouth,
taking it in.

"Wasn't she the one who was full of gossip about
Margot? Dark hints, you said," Birdie reminded her.
"And she hasn't lost an opportunity of spreading ru-
mors about Margot and this place since she got here."

"I just thought she was—just a natural gossip, or
something. People are. She seemed to enjoy . . ."

"Stirring. Yes. And despite all the blundering
about, there was something cocky about the way she
went on, wasn't there? As though she knew something
no one else knew? If she had something on Margot and
had come to make her pay up . . . Remember the
shouting match Belinda heard?"

"But Margot was talking to a member of staff."

"Was she? She said something about staying out
the fortnight and then getting out. And something
about telling no one. And something about not paying
out another penny. Think about it. She could have been
talking to a staff member. But she could just as easily
have been talking to her blackmailer, here posing as a

guest. Josie could have decided to confront her. Margot must have decided to tough it out. But she must have been frightened all the same."

"That would account for her terrible temper yesterday morning, all right," Edwina reasoned slowly. "And for her losing no time in talking to me about the money. And then Josie put that letter in her hand at lunchtime. Anyone could have seen. Josie was trying to—" She broke off mid-sentence. Her jaw dropped and her eyes widened. She was staring over Birdie's shoulder. Birdie whirled around. The door was opening, swinging on its hinges without sound.

"If you're going to talk about me," a harsh voice said, "you can bloody do it in front of me, you bloody cowards." Josie stood glaring at them, hulking and puffy-eyed in the yellow light. "Well?" she demanded. "Dried up, have you, now you can't mean-mouth me behind my back?"

How much had she heard? Birdie's thoughts twisted and turned for a split second. But another look at that thunderous, uncompromising face and she knew what had to be done. She held out the pink letter.

"You wrote this," she said flatly.

With a strangled exclamation Josie came at her, holding out her hand. "Give me that!" she ordered. From the corner of her eye Birdie saw Edwina jump from her seat. But she'd never get round the desk fast enough to stop Josie. Birdie put the letter behind her back and forced herself to be still as she looked up into the other woman's working face. "You can't have it," she said in a hard voice, not giving an inch of ground. "It's police evidence. You're in a lot of trouble, Josie. You know that. A lot of trouble."

"Who says?" hissed Josie through clenched teeth. "You can't prove a thing about me. You're the one who'll be in trouble, slandering innocent people. You're—"

"We've examined Margot's accounts, Josie," Birdie interrupted loudly, holding her gaze.

Josie hesitated, and with the hesitation, she was lost. Birdie had seen fire and rage die from Josie's face when Toby had stood up to her in the sitting room earlier that night. Now, as she had hoped, the tactic worked again. Josie deflated like a pricked balloon. She swallowed. "Are you police?" she asked dully. She plucked at her sleeve.

"I am assisting the police at present," answered Birdie with what she hoped was lofty assurance. She watched fear flit across the other woman's face and felt it was time to unbend slightly. "I don't want this to be any more unpleasant than it has to be, Josie, believe me," she said. "I think the best thing would be for you to just tell me exactly what happened between you and Margot Bell. Your version, I mean," she added quickly, realizing her mistake and seeing the flash of surprise and relief in the other woman's eyes. "You must have had good reason for what you did."

"I . . ." Defeated, Josie glanced around the room, as if looking for a way to escape. Her plump fingers fumbled with the clasp of her bulky handbag. She opened it, pulled out a damp handkerchief, and blew her nose. The familiar tang of eucalyptus filled the air.

"Just tell us, Josie." Birdie's voice was soft, tempting. "It will be a relief, won't it? To tell someone." She pushed out a chair and Josie sank down on it, the handkerchief still clutched in her hand. Watching her intently, Edwina also sat down.

Birdie exchanged glances with Edwina, and wondered where to begin. This would be delicate. If Josie guessed how little she knew she'd just sniff and walk out of here, and they'd be worse off than before. Birdie had already made one mistake, and got out of it by the skin of her teeth. She couldn't afford another.

"You'd better start at the beginning," she said firmly and waited, holding her breath. She leaned against the mantelpiece, trying to appear as casual and confident as possible. This was obviously the key to dealing with Josie.

Josie snuffled, and wiped her nose. Then she tucked her handkerchief into the sleeve of her dress, took a deep, shuddering breath and ran her tongue over her even, white teeth. She had decided to talk. Birdie could feel it. She held herself very still, unwilling to betray her eagerness.

"Eight and a half years ago," Josie began, "I got my front teeth broken off." She paused and looked at them defiantly.

What? Birdie preserved her relaxed stance and stern expression with difficulty. She didn't dare look at Edwina. Was the woman crazy? What did this have to do with anything?

"One of the boys whacked me with a cricket bat—by accident, it was, of course, but it gave me a fat lip and broke my two front teeth, one almost clear off and one half off. It bloody hurt, I can tell you."

"I can imagine," said Birdie carefully.

"Yes, but that's nothing to the way it looked. I wasn't any oil painting even then, but with broken-off teeth I looked like nothing on earth. Nothing on earth." Josie's voice was low. Gone was the raucous, jolly fat lady. There was a terrible hurt in the watery eyes when she raised them, and the mouth trembled.

"Doesn't sound like a great tragedy, does it?" she said, with an attempt at a smile. "Well, it wasn't, to anyone else but me, I suppose. The kids got used to it. And Glen—well, I s'pose he got used to it too. He was used to only half-seeing me anyhow." The smile grew bitter, the corners of the mouth turned down. "There was no money to fix my teeth then, you see. Glen was working himself half to death, starting up his business. We'd had a couple of thousand put away for emergencies, and at first I thought maybe we could use some of that. But when I mentioned it to Glen—just casually, because I didn't want to ask for it, I wanted him to offer —it turned out it was all gone. So there was no money. We had hardly enough to feed and clothe ourselves and the kids, let alone spend a fortune on the dentist for me. I pretended I didn't care. I never made much of a fuss about my looks, so he thought I really didn't. Or maybe he just thought what he wanted to think. I don't know."

Josie ran her tongue over her teeth thoughtfully. Her face was somber. The room was very still. "Anyhow," she went on, after a while, "for eighteen months I went around looking like a bag lady, trying to remember not to smile, and not looking in mirrors, and pretending I didn't care. Then things started to pick up with the business, and there was more money, and when I could see we were out of the woods I told Glen I wanted to have my teeth fixed. I did it on credit, and paid it off bit by bit."

She grimaced. "I'll never forget the feeling. To be able to smile at people again without making an exhibition of myself. To feel like a woman again. Like I said, Glen and the kids hadn't worried about it too much, but the way I went on after it was done—well, they couldn't help realizing, or at least Glen couldn't, how much it had mattered to me. He was shattered. That's the only way to describe it. Shattered. Guilty he hadn't realized, and ashamed he hadn't had the money to give me before. I told him I didn't blame him—and I didn't, not at all—but he went on and on about it."

Josie pulled out her handkerchief and wiped her nose again. She looked steadily at Birdie. "If you know all about it you know why he did," she said. "And you know how I must have felt about Margot Bell when I found out. Any woman in my position would've felt the same." Her chin lifted. "I'm not sorry for what I did. She deserved it. She was a bitch. A calculating, vicious bitch."

19

Birdie realized she'd been holding her breath. She breathed out and looked at Edwina, sitting rigidly behind Margot Bell's desk. Edwina's face was pale and fixed. It was impossible to tell what she was thinking. What now? Where did they go from here? *Keep Josie talking—* the answer came to her rapidly. *Toby will wake soon. Or Milson. Keep her quiet and talking till then.*

"How did you find out, Josie?" she asked.

Josie's lips curved in a bitter little smile. "Oh," she said drearily, "it was like in all the books. I found a letter in a suit of Glen's I was taking to the dry cleaners." She opened her handbag and rummaged in its depths, finally pulling out a battered envelope from which she took a folded sheet of paper. "Here you are," she said, holding it out to Birdie. "You may as well see it. I meant to show it to her, but of course I never got round to it. Not that it matters now."

Birdie took the paper and unfolded it. It reeked of eucalyptus from Josie's handbag—far more strongly than the other note. She had obviously been carrying it around for quite a while. It was thick, cream Deepdene stationery, with the butterfly motif embossed in one corner. Margot's flowing, elaborate script covered the page. It was dated six months before. Birdie read silently.

> *Dear Glen,*
> *Just a little note to remind you. I know how busy you are, but the check was due last week. Could you be a darling and send it on asap? If it's hard for you I could always pop in to see you at home one weekend. You know I've always wanted to meet Josie and the kids. I'll wait a week and if I haven't heard I'll know you're expecting me.*
> *Much love, as always,*
> *Margot.*

Controlling her expression with difficulty, Birdie nodded and passed the letter to Edwina with a warning look. Edwina read, paused, and put the letter face down on the desk, pushing it away from herself with a fastidious hand. Her mouth thinned with distaste.

Josie smiled again, wryly this time. "Pretty bloody obvious, isn't it? I suppose you'd've seen what it all meant straightaway," she said. "Any fool would've—except muggins here. It never occurred to me. I just asked Glen about it that night out of curiosity. He could've put me off—told me some tale. I'd have believed him." She gave a short sniff of joyless laughter. "You know, sometimes I wish he had. Ignorance is bliss. But I'll never forget his face, when I held out that letter to him. He got such a shock. It was in the bedroom. He had a drink in his hand. He saw the letter and his jaw dropped, and he went red, all over his face, and his hand opened and the glass dropped and whiskey went all over the white carpet, and he didn't even look at it. And after that even I couldn't miss the point."

She looked down at the plump, worn hands

clasped on the expensive handbag. "So then he had to tell it. All of it. He cried like a baby. I'd never seen him do that before, not even when the kids were born, or when things were going badly in the business." She nodded slowly. "I've thought since it wasn't just the shame. It was the relief. To be able to tell, after all those years of keeping quiet, and paying her to keep quiet. Paying her to keep quiet for years and years, because he was so scared, so scared, that if I knew I'd leave him and take the kids and it'd be all over."

Her chin lifted proudly. "Because he really loves us," she said. "He loves us, and he loves me. He told me then. He said he was crazy. That the affair they had was like being drunk. They met at some function. They started meeting for drinks after work. Glen's a good-looker, and knows how to impress people. He's a big talker. She probably thought he was loaded. He thought she was beautiful. He kept saying that over and over. 'She was so beautiful. So beautiful.' Like that. They started having an affair. They used to go to her flat in Double Bay. I thought he was working late. All that time I'd been so sorry for him, because he was working so hard, he'd been seeing her. God!

"He said he nearly went mad with guilt. He thought of breaking it off hundreds of times, but somehow she always got round him, and he didn't. Just kept seeing her, and spending money on her, sending her flowers and buying her presents and expensive dinners and things because that was what she wanted, and expected, and he couldn't make himself tell her he couldn't afford it. But all the time we were struggling, because all the money was in the business. He used up all the cash in the emergency account, and went into debt, and then he couldn't keep up the front anymore. So he told her, and she ditched him. Just like that."

Josie pulled out her handkerchief again and began folding it on her knee—over and over, into a small, damp square. Her blunt fingers stroked the white cotton while she stared past Edwina into space. "Glen said he was bowled over at first. Then, after a few days, he realized that what he really felt was relieved. Relieved, you know? As though he'd got better after being sick. He really got down to work then, and things started picking up in the business, and of course that drain on the money had gone. That was when I got my teeth done." She paused.

"About a year after that, the business started going really well. Glen got written up in the paper a few times, and once he was on TV. Margot Bell must have seen that, because it was just after that, he said, that the letters started coming. She asked for a little loan, first, to help her with this place, then another one, to tide her over something or other. He said she was always hopeless with money. Spent whatever she had like water. The model agency she ran was on its last legs by the time she got out and came here. He sent the money. She made it clear that if he didn't, she'd come to me and tell me about the affair, and the things they'd got up to, whatever they were. I didn't ask him then, and I don't want to know now. Men are fools about sex, and she was obviously a nymphomaniac. A dirty-minded nympho—that's all she was."

She smiled grimly. "After that, of course, she just kept asking, and he kept paying. As you've seen from the accounts, I suppose. It went on for years and years. Till I found that letter six months ago, and he told me. That was the finish. She got no more money out of us. Glen wrote and said he'd told me, and I forgave him, and it was finished. That shut her up. There were no more letters after that." She looked down at the handkerchief again, and her fingers patting and stroking, patting and stroking.

Birdie's thoughts were racing. This wasn't what she'd been expecting. It turned everything around.

And yet, of course, it was far more likely than the alternative, given the personality of Margot Bell. So much more likely that she'd be a blackmailer than the one blackmailed. "That was six months ago . . ." she began. She noticed that Edwina had started quietly looking through one of the account books again, comparing receipts and check stubs, running a pencil down lines of figures. She looked again at Josie's bent head and went on, feeling her way: "You forgave Glen, you said. Yet you came here and . . ."

Josie looked up. "I married Glen when I was eighteen," she said simply. "I know him as well as I know myself. He's a big, strong man, but he's a little boy, really. He'd paid for years to keep me from finding out about what he'd done. That proves how much he cares, and how scared he was. He depends on me. He loves me. I had to forgive him." Her voice hardened. "But I didn't have to forgive her, did I?"

"No."

"No. And whenever I thought about her, leeching on our family, cavorting with my silly husband in some luxury flat while I struggled on at home with the kids —no decent clothes, no money for fancy creams and cosmetics, going round with hideous, gappy teeth for a year and a half because she'd got all the money that would have fixed them, I just got angrier and angrier. I couldn't see why she should get away with it scot-free. I couldn't see why she shouldn't pay. So I booked myself in here, and I came. And when I finally met her, and saw what she was like, I hated her even more. Oh, she was a nasty piece of work. A dirty, nasty piece of work. I wrote the letters, and I left them round for people to find. I wanted everyone to find out what a nasty piece she was. I wanted her to worry, and be scared."

"She didn't get the first letter," Birdie said.

Josie laughed. It wasn't a pleasant laugh. "No. It was found, all right. It wasn't where I left it when I looked. But she hadn't seen it. She was in a black mood in the morning, but it wasn't because of the letter. Someone else had got it, and not told her. I could tell that, because she was so surprised when I finally gave her one myself—straight into her hand. I said I'd found it in the ladies'. She opened it straightaway. She wouldn't have done that if she'd seen the other one. Ah —she was rocked, all right, when she opened that letter. I'd heard her laughing away in her office before lunch. That poor little sod William was with her. They were supposed to be working, but she was having a lovely time. I'll wipe that smile off your face, bitch, I thought. And I did. She got the shock of her life. And then she had to go and do my makeup. I had almost an hour with her. I could watch her all the time. She was rocked, and she was scared. You could see it, under that mask of cosmetics. I watched her all the time. She didn't know where the letter had come from. She didn't know who it was who was here, and out to get her. She didn't have the faintest!" Josie laughed again, and suddenly yawned, hugely. "I had some more planned for her," she said, rocking in her chair. "And a few other things. But I never got to do them, as it turned out. Pity."

"Death intervened, you might say." Edwina had looked up and was gazing at Josie with detached interest, as though she was a scientific curiosity.

Josie returned her stare impassively. "That's right," she said. "I was thinking—now Glen'll find out where I've been. He'll get a shock, won't he?" She stuffed the folded handkerchief back into her sleeve and abruptly heaved herself from her chair, her handbag clutched under her arm.

"I'm going back to the sitting room to get a drink," she announced, watching them. "I'm parched. I've told you what you want to know. Any woman would have done the same, if she could. The bitch deserved everything she got. I'm glad she was scared. I'm glad that just for once she got to feel what she'd made other people feel. And if you want to know, I'm glad she's dead. Helen did the world a favor with that one, anyway."

She turned on her heel, and walked out of the room, leaving the door gaping wide behind her. Birdie and Edwina saw her cross the hall and go into the sitting room. They looked at each other. Birdie moved stiffly from the fireplace and slumped into the chair Josie had vacated. It was unpleasantly warm, and the eucalyptus smell hung around it. She squirmed a little.

"She didn't do it," said Edwina slowly. "She wrote the letters, but she didn't kill Margot Bell. Did she?"

20

Birdie was suddenly bone weary. Josie's sordid little story lay like a dead weight in her mind. Sacrifice, selective blindness, folly, greed, the primitive tie created by a lifetime's service and familiarity . . . she understood none of it. She'd seen it all so many times, in so many forms. But it was still alien, incomprehensible, and indescribably depressing to her.

Edwina leaned forward. "Josie didn't kill Margot," she repeated. "That line about Helen doing everyone a favor was absolutely natural. She really believes Helen is the killer. And she told us everything about her husband, and why she wrote the letters. She gave herself an impeccable motive for killing Margot Bell. She wouldn't have done that if she was guilty, or if she thought for a moment we didn't have the killer pinpointed already."

"We knew all about the letters. Or she thought we did. And she thought we knew about her husband's payments to Margot, too. She had to tell us something, at least. And as you say, she thinks we still believe Helen's the killer. She's not too bright, but she's cunning. She could have been double-bluffing—being absolutely straightforward about the crime she's forced to admit, and acting her socks off about the crime she's not."

"I don't think so." Edwina tapped her strong, white fingers on the desk.

"Josie could have gone to the makeup room as soon as you left it at quarter to six. She could have been watching for you to leave. For all we know she could have told Margot who she was during their session just after lunch, and arranged to see her after her last appointment. That might be why Margot didn't organize Angela to do her massage. Did she actually tell you she was waiting for Angela?"

Edwina frowned. "No. I think her actual words were, 'Tell Alistair, will you, that I'm waiting for a neck massage. I've got a frightful headache.' Or something like that. Something very high-handed. And after being buttonholed by her at every opportunity all day about their financial situation, the last thing I felt like was being sent on messages."

Birdie half smiled. "But if she really said those words—and remember Angela claimed she was definitely *not* asked to give up her swim to minister to Margot—then she could have just been establishing an alibi for absence, couldn't she? She could have meant, 'tell Alistair that's where I am,' rather than 'tell Alistair to get off his bum and make my massage happen,' couldn't she?"

"Yes, she could. That hadn't occurred to me." Edwina looked thoughtfully at her. "She could have been clearing the way for a private hour—for a meeting with Josie, or anyone else, for that matter, Birdie. And it would be unlikely to cause her any problem afterward, would it? If anyone tumbled to the fact Angela hadn't done her neck, she could just say she had asked her, or asked William or Conrad to ask her, and then she'd been left waiting. That'd be her form."

"But you misinterpreted her message. So the meeting could have been interrupted, or the murderer caught red-handed, if you'd gone straight to drinks. But you didn't. You went upstairs instead."

Edwina looked impassively at her. "Yes I did. I was hardly to know, was I?"

"Don't be bloody silly—I didn't mean that! But anyway, Josie—or, yes, anyone else—could have joined her after you left, killed her, and still been at drinks more or less on time. And if you hadn't put the wind up Alistair, the body wouldn't have been found till at least dinnertime. Not that it would have mattered— except that presumably more people might have been implicated, if it hadn't been found till dinner, say."

"It would have been fine timing. Bloody risky."

"Maybe." Birdie was trying to think, her chin resting on her hand. "And we mustn't forget that this is all conjecture anyway. That scenario fits if Josie is the killer. But after you came back into the room and told everyone where Margot was, quite a few people went out. Nothing to say the murder wasn't done then, as we thought at first. Oh, God!"

"Someone's coming," warned Edwina suddenly, looking over her shoulder.

Birdie turned to watch as Alistair crossed the hall toward the office. He looked anxious, and his soft mouth was set. Once he glanced back over his shoulder, but no one was following. He reached the office door and hovered there uncertainly, thick fair eyelashes blinking against the light.

"What's going on?" he asked abruptly. "What's happened to Josie? She came back looking like death and she won't say a word now, to anyone. She was with you two, wasn't she? Did something happen?"

"What are the others doing?" countered Birdie. "Are they asleep?"

"No they're not!" Alistair shook his head despair-

ingly. "They're whispering and talking and driving
themselves and me crazy. William and Belinda, anyway. Conrad just sits there. Look, I think this has gone
on long enough. I'm going to get them all off to bed."

"No, don't do that," said Birdie bluntly. "Betty
Hinder hasn't rung you from upstairs, has she?"

Alistair's pale face suddenly flushed with anger.
"Listen!" he hissed, and took a step into the room.
"Listen, you just stop this, and answer a few questions
yourself, will you? What's going on here? Why are you
two huddled away like this? What did you say to
Josie?" He glanced at the account books and papers in
front of Edwina and his eyes narrowed with suspicion.
"Why did you really want to see those, right now? I
don't believe you wouldn't wait till morning, unless
there was some other reason. What is it?"

Edwina shrugged noncommittally. He turned furiously on Birdie. "You're acting like there's something
you aren't telling. Why can't I let everyone go to bed?
They're dead beat. I've been thinking. There's no real
reason to keep them up now, is there? Unless there's
something you know that I don't."

"Like what?" Birdie drawled, looking bored.

He hesitated. "You . . . you might . . . for some
reason, think Helen isn't the one. You might think—it's
one of us. You might be trying to keep us all up, and
together, in case . . ." His voice trailed off. His face
was very white. The fair lashes blinked over pink-
rimmed eyes.

Birdie spoke quietly. "Have you said anything to
the others about this?"

"Of course not." Alistair swayed slightly and
gripped the door handle to steady himself. "Look,
you've got to tell me what's going on. This is my place
—my place, d'you understand?" He was almost pleading now. "These are my people. My partner and a

member of my staff are dead. You can't shut me out. You can't!"

Birdie made a quick decision. "All right," she said. She went over and took his arm, leading him to a chair. "It seems the cops have been barking up the wrong tree. Helen couldn't have killed Angela. Her ankle is so bad that she can hardly walk. She couldn't have done it in the time."

Alistair looked astounded. Confusion and panic crossed his face in quick succession. "She . . . I'd forgotten . . . she twisted her ankle on the stairs. Was it so bad? . . . I'd completely forgotten. How could I have forgotten?" He put a trembling hand to his forehead.

The phone on the desk buzzed. Edwina picked it up and listened. "Mrs. Hinder," she said briefly, and held the receiver out to Birdie. Heart thudding, Birdie grabbed it.

"That Toby's stirring." Mrs. Hinder's reedy voice vibrated in her ear. "You said to let you know."

"I'm coming. Keep him awake, Betty. Please try. It's vital!" Birdie slammed down the phone and made for the door. As she reached it a thought struck her and she spun around. "Go back to the others and stay there!" she said firmly to Alistair and Edwina. "Nothing can happen while you're all together. All right? Don't let anyone go anywhere alone, even to the toilet."

"Birdie . . ." Edwina began, but with a wave of her hand, Birdie had gone.

She took the stairs two at a time, confused thoughts racing around in her head. All very well to act decisively with them, but what on earth did she think she was doing? Running up to Toby because she couldn't cope, that's what. There was no rhyme or reason here, that was the trouble. No pattern. Nothing fitted. She slapped her cheeks impatiently with her hand.

She was so tired. She couldn't think! She'd wasted such a lot of time. How could she have believed Margot was being blackmailed, whatever little shreds of evidence had pointed to it? Margot was the one dead. Blackmailers didn't kill their victims—they were only useful to them alive. But victims killed blackmailers, to stop the torment. Margot had been a blackmailer. She'd blackmailed Josie's husband. Margot had been killed.

But in Josie's case the torment had ceased. No need to kill for that. Revenge, then? Maybe if . . . Birdie forced her mind away from that particular hare. Stick to the point. Work it through, she told herself. She stood at the top of the stairs, grasping the balustrade, and forced herself to concentrate.

Margot had lost the income she'd been used to receiving from Josie's husband. And—Sir Arthur Longley. Sir Arthur had written to Margot very regularly. Every month, without fail, William had said proudly. Fairly unusual, in this day and age, wasn't it? Unless each of Sir Arthur's billets doux was accompanied by a check. Unless he'd been another victim. A victim released, in his case, by death. He'd died a year ago—and he'd left less money than had been expected, remember?

If Birdie was right, Margot Bell had lost two tidy sources of income in the last twelve months. And her needs were great. You could tell that just by looking at her. Those looks, those clothes, were expensive. As were overseas holidays, good hotels, nice cars—all the good things of life. Margot wouldn't have gone without the goodies with which the blackmail money had provided her. When it dried up she'd started milking the Deepdene business to make up the loss—that was obvious. But just as obviously things were coming to a head. She couldn't keep it up. Alistair, for one, would eventually find out, and there'd be hell to pay. Margot, then, had to find another victim, fast. Someone with money. Someone with something to lose. Someone with something to hide, that Margot had found out about. Someone who'd pay to . . .

Birdie's heart leaped. She pounded along the gallery and arrived at Helen's room, panting. She pushed open the door. Betty Hinder had Toby sitting up on the couch. She was holding a cup to his mouth. Black coffee was dribbling down his chin and he was mumbling impatiently. But his eyelids were fluttering. He was awake.

"Dan!" She ran forward and crouched on the floor beside him. She gripped his arm and shook it. His eyes opened a little. Vague-looking gray-blue slits tried to focus on her. A half-smile trembled on his lips. He mumbled.

"Dan! You've got to wake up. Dan! It wasn't Helen. Helen didn't kill Margot!" whispered Birdie urgently. Betty Hinder made a small, choked sound. Birdie glanced at her rapidly, then turned her attention back to the man slumped in front of her. He began to mumble again, and desperately she put her ear close to his mouth, striving to hear the words. "I can't hear you, Dan," she pleaded. "Speak up!"

Toby licked his lips and made an obvious effort to enunciate. "Knock it off, Birdwood," he said clearly. His eyelids fluttered closed.

"Oh, Dan! Oh, God, Dan! Listen to me. You've been drugged. Angela's dead. Dead, like Margot Bell. You've got to wake up and help me. Do you hear? There's been another murder."

Toby's head lolled back. His mouth fell open and his tongue licked again at his lips. He struggled to open his eyes. "Angela? Dead?" The slurred words were loud in the room. "How dead?"

"Just like Margot, Dan. Same method exactly. Out in the annex. And it wasn't Helen."

"Yes. Must have been . . . Helen . . . Laurel

Moon." Toby was frowning now, rolling his head from side to side.

"Not Helen. She couldn't have made the stairs. Her ankle, remember? She can hardly walk. Listen, Dan. Margot was a blackmailer. She was blackmailing Josie's husband. I think she tried to blackmail someone else, and . . ."

"No!" The word bubbled from Toby's lax lips. His hands balled into loose, frustrated fists. "Birdie—listen. No . . . wrong . . . no doubt . . . Gray Lady murders." His heavy head rolled helplessly from side to side against the soft floral fabric of the couch.

"That's what someone *wants* us to think, Dan. Someone drugged you, to frame Helen for Angela's murder as well as Margot's. The killer just copied the method. It was a copycat murder. Do you hear me?"

He was still rolling his head, trying to force his eyelids open. His hand lifted and fell heavily onto her shoulder. His mouth opened, closed, opened again. "Not blackmail," he slurred painfully. "Not nothing else. Laurel Moon." He breathed deeply. "Birdie, ask Milson. Milson knows. Should've told you . . . smartarse . . . teach lesson, I thought . . . might have known . . . backfire. Get Milson. He's got them . . . show you . . ." His eyes closed. His breathing grew loud and regular.

"Milson's unconscious, Dan. Dan, wake up! Please wake up! It's not Helen. It's someone else, and I need you. I'm scared!" Birdie was shaking his arm desperately now, hardly knowing what she was saying. She grabbed his chin and pulled it roughly from side to side, willing him to wake. But he didn't stir.

"It's no good," said Betty Hinder flatly. Her small, black eyes were fearful. "He's gone off again."

"Oh no!" Birdie pulled off her glasses despairingly and scrubbed at her eyes. "What'll I do now?"

"He's coming on. He'll stir again in a minute. If

you've got any more questions for him have them clear and ready. No good just blathering at him." Betty stood very upright, arms tightly folded against her narrow chest. "He seems to think you've got it wrong, anyhow," she rasped, and cleared her throat. "Maybe you have."

"He's a stubborn old . . ." Birdie put her glasses back on and ran her hands through her silky, cropped hair. She couldn't just sit here. She had to do something. *Ask Milson,* Dan had said. *He has them.* Has what? The answers? Her eyes drifted to Milson, lying on his side in approved Red Cross recovery position on the floor on the other side of the room. He showed no signs of waking.

As Mrs. Hinder watched curiously Birdie went over to Milson and knelt beside him. She slipped her hand into his shirt and trouser pockets. One crushed white handkerchief; a small bunch of keys. Nothing else. But his jacket hung neatly over the back of the chair. Inside breast pocket: wallet, containing two credit cards, identification, money; another handkerchief, clean and crisply folded, and his notebook. She seized the notebook and began flicking through it, her eyes darting over Milson's neat shorthand. Her own record of interview—God, how long ago that seemed! —broken off at the point at which they'd all rushed to the sitting room in response to Helen's cries. Notes on Helen! She read avidly. Physical description—old scarring on wrists and stomach noted—then the first rambling phrases. "They'll send me back," Milson had recorded in unemotional dots and squiggles. "I don't want to go back." Birdie flicked over a page. Something fell from the back of the notebook, where it had been slipped for safety.

She picked it up. It was a small plastic envelope with two pale-colored fabric-covered buttons inside. She stared at them, recognized them for what they

were: the buttons missing from the waistband of
Margot's cream wool trousers. Little round buttons,
each bearing its neat circle of fabric at the shank, en-
closed in plastic, bearing mute testimony to violence,
terror, struggle, indignity, and the bizarrely humdrum
routine, the literal grasping at threads, associated with
murder investigation. She thought of Margot, lying
on display in the beauty therapy room, of Angela
sprawled horribly on the floor in her neat, white-
painted bedroom.

"I'm going downstairs to make more coffee."

Birdie looked up, startled. She'd almost forgotten
Betty was with her. "Wait a minute—can you wait?"
she gabbled, sticking the plastic bag into Milson's wallet.

"Coffee's cold," said Betty firmly, edging toward
the door. "Looks to me as if you could do with some
yourself."

"I . . ." Birdie rubbed her forehead with the back
of her hand. If only she could think! Get something
other than pictures, vivid and horrible or totally mun-
dane, distorted by her exhaustion, flickering across her
mind like movie shorts. Just pictures—people saying
things, faces—no pattern or purpose. Betty Hinder on
that first night, curling her lip, talking about madam.
Belinda balancing a brimming, slopping cup of tea in a
delicate china cup. William's tragic face, talking about
the past. Helen, radiant on Conrad's arm. Helen, stag-
gering against Edwina as she hauled her to "Juliet."
The coffee tray, unattended by the stairway, big silver
pot gleaming in the lamplight. Mrs. Hinder complaining, sticking out a red, wet stockinged toe. The
closed doors of the annex corridors. Angela, sprawled
on her back, baby-blue pajama top gaping, white nylon
biting into her neck. William's disapproving face: "Angela *always* swims from six to six-thirty."

The beauty therapy room, as she had seen it—as

Angela had seen it. A pink gown draggled in blood. Pictures. Belinda whispering, whispering to William. Edwina poring over account books behind a gleaming desk. Margot Bell, on edge at drinks, thunderous at breakfast, brittle during the Deepdene tour, laughing in her office with William by noon. Josie's pudgy hand handing over the letter she'd found in her husband's pocket. Margot Bell. Conrad smiling wolfishly. "She knew what she wanted." Two buttons in a plastic bag. Alistair's shocked face in the kitchen as Edwina talked about something she thought he already knew. The article she'd read about the Gray Lady murders so long ago. Copycat murder.

Shorts—no full picture. Movie promos took the best bits, cut them together, to give you a taste of the story. But they could be misleading. They could make you think the story went one way, when it really went another. They could focus your attention on one aspect of the whole, and make you think the movie was based on that, when it could be far more complex. Or it could be the other way around. The story could be very simple indeed, but the shorts could confuse you, creating complexity where none really existed.

The Gray Lady murders—the sensational motif that had run like blood through the last few days: madness and terror in the warm, claustrophobic world of Deepdene. The facts had been overwhelmed by the fear. With an almost audible click, the pictures stopped their headlong rush through Birdie's mind. The facts: what were the facts? The facts—not the words of just one person, but the provable, observable facts. The facts. Birdie felt the phrase run like icy water through her brain, clearing it. Felt her feet touch solid ground. Saw the world come back into focus. Strip off the terror; strip back the blood; strip away the nightmare. What was left? Some pictures. Some personalities. A timetable. A few sentences, unimportant, disregarded.

Birdie looked up. Betty Hinder was standing rigidly by Toby's slumped form. One hand still held the coffeepot, the other rested on Toby's shoulder. Her eyes were full of fear. "Can I go now?" she asked, through dry lips.

Toby mumbled and stirred.

"It's all right, Betty," said Birdie gently. "Soon you can go. But I've got to ask you a few things first." She moved to the small woman's side. "Listen carefully, Betty," she murmured. "There mustn't be any mistake."

Mrs. Hinder nodded, biting her lip. She bent her head as Birdie started talking.

21

They came silently up the stairs together. Alistair, Edwina, Conrad, Josie, William, and Belinda. Behind them, soft-footed in her spare shoes, came Betty Hinder, carrying coffee and extra cups.

Birdie was waiting for them in her room. She'd done what she had to do. She knew now that she was right, but she felt no elation. Only a sick tension. In the morning the police from Windsor would come. By boat, by helicopter—somehow they would be here. She was so tempted to wait. But she knew she couldn't. Murder was habit-forming. Too many people were thinking now, too many people were at risk—she herself most of all. This killer wouldn't hesitate to strike again. There was so much to lose. Shared knowledge was the only protection any of them had.

She looked for Betty Hinder as they gathered by the door. She wondered briefly whether that deter-mined little woman had in fact done her bidding, or decided, once safely out of the room, to follow her own path. There was no way of knowing. She would have to proceed as if all was well. She nodded reassuringly to the haggard figure lying propped up on her bed. Helen stared back, silent. Her big hands twisted in her lap. Her huge gray eyes seemed to have sunk even further into their sockets and great shadows creased her face from nose to chin.

Quietly Birdie went to the door and ushered her guests into the room. They filed in, unexpectedly docile, then with a couple of exceptions started violently to see Helen unfettered and apparently unattended on the bed.

"Shit, man!" muttered Conrad, backing against the wall beside the couch as Belinda and William, wide-eyed, felt for each other's hands like Hansel and Gretel confronted by the wicked witch, and sank into its soft cushions together.

"Where are the police? Why did we have to come up here?" shuddered Belinda, looking everywhere but at the bed.

"We're meeting here because Helen is injured and can't handle the stairs. I wanted her to be at this meeting. More than anyone, Helen has the right to hear what I have to say." Birdie avoided Edwina's questioning eyes and looked instead at Conrad, slouching against the wall beside the couch, and at Alistair, white-faced, perched uncomfortably on its arm. She showed the reluctant Josie to an armchair, then went to sit beside the desk. Edwina looked around, found all seats taken, and coolly settled herself on the coffee table. All of them looked expectantly at Birdie.

Birdie was aware time was ticking away. It couldn't go fast enough for her. With every minute that passed, first light drew closer. With every second the likelihood grew stronger that Toby or Milson, and with them the authority of the law, would walk through the door.

She began to speak in a slow and measured voice, demanding their exhausted attention.

"On the night I arrived here with Josie, Belinda,

Helen, and Edwina, we all heard, at the late night drinks, the story of Laurel Moon and the Gray Lady murders: a story we were all familiar with, but hadn't heard much about for a decade. William had just been notified that Laurel Moon had been released from the psychiatric institution where she'd been held for ten years. He was almost hysterical with fear about this because, as we were to find out later, his informant had also told him that Laurel Moon was on her way to Deepdene, and he took it that she was coming to revenge herself on him for his statements following his fiancée's murder. The discovery of an anonymous, obviously threatening, letter confirmed his belief that Laurel Moon was not just on her way, but was actually here, masquerading as one of the guests."

Out of the corner of her eye Birdie saw a black shadow flitting silently out the door—Betty Hinder, slipping from the room unnoticed by anyone else. She made no sign, but went on: "Margot Bell, who William was sure would protect him from Moon by identifying her and sending her away, in fact wouldn't talk to him that night. Eventually he was persuaded by Alistair not even to try to tell her about Moon's presence. Alistair gave him the impression that he would do that, and William let it go on that understanding. In the event, no one at all appears to have told Margot Bell that Laurel Moon could be here at Deepdene. It seems she met her death without knowing."

William buried his face in his hands. Alistair stared steadily at Birdie, only a slight tremor of the lip betraying his tension.

"Once the police got here," Birdie went on unemotionally, "it wasn't long before they reached what was, to them, an obvious conclusion—that the woman we know as 'Helen' was responsible for the crime. Margot Bell had been killed in exactly the same way as the Gray Lady victims. 'Helen' was, the police quickly realized, almost certainly Laurel Moon. The fact that she had ample opportunity both before the six o'clock drinks party and during it, when she left the room for some time, coupled with her collapse while waiting to be questioned by the police, were taken to be the final proofs of her guilt.

"I must say I had some reservations." Birdie glanced at the woman sitting propped up on her crisp, white pillows. "It seemed very pat. But then, what could be simpler or more easily understood? Laurel Moon, coming here for vengeance or simply peace and help, finds herself confronted not only by the hysterical boyfriend of one of her victims but by the highly colored story of her previous madness and violence as told to us all by Josie. She is further confronted by the very dominating personality of Margot Bell, so like the dominating women of her past. It's not hard to believe that these circumstances might drive her to madness and violence again."

Helen opened her mouth, but no words came. Her hands twisted in her lap.

"Then Angela died—in exactly the same way as Margot. Not because she fitted the Gray Lady murder type, because of course she didn't, not at all. She was a pleasant, healthy, rather simpleminded girl who was unfortunate enough to present a danger to a killer."

"What danger?" The words burst from Josie's lips involuntarily. She flushed and blustered. "What possible danger could that poor kid have been to anybody?"

"I think she saw something," Birdie answered. "In the beauty therapy room, when she discovered Margot's body. She saw something, registered it unconsciously, but didn't think about it till afterward. Then she remembered, and it puzzled her."

"She *did* say something like that!" exclaimed William suddenly, leaning forward. "Didn't she, Belinda? When she came back after talking to the police."

"Did she? I don't really remember," whispered Belinda fearfully. "She said such a lot—I wasn't really listening to all of it. Then you and Conrad took her to bed . . . to her room . . . and she was talking all the way out the door."

"Yes! You remember, surely. She said she'd been thinking," persisted William, "and there was something she didn't understand. She wanted to go back and talk to the policeman again, but the office door was shut and we thought she was just . . . you know . . . and just took her off to bed—" He broke off, looking horrified.

"Fair enough, too," Josie cut in. "She was carrying on like a two-bob watch, poor little creature. No one could take her seriously."

"Someone did," said Birdie bluntly. "Someone went to her room and killed her. And drugged the coffee being sent up to Helen's guard. Someone was very arrogant, and very stupid."

Josie stirred. "Someone?" She glanced at Helen and looked away quickly.

"Someone gilded the lily. Someone saw that coffee there, sitting at the bottom of the stairs, waiting to go up to Helen's guard, and suddenly saw they could use it. They knew Helen didn't drink coffee. They drugged it, so only the police would go to sleep, and Helen would have no alibi for Angela's murder. But they were too smart for their own good. They didn't know that Helen had hurt her ankle, and was only able to move very, very slowly. They didn't know the lights were going to go out. And they didn't know I was expecting Dan Toby to call within thirty minutes, so would be bound eventually to go up and check on him, and discover what had happened."

She looked around the room. "Helen's bad ankle, combined with the blackout, meant that she was physically incapable of getting to Angela in the time required, let alone overpowering her. She couldn't have carried out that murder—though the drugged coffee proved that someone had tried to frame her for it.

"So Helen was innocent, and someone else was guilty. Thinking about that, I went back to the theory I'd had at first. That it was a copycat murder. That someone had used Laurel Moon's method, as described on our first night here, to kill Margot Bell. Maybe to confuse the police. Maybe to take advantage of Laurel Moon's supposed presence here to divert suspicion from themselves. Maybe to satisfy some morbid need of their own."

"You mean—one of *us* killed Margot?" William's voice quavered. Conrad shifted impatiently, but said nothing. Josie's eyes darted from face to face.

"One of us," agreed Birdie quietly. "As it happens, we all had the opportunity to do it. I thought at first that from six to six-thirty, during the drinks party, was the critical time. That would mean that anyone who left the sitting room during that time was suspect, and anyone who didn't was in the clear. Simple. But I've since found out that the quarter-hour before six was also a possibility, so even the people who stayed in the room from six on don't have an iron-clad alibi."

"You mean Edwina and me, I suppose," Josie burst out, "since we're the only ones who stayed put except you, and you're obviously leaving yourself out of all this. As if—"

"Calm down, Josie," said Edwina wearily. Josie shot her a reproachful look, but subsided into awkward silence.

"I simply mean to explain," Birdie plodded on, looking around blandly and trying to catch, as she did so, any movement from the door, "that we all had the opportunity to do the first murder, and in fact, with a couple of exceptions, the second. I had to, then, start thinking about motive. And here again, the field was fairly rich.

"Edwina reminded me earlier tonight that money is one of the best motives for murder. That's true. But passion is another." Her somber gaze swept the room, her glasses flashing where they caught the light. "What about when money and passion are united? As they could have been in Alistair's case." She turned to the still figure perched on the arm of the couch.

"Alistair was Margot Bell's silent working partner. He was continually overlooked by outsiders, yet the idea for this place was his, and he is passionate about it and all it stands for. He put all his savings into the fulfillment of a long-term personal dream, and he obviously did most of the work and organization associated with its running. This was plainly something he accepted without much trouble, knowing the PR value of Margot's name and glamorous image. What he increasingly couldn't accept was her assumption that she had a right to make decisions without consulting him, her irresponsible behavior and moodiness, and most important of all, as I learned only a few hours ago, her plan to pervert his dream by turning it into a quick turnaround money spinner instead of the carefully structured, labor-intensive personal service he'd created."

Alistair sat with his head bowed and his hands clasped. He didn't move or speak. On the couch behind him Belinda drew breath and felt for William's hand again.

"Alistair seems on the surface a gentle man, but as is so often the case, and as we've all seen in the past couple of days, he's perfectly capable of strong, decisive action and great self-control.

"Edwina found out earlier tonight that Margot Bell had been writing cash checks with increasing regularity over the last nine months or so. In the last six months particularly. Margot told William, and presumably Alistair, if he ever asked, that these were checks given to tradesmen to help them avoid tax. But in at least two instances it's clear that the tasks she claimed were being paid for weren't done. The generator, for a start, had not been serviced as she claimed it had. Betty Hinder will attest to that. Two dozen bottles of brandy she arranged to have delivered seem to have disappeared."

Birdie paused to draw breath. Silently the other people in the room digested this new view of Margot Bell. Conrad was shaking his head and smiling. Josie was stony-faced.

"What's she saying?" William was shaking his head in bewilderment. "Is she . . . are you saying Margot was taking the money for herself? But . . . that's ridiculous! Alistair, tell her! Margot didn't need money. She had lots of money of her own. And anyway she wouldn't take Deepdene money. Would she, Alistair? *Alistair!*"

Alistair rubbed his face with trembling hands and didn't answer.

"Margot didn't in fact have money of her own," Birdie went on remorselessly. "Her modeling business left her with very little, and that little she put into this place. But I think she found two extra sources of income, and they served to help pay her considerable personal expenses for a long time. Then a year ago one of these sources of income died, and six months later the other dried up. She was left depending on her Deepdene salary, which could in no way allow her to indulge her expensive tastes. So she began to dip into the till."

"No!" William clenched his fists. "Alistair," he almost shouted at Alistair's unresponsive back, "you don't believe this, do you?"

"No one is saying you knew anything about it, William," soothed Birdie. This extreme reaction was almost certainly rooted in paranoia rather than affection for Margot Bell. William's affections seemed to be fairly shallow rivulets when it all came down to it. It irritated her to have to placate him, but hysterics were something she very much wanted to avoid at this point. "You had no reason to suspect anything, given Margot's . . . adept handling of things."

"Of people, you mean," muttered Alistair. "Of William—and me. Oh yes. Margot could handle us all right. She got away with murder."

The word fell from his lips like a stone into a pool, spreading ripples of horror through the room. Birdie dropped her eyes and continued, speaking more rapidly now.

"If Alistair discovered the swindle—which, despite his proclaimed lack of business knowledge, he easily could have done—this, combined with Margot's threat to the Deepdene dream, could have tipped him into murder. The presence of Laurel Moon, which he had every reason to suspect strongly, could have been the precipitating factor; the chance to kill Margot and inherit her share of the business without fear of coming to justice might have proved irresistible. It was Alistair, after all, who failed to tell Margot of Laurel Moon's probable presence here, who told William not to try to do so, who swore us to secrecy about the first anonymous letter. Why? Could it have been because, as William knew, Margot would have identified Moon and insisted she leave Deepdene immediately? If that happened there would be no convenient scapegoat for murder."

Alistair raised his head. "I didn't kill Margot," he said huskily. "I didn't. I needed her, to keep this place alive. I told you that."

"Yes," agreed Birdie. "You did. And it made a lot of sense. In one way your passion for this place made you the obvious suspect, as did your ability to think and behave very pragmatically when absolutely necessary. And in another, the same passion and the same personality traits made you the most unlikely. So I went on to think about other people, and other motives.

"William had been Margot's lover." She saw William jump a little in his seat, and his white face begin to color, and went on. "It was obvious to us all on Sunday night that he was still attached to her and very sensitive to her opinion. He was upset by her relationship with Conrad, who appeared to delight in tormenting him. I began to consider whether his jealousy could have become too much for him. In his highly nervous state the reappearance of a past horror in his life could have tipped him over the edge. Just like Alistair, he knew early about the anonymous letter. He also knew about Laurel Moon's presence in the house."

"Don't say those things." William whispered, trembling. "You can't say those things about me."

"Don't worry, Willy. Just hold onto little Bindy there. She'll look after you," drawled Conrad offensively. Belinda shot him an angry look, then turned back to the anguished William, her face creased with anxiety.

"But a couple of things made William a less likely candidate," Birdie went on, ignoring them. "William, for one reason or another"—she glanced at Belinda and looked quickly away again—"seemed to have calmed down quite a bit about Margot's reaction to him by Monday morning. Perhaps as a result of this, Margot was behaving graciously to him, and they were getting on well, laughing and talking and so on, as late as midday on Monday.

"There was also the matter of personality. Of all the people here William was the one most unlikely to do anything unexpected or new. He was an excellent secretary for Margot because of his compulsive respect for routine and attention to detail. It was hard to imagine him taking such a chance, actually *planning* to step outside the known—because there's no way this murder could have been an impulsive one. The murderer must have gone to the beauty therapy room with the scissors and a pair of tights, and almost certainly a pair of latex gloves too, knowing what he or she intended to do."

Birdie cleared her throat, gaining time. She looked up and with relief saw Betty Hinder slipping through the door. The small woman met her eyes and nodded slowly. Then, noiselessly, she again left the room.

"On the face of it, there seemed no real reason to suspect Conrad," Birdie went on. She watched as the other people in the room cast furtive glances at the figure slouched against the wall. Conrad inclined his head at her, smiling mockingly. He seemed completely relaxed but Birdie could see that his muscles were tensed with the effort of holding himself still. He was prepared for action if necessary.

Birdie drew breath. "But I had to take into account that Conrad was on intimate terms with Margot Bell, and statistically this meant he was someone I had to consider. So I did, and in the course of this I remembered one oddness relating to their relationship on Monday. Margot apparently canceled her usual evening massage appointment, without telling anyone but Conrad himself, or even making alternative arrangements with Angela. Since Margot always made a great issue of her Monday massage, this seemed very strange. But of course we only had Conrad's word that the massage *was* in fact canceled. What if it wasn't? What if the appointment was kept? How easy would it be for a masseur to kill? The victim lying relaxed, and suspecting nothing. Very easy indeed."

"Dream on, dear," drawled Conrad. "She wasn't even in the massage room, was she? What was I supposed to have done? Carried her into beauty therapy, scissors, blood, and all?"

Josie and Belinda both let out little gasps of horror, and even Edwina shuddered slightly. But Birdie saw that Helen's face was unmoved. She simply went on looking at Conrad with fixed gray eyes. William and Alistair seemed beyond reaction. Neither of them even raised their heads.

"There's no doubt that Margot Bell died where she was found," Birdie said dryly. "But the beauty therapy couch reclined completely, if required. It was as good for a neck massage as the massage room table. Margot could easily have been persuaded to be worked on there. And of course you wouldn't want to have her found in your workplace, would you, Conrad? That would all be a little too obvious."

His long fingers tapped the wall, but his face gave away nothing.

"I couldn't see a motive for Conrad, though," Birdie went on, "until Belinda told me earlier tonight about an argument she heard early on Monday morning. Margot was shouting at someone in her room—she was bitterly angry. Because money was mentioned I thought at first someone was trying to blackmail her."

Alistair closed his eyes and shook his head. A rueful smile curved his lips.

"Yes," said Birdie, watching him, "I was stupid. Margot wasn't the type to be bullied. Quite the reverse. And of course once I started thinking about her personality, Conrad's obvious proclivities and what else happened that morning, a much simpler alternative occurred to me."

"Nothing else happened," said Alistair blankly.

"Oh yes it did. One of the maids was sacked, wasn't she? She left immediately, in floods of tears, leaving Mrs. Hinder shorthanded. Margot sacked the girl personally. A 'pretty little thing,' she was, Betty Hinder said."

She shrugged. "Margot Bell was obviously not the best-tempered woman in the world, and she liked to get her own way. I'd seen and heard her angry. She went cold, and said biting things. But what, I thought, would really make her go off her head? Swear and scream? A serious blow to her pride and vanity, that's what. Being diddled. Tripping downstairs to the massage room early and unannounced after a passionate night, looking for a little more of the same, only to find the man she'd so honored having a pre-breakfast tumble with a pretty little thing in a frilly white apron."

Josie rubbed the back of her hand over her mouth. Edwina's lips tightened.

"So?" Birdie looked over her glasses at Conrad, and raised her eyebrows.

He looked resigned and slightly bored. "So what? It's no big deal."

"Isn't it? I always did think a member of staff was the most likely person to have killed Margot, because you all know your way around so well, know about people's habits, and the timing of things. And you had it pretty sweet here, didn't you, Conrad? You wouldn't want to be thrown out without a reference, I shouldn't think. Especially if you left Right-Moves under a cloud —which somehow I think we'd find, on investigation, you had."

He shrugged. "So what?" he repeated. "So she sprang me with Rachel and threw a fit. So she told me to get out. So I tried to talk her out of it. She wouldn't listen. She wouldn't even agree to pay me out the month. Said she wouldn't pay me the fortnight if I let on to anyone else what had happened. God, she was a tough old tart, Margot Bell." He smiled reminiscently. Rueful admiration, and even affection were in the smile. Then he looked Birdie straight in the eye. "O.K. I screwed round on her. She'd have done the same if she had the chance. O.K., I didn't want to lose this billet. I like it here. It suits me. But I didn't kill her. I'm not the type."

"No, I think that's true." Birdie risked a glance at the door again. She cleared her throat, gaining time. Her ears strained for the sound of movement from the room next door. How much time had gone by? How long would they sit here and let her talk?

"Anyhow, why pick on the workers?" Conrad drawled. "We're not the only ones here, you know. And we're not the only ones Margot played around, either."

"Quite so. I'm coming to that. I thought about the guests. Very carefully." Birdie pushed at her glasses and took a breath. "Belinda, for example . . ." She watched as the small dark figure on the couch jumped nervously.

"Belinda is here as the sister of an old friend of Margot's. On the surface there seems no reason whatever for her to want to hurt anyone. She tends to be timid, easily frightened, and clinging. Margot hadn't seen her friend Roberta for twenty years. She's been in Europe. Margot didn't even know Roberta had a sister. I couldn't see any past knowledge, relationship, or connection that might lead Belinda to want to kill Margot."

"Of c-course not!" Belinda burst out. She giggled hysterically, her hand over her mouth. William gripped her arm.

"But the fact remained that there were some odd things about Belinda's story," Birdie went on. "She was here, she said, because her husband had left her. She talked about that a lot. She gave the impression she was freshly separated or divorced. But she told William she'd married very young, just after Roberta went overseas, and the marriage only lasted a couple of years. He didn't think much about this, but I did.

Roberta went overseas *twenty years* ago. So Belinda's been a single woman for at least fifteen years. And what she's been doing during that time, she and Roberta obviously decided to keep to themselves. Belinda feared and disliked Margot Bell, who was a natural bully and recognized in Belinda her natural prey. I began wondering about Belinda . . ."

"Oh!" Belinda's face crumpled. "Oh! Don't say those things! You can't . . . What are you trying to say about me? Just being scared of someone isn't a motive for . . ." The words choked in her throat and she felt for William's hand. He let her take it but glanced quickly sideways. A slight frown puckered his smooth forehead.

"No, it's not a motive," Birdie said calmly, her eyes on the door. "And I'm not saying anything about you. I'm trying to get at the truth, that's all. And I'm pointing out that here, that's not easy. Deepdene is a very discreet place. It keeps secrets. Its own, and other people's. And the people in it keep secrets too. We're none of us exactly what we seem."

"Birdie, what's going on?" Edwina's cold voice cut through the silence. "Can't you get to the point?" She stood up. "These games are getting a little wearing, wouldn't you agree?"

"I am getting to the point, Edwina." Birdie sat still on the desk chair, aware that she was holding these people by a thread. "I simply want it to be perfectly clear to you all how I came to the conclusions I eventually came to. I don't want there to be a shred of doubt in anyone's mind. So I'm going through it step by step. I'm sorry if it's boring. It's necessary. Please sit down again. It won't take much longer."

"Boring's hardly the word for it, is it?" Josie mumbled through her handkerchief. She blew her nose lushly. With a barely controlled glimmer of distaste,

Edwina sank back onto the coffee table and sat there, stony-faced.

"I said earlier," Birdie continued, "that I had played with the idea that Margot was being black-mailed. The anonymous letters, once I knew they weren't from Helen, gave that idea some legs. As did the sums of money Margot was nicking quietly from the Deepdene account. But I soon realized, as I said before, that Margot was taking that money as a substitute for at least one, and possibly two, other money sources that had dried up. Those sources were men who Margot was quietly blackmailing. Now she needed another victim—fast. And if Margot was a tough old tart, as Conrad put it, her vanity made her a rather naive one too—as her experience with him shows. If she seized upon a possibility here, one less biddable and more dangerous than the poor confused men she'd dealt with before, she might have found her-self in very deep water indeed."

Alistair leaned forward. His face was anguished. "You're saying that Margot—Margot was a *blackmailer*? That's impossible! You don't know what you're say-ing."

"Impossible my fat aunt!" Josie burst out impul-sively. "It's bloody true!" The folds of her cheeks flushed red. "Take my word for it if you don't take hers. It's bloody true—the smarmy, snobbish bitch was a dirty blackmailer. She turned that madeup face to the whole world, so gracious, so up herself, and inside she was a blackmailing, devious trollop. What d'you think of that!" She flung herself back in her chair, panting, her top lip beaded with sweat, her sandy hair sticking to her forehead in draggled tails.

Alistair wiped his mouth with the back of his shaking hand. "I thought she had shares. I thought she had a packet stashed away. Those trips—the clothes, the jewelry, the cars—all that was . . ."

"Bought with other people's money, yes," said Birdie calmly. "And just lately, with the business's."

"Who'd she try to bite next, then?" asked Josie. "Wasn't me, I can tell you that. She'd had all she was going to get from my family, and I couldn't care less what people said about me. Whoever it is may as well own up. If they knocked her off, they did the world a service."

"Oh, stop!" Belinda buried her face in her hands. Edwina sat impassive, unmoving.

Birdie looked at the door. Betty Hinder was again standing there, her face in shadow. But Birdie could see the nod. Her heart leaped into her throat. It was time.

22

"I came upstairs a little while ago to try to tell the police what I suspected, about my blackmail idea," Birdie said. Her chest felt tight. She could hear her own voice echoing in her head. She wondered that it sounded so flat and laconic. "And then I found out why it was that they'd been so convinced that Helen had murdered Margot Bell. Why they wouldn't even consider any other theory. They're not completely stupid, and they're not that stubborn. I know. I've dealt with them before, many times. I should have realized that they must have had a very good reason for what they were doing and saying. They wouldn't consider any other alternative because they knew something I didn't know.

"I haven't done much reading on serial killers, but one article I did read years ago talked about the phenomenon of the copycat killing. I remembered that clearly, and obviously it affected the way I thought about this case. But there was one detail I didn't pay enough attention to. The article also said that when investigating serial killings, the police often suppress some of the information available to them. They fail to report to the press some characteristic detail of the real serial murderer's calling card, so that they can tell copycat killings from the real thing. Just half an hour ago I realized that this could be the reason for Toby and Milson's being so sure that Laurel Moon was the killer. They would have had access to police records on the case at the time. And if there was a detail that was never released to the press, they would have known about it. And if they saw that characteristic detail here, they would have had no doubt about the murderer. I thought about that. I thought about the deaths we'd seen, and something William said. And then I thought I knew."

The room was utterly still. Only the rain on the roof drummed on outside in the cold, black dark.

"Dan Toby's still a bit drugged up. That's why he's not with us—yet. The first time I tried to talk to him I got nowhere. But once I knew the right question to ask, I was able to get a straight answer the next time he stirred. He confirmed my guess. I now know that the scissors used to kill the Gray Lady victims weren't only used to stab and kill. Before that, while the victim lay unconscious, they were used to remove every button from her clothes. If there were no buttons, then hooks, press-studs, and even the tops of zippers were cut off and left by the body."

Birdie paused. Her amber eyes behind the thick glasses swept the room. "The police found two buttons in the beauty therapy room. I thought they'd been torn from the waistband of Margot's slacks in the struggle but the holes were too neat, of course. They'd been cut off. As were the buttons from Angela's pajamas, so the jacket gaped. We all saw it. But we didn't know what we were seeing."

William was trembling all over. His great brown eyes were swimming. "Lois—her cardigan. The buttons were all over the grass. Red buttons. Like little buds, they looked. I remember . . ."

"I remember you telling me, William," Birdie said softly. She watched Belinda press his hand and put her other hand to his face, intensely tender.

"So . . ." Alistair's face was wrinkled with anxiety and concentration. "You're saying—the blackmail, all that . . . was nothing? That . . ."

Birdie lifted her chin. "I'm saying that the killing of Margot Bell wasn't a copy of the Gray Lady murders. It was the genuine article, by the same hand. As was the killing of Angela."

"But . . . you said before . . . you said Helen couldn't have done the murders. You said . . ."

Birdie looked at the still, watching figure on the bed. "That's right. Helen couldn't have done the murders."

The people in the room looked at her, and each other, first wonderingly, then wildly, as the meaning of her words sank in.

"She's not Laurel Moon at all," Edwina said slowly. "We locked up the wrong person. But then . . . who else . . . ?"

Birdie watched the door. The woman on the bed stirred, and spoke.

"Who else." Helen's flat, dead voice drew all eyes but she stared into space. She might have been alone in the room, talking to herself. "There was no one else it could have been, was there? Who looked like me? Who didn't fit in, like me? Who was strange, like me? Who had my memories, to burn them out, kill them inside? Who else could be Laurel Moon? Why have a minute's doubt?"

"Helen . . ." Alistair leaned forward, his face anguished.

"No. Don't apologize." Grotesquely, Helen smiled. "I'm not surprised you picked on me, Alistair. You and

William and the police and everyone else. I'm not blind. I can see myself in the mirror. I can see myself in the mirrors of other people's eyes. I came here for just that reason. I wanted to be remade—show the world a different face. But that didn't help me. When it happened I knew what you were thinking. What you were all thinking. And why should you look further for a murderer? Or even for a serial killer? Why should you? Why should I? Why should anyone, ever?"

"But there's no one else who could be Laurel Moon. No one else," whispered William, as though he was repeating a lesson by heart. "We've seen Edwina before—in the paper. Verity's from the ABC. Josie rang her kids the first night. I put her through. And that only leaves Belinda. And it couldn't be her, because she's the sister of an old friend of Margot's."

The door swung open. Bleary-eyed and pale, but with hair slicked back and tie in place, Detective Sergeant Dan Toby walked unsteadily into the room, with a grim-faced Betty Hinder at his side.

Helen turned to look at him and smiled again, infinitely weary. She turned back to William. "People can keep secrets, William. Especially secrets they're ashamed of, and that could hurt them. You know that. And even murderers are human. They have mothers, and fathers, brothers and—even sisters."

William's eyes bulged. He jerked his head around to Belinda. She looked at him blankly, her mouth stretched in a travesty of a smile. She put out her hand. He screamed—a shocking, shrill cry, and still she reached for him. And then Alistair had seized her arm, and Conrad had pulled William away from her with one strong hand.

Helen smiled again, at William this time. "But you were right, William. You can take consolation in that. There was no one else. I am Laurel Moon."

Dan Toby moved to the couch, and spoke.

"William Dean, I arrest you for the murders of Margot Bell, Angela Fellowes, Lois Freeman . . ."

There was more, a lot more, but William's screaming drowned it out.

It was Conrad and Alistair who finally dragged William away. Toby could only follow them slowly and painfully, like a priest attending an execution. Now the rain on the roof and Belinda's quiet sobbing against Josie's shoulder were the only sounds in "Juliet."

"Thank you, Betty," said Birdie quietly.

The small woman in black nodded. "Glad to help. Thought you were nuts to depend on that Conrad, I must say. Still, he did all right, didn't he?"

"Yes. And so did Alistair. And you. Especially you."

Mrs. Hinder shrugged. "Just followed orders, didn't I? Tell Conrad and Alistair to stay near William and Belinda and separate them when you gave the nod; get into William's room and find the pills and a wet dressing gown and pajamas; get the copper on his feet. Not so hard."

Edwina had been staring into space. Now she roused herself. "Wet pajamas? Listen, Birdie, I don't see how you worked all this out," she said. "William . . ."

"It was incredibly simple, Edwina. It really was." Birdie leaned forward in her chair, hands clasped between her knees. "I found out that Margot and Angela had definitely been killed by the same person who did the Gray Lady murders. But I knew that Helen hadn't killed Angela, at least. And I knew that Helen was Laurel Moon. Therefore, as a matter of logic, Laurel Moon was not the Gray Lady murderer."

"But she was seen." As Edwina forced out the words she couldn't look at Helen. She looked intently at Birdie instead. But it was Helen who answered her.

"Yes, I was seen," said Helen. "I was seen killing

my aunt. And I did kill her. I did. The blood . . ." Her eyes closed. Her big hands twisted on her lap.

"Helen had been—ill, Edwina," Birdie explained. "For a long time. You've read about her history. Her aunt, with whom she lived, was a tormenting, bullying woman. The papers, TV, radio were full of the Gray Lady murders. No one talked of anything else."

"I had voices," Helen said. "In my head, but they seemed so real. I'd had them for a long time—since I was in my early twenties—but they were getting worse. They would shout at me. I couldn't believe no one else could hear them. I couldn't work. I couldn't think. I had times when I didn't know where I'd been or what I'd done, for hours at a time. Days, sometimes. I started to think about the Gray Lady murders a lot. They were happening in our area. I started to wonder whether I . . . I couldn't remember, you see. I couldn't remember, quite often. There were big patches of blank, black space. And Auntie Meg . . . wouldn't leave me alone. She said I was hopeless, lazy, bad, mad —everything. Over and over. She had these moods when she'd go on and on and on at me. I used to think about killing her, to stop the noise. I used to look at her little red mouth, making shapes, and the little bit of dribble she always got in the corners, and I'd think, I'll kill you. And one day I did. On the back veranda. With a pair of tights and the sewing scissors. Just like in the paper. And then I tried to kill myself. But they wouldn't let me die."

"They took Helen in," Birdie said. "She hadn't cut off her aunt's buttons, but she'd been disturbed— caught in the act. It was just taken that the pattern had been thrown out by that. No one had any doubt she was the person they were after. And neither did she. She was examined by psychiatrists and judged not fit to plead. She was put away, and the case was closed. But she wasn't the Gray Lady murderer. She was a copycat killer. The Gray Lady murderer had claimed his last victim with Lois Freeman, the mother figure for whom all the others had been symbols, and was safely recovering from a nervous breakdown, pitied, cosseted, and completely unsuspected.''

"But how did you know that it was William?" demanded Josie, over Belinda's tangled hair.

"Think about it, Josie." Birdie sighed. "I knew, because of the buttons, that the Gray Lady murderer was here. There've been quite a few coincidences in this case, and that's life. Coincidences happen far more often than we realize. But the biggest coincidence here was that we had, under the same roof, two people who'd been intimately connected with the Gray Lady murders: Helen, or Laurel Moon, and William. The odds against there being yet another person secretly involved would be astronomical. So once Helen was out of the running as the killer, William was the obvious choice. And once I started thinking about him, everything fell into place.

"I suddenly remembered something he'd said about his discovery of Lois Freeman's body. He said her red cardigan buttons were scattered all over the grass, like little buds. But he was supposed to have found her after work, at night. He'd been working late. And remember he said it was this time of year—winter. It would have been quite, quite dark. He couldn't have seen red buttons on the grass then. He must have been remembering something he saw earlier in the day. As he stood over her, perhaps. After he'd killed her.

"Margot Bell's death, then. How had he managed that? Margot was too fond of her own comfort to cancel a massage without arranging for another. And she never ran her own messages. Who did? William. This time was no exception. She asked William to organize Angela for her, but William didn't say a word to Angela or anyone else. William knew this place's routine, and trusted in it completely. He knew Margot would be finished with Edwina by a quarter to six, because she told him to order Angela for then. He knew Angela would go off for her swim at five-thirty, because she always left her room just after he did, and he always left in time to put in half an hour in the office before drinks."

"Wait a minute. I thought it was six to six-thirty that she swam," Edwina interrupted curiously.

"Angela was a very simple, literal-minded girl. She *swam* from six to six-thirty. The half-hour before that was spent changing, meditating, and doing warm-up exercises. When I thought about what she'd said at her interview I realized we'd had enough hints that this was the case. If we'd only asked her a few more direct questions we'd have seen it.

"She told us she heard William leave his room. She, and we, assumed he'd then gone into the main house as usual. But he hadn't. He'd simply ducked into the annex storeroom. All the permanent staff had keys to it, because that's where the spare therapy equipment was kept, as well as the sample clothes. And it's right next to his room. I should have seen it—at drinks he said he'd seen Angela go off for her swim. He was scoring points off Conrad, and made a slip. Because Angela took a short-cut through the massage room to the pool changing room that night he couldn't possibly have seen her unless he was still in the annex corridor. Or hidden in one of the rooms, watching. The storeroom was the obvious place, since he had to visit there anyway to get what he needed, and from there he had an uninterrupted view of all the therapy room doors.

"He helped himself to a pair of tights, one of the spare protective gowns, and some rubber gloves. He could have used one of the gowns from the beauty therapy room itself, but William's motto was 'be prepared.' He wanted to go into that room with everything he needed, risking no mistake. He waited till Angela and Edwina left and Margot went to the beauty therapy room. He knew that Conrad always had a spa after he'd cleaned up, and would certainly go on up to the house after that. He knew that Alistair never finished his last appointment till just before six. He told me that Alistair always used his full time. He had about fifteen minutes to do what he planned. He went into the beauty therapy room where he knew Margot would be waiting, laid out ready for Angela. She'd be quite relaxed with William. She probably already had the pads on her eyes, or maybe he helped her do that. She'd be grateful to him when he locked the connecting door into the massage room, to prevent unwanted intrusion —from Conrad or anyone else. Then, while she relaxed, blind in both senses, he put on the protective gown and the gloves, and killed her. A matter of moments."

Belinda began to sob again, shuddering all over. Josie patted her back mechanically, murmuring.

"The gown protected him from the blood," Birdie went on, "and when he'd finished he just dropped it on the floor. He pulled off the gloves so they turned inside out, and walked straight on up the corridor with them in his hand, stuffing them into the toe of the spare pair of gum boots in the kitchen on his way through to the sitting room. Safer than the garbage, where the police would be sure to look. And unlikely to be used, he thought, before he could retrieve the gloves. I suppose he was scared of fingerprints. He was having drinks with Josie, Helen, and Belinda and Conrad by the time Alistair and I got there."

"But why?" Belinda raised a swollen, piteous face. "Why did he kill her? He was getting over her. You could see that. Wasn't he?"

"They certainly seemed to be on good terms," Edwina agreed. "Josie heard them laughing together only that morning."

"She heard *Margot* laughing," Birdie corrected. "There's a difference. An important difference if—"

"But why kill Angela?" interrupted Josie fiercely. "Why that?"

"Because Angela knew all about the beauty therapy room and its equipment. Once she thought about it, she realized that the gown on the floor was an old one, from the storeroom. I saw it myself, the strings all draggled with blood. The new ones, the ones in use now, have Velcro tabs. Only the old ones kept in the storeroom for emergencies have strings. So Angela turned this over in her mind and puzzled over it.

"I'd say she heard William come back to his room after his interview and decided she wanted to talk it over. She was a great talker, Angela, and she wouldn't be scared of asking a pussycat like William to her room. So she talked, and he realized he had to act fast, before she talked to anyone else, because what she was saying effectively implicated a member of staff with access to the storeroom, not Helen, and that meant trouble for him. So when she turned her back on him, he caught her round the neck with a pair of her own white panty hose and strangled her, and cut off her pajama buttons and stabbed her over and over in the neck with her nail scissors."

"Ugh! Oh, God!" Edwina turned her face away.

"But he wasn't prepared, you see. He was in his dressing gown, and he got blood all over it. And on his pajamas. He raced back to his room, stripped them off, and put them under the shower. He knew all about blood washing off in cold water. He wrung them out and hung them up to dry. With the heating like it is in this place he thought they'd be pretty well dry by the next day."

"I found them in his room, just like she said," Betty Hinder mused. "Like magic, it was. She told me, 'Look for this and this . . .' and there they were. Dark blue silk. Very nice."

"When we got him up, you see, he had to put on a dressing gown," Birdie explained. "This place must have got to me because I couldn't help noticing how old and tatty it was. A big contrast to the pajamas, which were very classy. A gift from Margot, I'll bet. He had a spare pair of those, see, but he had to put on his old warm dressing gown—the one he had when he first came here, I suppose. The way the air-conditioning is in this place, he must have nearly roasted in it. He certainly looked hot. Anyway, there'll still be traces of blood on the wet gown and pajamas, for forensic to find. And they'll convict him."

"He used his own sleeping pills in the coffee, I suppose. Pretty silly, that," pondered Betty, enjoying her Watson role.

"I think he'd pretty much lost his head by then," said Birdie. "He was fixated by the idea of pinning the whole thing on Helen. After all, it had worked before, and William was a creature of habit. But that meant he had to immobilize or distract her guard. He obviously came skulking back into the house to see what could be done, and heard about the coffee. So he ran back and got the drug, and Toby played right into his hands by leaving the tray unattended by the stairs. William must have thought all his Christmases had come at once."

Edwina fixed her with stern eyes in which a slight twinkle lurked. "You didn't play fair, you know," she teased. "You said you'd ruled William out as Margot's murderer because he was the last person to deliberately step into the unknown. Stickler for rule and routine. Afraid of anything new. All that."

Birdie smiled grimly. "I said Margot's death was a

planned crime, and I didn't think William could have
planned a leap into the unknown. But he didn't, did
he? He did only what he'd already done five times before. He followed a tried and true routine. He'd had
lots of killing practice, before he got to Margot Bell."

Downstairs in the office, William was talking. He'd
been talking for some time. His long, slim fingers
played with the frayed cord of his tartan dressing
gown, but his great brown eyes ranged aimlessly
around the room. He appeared to have forgotten that
Alistair and Conrad stood behind him. But sometimes
his blank stare would focus on the figure of Dan Toby,
sitting in front of him with his chin propped up on his
hands behind the big, gleaming desk. Then he would
hesitate, and a slight frown of puzzlement would
crease his brow before he went on.

    ". . . so then of course when she told me, so
sweetly, so calmly, that she'd told Conrad to go and
asked me to arrange for Angela to look after her neck
that night I thought she'd finally seen through him and
come to her senses, and everything would be all right
again, like it was before. And I was so happy. I nearly
told her about Laurel Moon then. Because I thought she
was my Margot again. But I didn't want to spoil things.
I felt very close to her. I thought the time was right. I
asked her to marry me. And you know what she did?"

    "What did she do, son?" Toby spoke quietly, reas-
suringly.

    "She laughed!" The brown eyes burned. "She
laughed, and laughed and laughed! She laughed at me!
Just like Lois, when I asked her. Just like Mother, before
she went away. She was just like them. She didn't love
me! She was evil, and bad. And then I knew that Laurel
Moon coming here was a sign. And I knew what I
would do." William's lip quivered. His long black

lashes were wet. "She shouldn't have laughed at me, should she?" he whimpered.

Alistair shut his eyes.

"No, son," said Dan Toby heavily. "No, she shouldn't. That was her big mistake."

Dan Toby turned back to the house, held up his arm, and
waved, just once. It was like a salute. At the sitting
room window Birdie raised a hand slowly in response.
"You're welcome," she murmured. She looked around
quickly to find Edwina watching her in amusement.
They both watched through the curtains as the police
boat moved off through the drizzling dawn. Then they
closed out the gray, and turned away from the window. The sitting room was warm and brightly lit, and a
newly laid fire crackled brightly in the grate, sparking
and popping. The dining room and kitchen doors were
wide open, and they could hear Betty clattering around
in the kitchen. The smell of hot toast and bacon drifted
in the air.

Alistair came in from the hall and went to the fire.
He threw on another log and turned his back to it, rubbing his hands. "They've gone," he said. "Did you
see?"

The women nodded. "He'd stopped talking,"
Birdie said.

"Yes, thank God. As soon as he got outside. It was
like a tap had been turned off. He stopped talking and

went limp. Dan Toby and the other cops had to practically carry him to the boat. But he'd said it all. Over and over. His mother, those other poor four women, Lois, Margot . . . Angela . . ." He rubbed his eyes vigorously with his knuckles and looked up at them. "I can't believe it, you know," he said simply. "Any of it. It's like some terrible dream. I didn't know them at all. Margot, William—I was completely wrong about them. Neither of them was what I thought."

"They were, you know," Edwina said thoughtfully. "They were just other things as well, that they kept hidden."

"Maybe." He stirred. "Look, I'll go and give Betty a hand. It's just us, isn't it?"

"Yes. Everyone else is asleep, I think."

"O.K. I'll be back. We'll eat in front of the fire."

Alistair wandered off into the dining room and Birdie and Edwina sat down by the fire.

"In all this ghastly business at least one person's better off," said Birdie. "Helen. It's like she's woken up after a nightmare. Now maybe she can get on with the rest of her life. Belinda's a different story, unfortunately. Years of pill-popping behind her, I'd say, and more to come, by the sound of that sister of hers. But Josie'll be all right. Though I bet she hasn't had the last trouble she's going to have with that husband."

"My sentiments exactly," said Edwina. She stared fixedly at the leaping flames. "You thought it was me for a while, didn't you?" she asked abruptly.

"Just for a while," Birdie said, and grinned. "Still, don't take it to heart. I thought it was everyone at one point or another. Even Betty, till she got that blood on her toe and showed us all. That put her right in the clear. And you must admit that as a candidate for blackmail, you were the best prospect."

"I may have money and position, but I have led a

blameless life," retorted Edwina with dignity. "Practically." She sighed. "Worse luck."

"Ah well, you're not dead yet. Still time to blot your copybook if you feel inclined," said Birdie lazily.

"Actually, I was thinking about that." Edwina leaned back, stretched out her legs, and put her hands behind her head. She smiled to herself. "Not to say blotting, you understand—but branching out. Because I've led such a blameless life I've never spent much on myself. I've got all this money invested here and put away there and rolled over somewhere else. I'll never spend it if I live to be a hundred and twenty. And this place . . ." She put her head to one side. Her eyes were dreamy.

Birdie looked at her in amazement. "You're thinking of buying Deepdene?"

"Oh no. Not buying. Only buying in as a partner. As an investment. Alistair runs this place. It'd be nothing without him. It's him, not Margot Bell, that made it such a success. She had him bamboozled. Deepdene's got such a reputation now, he doesn't need a glamorous figurehead. But he does need cash, and some good advice. Well, I can supply that. And it's a bloody good business. I wouldn't lose by it." She hesitated. "It's unusual. I'd have to do it reasonably quietly, of course."

"Oh, of course." Birdie grinned to herself.

"Do you think I'm nuts? Do you think he'll be interested?" Edwina looked at her anxiously.

"No, and yes, like a rat up a drainpipe."

Betty Hinder appeared wheeling a trolley from which delicious smells arose.

"Betty, you're a truly wonderful woman," cooed Birdie, reaching uninvited for a plate.

"Get away with you. Cupboard love, that's all that is." Betty grinned.

"You know, Edwina," Birdie went on serenely, surveying the pile of crisp bacon with relish, "I've been thinking. If I'd only listened to Betty, this whole case would have been solved in about two minutes. She said Margot Bell was the problem with this place, and that turned out to be true. She said William was a basket case, and that turned out to be true. She said Belinda was a wrong drummer who'd always choose the wrong man and *that* was true, too. She's a witch, I think. She's got magic powers." She selected three large, curly rashers and licked her lips.

"What I've got, Miss Birdwood," responded Betty Hinder severely, "is common sense. More than some people I could name. Don't forget to leave some for Alistair!" she warned as Birdie started on the toast. "And speaking of him . . ." She lowered her voice to a stage whisper and leaned toward Edwina. "Before he gets back, love, I thought I'd put something to you. You'll think I'm cheeky, but have you ever thought of branching out, like?"

"Mmm?" Edwina jerked up her head, her eyes startled, her mouth full of bacon.

"Like . . . we'll have to close Deepdene down for a few weeks now, won't we? But after that we'll be going on," Betty said firmly. "And Alistair needs a partner—someone with money and a bit of sense. I was thinking maybe you . . ." she broke off.

Edwina was speechless.

"Told you," crowed Birdie. "Magic. Betty, could you pour the coffee? Or will I?"

"I'll do it," said Betty. "Hold your horses." She had raised her head and seemed to be listening to something. "There," she said triumphantly. "What did I say?" She turned to the trolley and grasped the coffee-pot in a small brown hand.

"What?" The other women looked around, bemused.

"The rain. It's stopped raining."

They sat on in warm silence. After a while, Alistair

joined them. The fire leaped and crackled, the embers glowed. Outside, the first watery rays of the morning sun hit the tips of the poplar trees. A couple of surprised birds squeaked. And below, on the softly rippling ground, by infinitesimal stages, the water began to withdraw, moving on through the valley to begin its long, inevitable progress to the sea.